DEIRDRE AND DESIRE

C

DEIRDRE AND DESIRE

Being the Third Volume of the Six Sisters

M.C. Beaton

WINDSOR
PARAGON

First published 1984
by Macdonald & Co (Publishers)Ltd
This Large Print edition published 2013
by AudioGO Ltd
by arrangement with
Constable & Robinson Ltd

Hardcover   ISBN: 978 1 4713 3378 1
Softcover   ISBN: 978 1 4713 3379 8

British Library Cataloguing in Publication Data available

Printed and bound in Great Britain by
MPG Books Group Limited

*For my sister, Tilda Grenier,
and her husband, Laurent, with love.*

SPECTATOR AB EXTRA

Parvenant

It was but this winter I came up to town,
And already I'm gaining a sort of renown;
Find my way to good houses without much ado,
And beginning to see the nobility too.
So useful it is to have money, heigh-ho!
So useful it is to have money.

There's something undoubtedly in a fine air,
To know how to smile and be able to stare.
High breeding is something, but well-bred or
    not,
In the end the one question is, what have you
    got.
So needful it is to have money, heigh-ho!
So needful it is to have money.

And the angels in pink and the angels in blue,
In muslins and moirés so lovely and new,
What is it they want, and so wish you to guess,
But if you have money, the answer is Yes.
So needful, they tell you, is money, heigh-ho!
So needful it is to have money.

Arthur Hugh Clough

Georgian menu used in this volume of *The Six Sisters* was taken from *Georgian Meals and Menus* by Maggie Black, published by the Kingsmead Press, Rosewell House, Kingsmead Square, Bath, England.

ONE

It had been a day of heavy rain, but towards sunset the clouds had broken, and an angry, yellow, glaring light bathed the village of Hopeworth and the surrounding sodden fields.

Little choppy golden ripples danced angrily across the village pond. The sun blazed through two huge purple-and-black ragged clouds, and the rising wind sent a shower of wet brown leaves dancing over the cottage roofs.

It was the sort of sunset which presaged a high wind; yellow sunsets always meant a wild night to come.

Squire Radford huddled his thin, old shoulders further into his greatcoat, feeling the heavy material beginning to flap against his spindly legs.

As he hurried in the direction of his cottage *ornée*, he cursed himself for having been stupid enough to accept Sir Edwin Armitage's invitation to take tea at the Hall.

Sir Edwin's haughty wife had been glacially aloof, as usual, and her plain daughters, Josephine and Emily, still unmarried, had giggled and pouted in turns in a most irritating manner.

The squire's thoughts turned from Sir Edwin to Sir Edwin's brother, the Reverend Charles Armitage, vicar of St Charles and St Jude in the parish of Hopeworth. For although the vicar was a close friend of the squire and usually came to call most evenings, Squire Radford found himself hoping for the first time that the ebullient fox-hunting vicar would decide to stay in the

1

comfort of his own home.

It was a sad and lonely feeling to see a dear friend so monstrous changed in character. The vicar had become so puffed up, so swollen in pride, that he seemed another man altogether.

The rot had set in, mused the squire, wincing as the first blast of windy rain tugged at his old fashioned three-cornered hat, with the marriage of the vicar's second eldest daughter, Annabelle.

His eldest, Minerva, had done very well for herself by marrying Lord Sylvester Comfrey, but the vicar had accepted that piece of good fortune with a comfortable sort of gratitude. Then Annabelle had become wed to the Marquess of Brabington and the vicar had accepted that piece of good luck with a comfortable sort of gratitude as well. But after Annabelle's marriage when she had gone off with her husband to the Peninsular Wars, the vicar had found his social standing much elevated by virtue of the aristocracy of his new in-laws. He began to spend as much time in Town as he could out of the fox-hunting Season, returning to the country only to plunge into more wild farming experiments, and more expensive purchases of hounds.

He was now the proud possessor of twenty couple of hounds, a ridiculous quantity for a country parson. Two years had passed since Annabelle's wedding; Lord Sylvester's steward, who had done much to put the Armitage farming land in good heart, was now back managing his master's estates; and once more the vicar was faced with ruin.

He had been faced with ruin before, but never before had Charles Armitage ignored the fact so blatantly.

And he still had four daughters unwed, and two sons at Eton whose future was a weighty matter.

Two whole years had passed since Annabelle wed the Marquess of Brabington. How old were they all now? The squire pushed open the tall iron gates leading to his cottage and murmured names and ages over to himself.

'Let me see, the twins, Peregrine and James, will be twelve. Minerva will now he twenty-one! Dear me. How quickly the time flies. Annabelle will therefore be nineteen which will mean Deirdre is just eighteen, Daphne is sixteen, Diana, fifteen, and little Frederica, fourteen.'

The squire's soft-footed Indian servant opened the door and relieved his master of his coat.

'Thank you, Ram,' said the squire. 'I am chilled to the bone. Bring some brandy to the library and if anyone calls—*anyone*—I am not at home.'

Even when the squire felt mellowed by his slippered feet on the hearth, the curtains drawn tightly against the rising storm, and the flames from a blazing coal fire sending golden flames dancing in his brandy glass, he was relieved to be alone.

He had had his cottage *ornée* built some twelve years before to replace the old insanitary Tudor hall which had served his earlier years. He had wanted something simple, and considered his fifteen charming rooms hung with French wallpaper and filled with fine furniture, paintings and china sufficient for his needs. His wife and his daughter had both died a long time ago. The ceiling was low and raftered and the gold lettering of the calfbound books which lined the library walls winked cheerfully in the soft glow from the oil lamps.

3

As an angry burst of rain struck the windows the squire smiled contentedly and snuggled deeper in his armchair, sipped his brandy, and opened a book.

Then, as the wind slackened slightly, he heard the clip-clop of a horse's hooves coming up his short drive.

The vicar.

He crouched a little further down in his chair, listening guiltily to the sounds of the vicar's arrival, the hammering on the door, the soft murmur of his servant's voice.

Then the closing of the door and no sound other than the howl of the rising wind.

The noise of the wind must have covered the sounds of the rejected vicar's retreat.

Suddenly, Squire Radford got to his feet and walked to the library window nearest his chair and pulled aside the curtains.

He let out a frightened little scream and backed away from the window, his wrinkled old hands to his mouth.

A hideous, squat, fat, distorted face was pressed against the glass.

Then the face retreated a little and resolved itself into that of the Reverend Charles Armitage.

He was mouthing something but the squire could not hear him because of the noise of the storm. Still too shocked to gather his wits together, the squire made flapping movements with his hands to indicate that the vicar should return to the front door.

Then he closed the curtains and sat down in the armchair by the fire, his heart still thudding.

In no time at all, the Reverend Charles Armitage

came striding in.

He was a short, round man who normally wore a shovel hat and a pepper-and-salt coat and gaiters. The squire had often thought a Union Jack across his chest would have turned him into the perfect John Bull.

But on this occasion, the vicar presented a very odd figure. His face was painted and rouged and he wore an elaborate cravat and evening clothes, his skin-tight trousers being shoved into hessian boots. As he moved, he unmistakably creaked and snapped.

'Corsets, Charles?' queried the squire faintly.

'Nonsense,' said the vicar, turning even redder. 'It's my bones creakin'. Being locked out in this demned plaguey weather don't do my old bones a mort o' good. Well, well, well. I'm here, and that's the main thing.'

He sat down by the fire opposite the squire and helped himself to a glass of brandy before removing his dripping hat and putting it down on the hearth where it started to steam.

His light brown hair had been teased and curled and pomaded so that it stood up on his head like a crest, giving him an air of perpetual surprise.

He tossed his glass of brandy off, shuddered, looked at the fire and sighed lugubriously.

The squire said nothing, so the vicar sighed noisily and eyed his friend out of the corners of his twinkling shoe-button eyes.

The squire resigned himself.

'What is the matter, Charles?' he demanded in his high precise voice.

'I have lost my faith,' mourned the vicar. 'Just like that. Just like the thingummy on the road to whatsit.'

He didn't lose it. He found it,' said the squire crossly.

'Who?'

'St Paul.'

'Oh, him? O' course, it was easy for *him,*' said the vicar with something like a sneer. 'But does He care if I've lost my faith? Does He send down lights or one small miracle? No. Couldn't even get me some decent hunting weather last year.'

'I do not see, Charles, how you can claim to have lost what you never had,' said the squire, becoming much flushed. 'You are turned exceeding arrogant. Without humility there is no faith.'

'Don't preach,' said the vicar huffily. He poured himself more brandy and sighed again.

The squire looked at him in a mixture of exasperation and compassion.

'You are a great child,' he said gently. 'Faith or lack of faith is not what troubles you. It is money, or the lack of *that.*'

'Aye, that's it,' said the vicar. 'You have it in a nutshell. Two rich sons-in-law and I can't get my hands on them. Brabington's in France and Comfrey has already gone to join him.'

'Indeed! I did not know Minerva and her husband had left the country? I did not expect it. She is soon to present you with a grandson.'

'Another two months,' said the vicar moodily. 'And it'll probably come into the world speaking French.'

'But what took Lord Sylvester to France?'

'I don't know. Went along o' everyone else, I s'pose. At least they're in Paris, and haven't gone to Waterloo to poke around the dead bodies with a

6

stick.'

'My dear Charles!'

There came a silence. The door opened and the servant came in and put two large shovelfuls of coal on the fire.

The vicar watched morosely as grey smoke began to curl up in long trailing wisps. Then little yellow flames sprang through the bank of black coal and green and blue ones danced in the spurts of coal gas.

The clock ticked sonorously in the corner. A great buffet of wind howled round the building.

'There is a solution,' said the vicar at last. 'When I was in London, there was a lot o' talk in the clubs about Lord Harry Desire.'

'The Earl of Carchester's son?'

'Him.'

'And?'

The vicar heaved a gusty sigh. 'Desire's got an uncle who's a nabob, Jeremy Blewett. He says he'll leave all his money to Desire if the man gets married. Blewett's said to be on his deathbed.'

'Has Desire no money of his own?'

'Not much. The Carchesters never knew how to keep it. He lives high, does young Desire. He spends more on his tailor than I spend on my pack.'

The squire did some rapid mental calculation.

'Impossible,' he said at last.

'True. He's a great dandy.'

'I do not see how this young man can aid you. How old is he?'

'Late in his twenties. Thirty, say.'

'You have met him?'

'Not I,' shrugged the vicar. 'Heard of him, though.'

7

'You cannot possibly be thinking of a husband for Deirdre!'

'Why not?' demanded the vicar crossly. 'Had enough trouble with Minerva and Annabelle. Arranged marriage will be just the thing.'

'Deirdre is a highly intelligent lady with a mind of her own.'

The vicar ferreted around in his waistcoat pockets until he found a goose quill and then proceeded to pick his teeth, much to the fastidious squire's irritation. 'Hark 'ee, Jimmy,' he grinned. 'Deirdre's been *told* she's the brainy one o' the family for so long, she's come to believe it herself. But she reads *novels*. So there!'

'I read novels myself,' protested the squire.

'Different for a man,' muttered the vicar. 'Lots o' vices are.'

'I think you are making a great mistake,' said the squire severely. 'I don't know what has come over you this last two years, Charles. You have wasted your money, you have taken to wearing *paint,* and, yes, you *are* wearing corsets.'

The vicar flushed and looked mutinous. '*I* haven't changed,' he said, whipping himself up into a fine anger. 'It's you who have changed. Demme, you're worse than the bishop. Always preaching and moralizing and argyfying. I'm off!'

'If our friendship means so little to you that you cannot take a piece of well-meant criticism ...'

'Fah!' said the vicar, rising, picking up his steaming hat and cramming it on his head.

'Let us not part in anger,' pleaded the squire. 'Join me for supper, I beg you, and let us talk this thing over.'

The vicar marched to the door and then turned.

' "Better a dinner of herbs where love is, than a stalled ox and hatred therewith." Proverbs, Chapter fifteen, verse seventeen.'

'Oh, Charles ...' began the squire, but the vicar had already made his exit.

A ride through the night did little to improve the Reverend Charles Armitage's temper. The squire's sorrowful, reproachful face kept rising in front of him as he spurred his horse in the direction of the vicarage. He had felt a new man these past two years. An important man. One of the peerage. By virtue of his daughters' successful marriages, he was invited to all the best houses.

He felt he had regained his youth. And if his corsets pinched and the paint on his face made his skin itch, these were mere pinpricks set against the heady exhilaration of feeling he was one of the bucks and bloods.

He stomped into the tiny, dark hall of the vicarage and was pulled up short by the sight of his daughter, Daphne. She was standing in front of the hall looking-glass, staring at her reflection with a rapt expression on her face.

'Go to your room, miss,' snapped the vicar, 'and stop endlessly preening yourself. And send Deirdre to my study.'

Daphne leaned forward, closer to the glass, and patted one glossy black ringlet into place.

'Yes, Papa,' she said vaguely as she drifted towards the stairs.

'Grumph!' said the vicar. He shoved his head round the door of the vicarage parlour. His wife was lying on a sofa. She raised a brown mask of a face in his direction.

'Gad's 'Oonds!' shrieked the vicar. 'What ..?'

'It's mud,' said his wife, moving her lips as little as possible. ' 'Tis said to be most beneficial.'

'Pah!' snorted the vicar, pulling shut the door and crossing the hall to his study. Mrs Armitage, when not suffering from some imaginary illness or other, was always trying our beauty remedies. He rang the bell for Betty, the housemaid, and demanded a bottle of white brandy and a jug of hot water. The maid went to light the fire but he growled that he would do it himself. As soon as the brandy had arrived, he poured a generous measure into a pewter tankard and added hot water. Then he threw another measure of brandy over the sticks in the grate and struck a lucifer. The fire went up with a satisfying *whoosh*, nearly singeing his eyebrows. He tossed on a log and settled himself behind his cluttered desk.

The door opened and Miss Deirdre Armitage walked in. The vicar looked at her, sighed, and looked quickly away again. Everyone called Deirdre a beauty but her father always thought, uncomfortably, that his daughter reminded him of a fox.

She had thick, shining red hair and green eyes, not the emerald green of Lord Sylvester, but a peculiar jade green like sea-washed glass. They were slightly tilted at the corners. This, together with her short straight nose, high cheekbones and pointed chin gave her an elfin appearance. She had a small, high, firm bosom, a tiny waist, and thin, fragile wrists and ankles. But there always seemed to be some inner joke amusing Deirdre and that was what made the vicar think of a fox. He sometimes thought her sly.

'Well, Papa,' said Deirdre, sitting down opposite

10

him, 'and how was Squire Radford?'

'How did you know I'd been to squire's?'

'Because your coat is in the hall, Papa, and it is wet, and you look guilty and in a bad temper which is the way you always look when you come from Squire Radford.'

'See here, my pert miss, it's time you guarded that tongue o' yours. No man wants a carroty-pated clever shrew for a wife.'

Those green eyes of Deirdre's that gave so little away studied him intently.

'I am to have a Season next year, Papa,' said Deirdre at last. 'Minerva has promised to bring me out. I ... am ... looking ... forward ... to ... it ... very ... much,' she added, slowly and clearly.

'Oh, ah,' said the vicar studying the bottom of his tankard.

'And 'I shall not put myself through any of the miseries Minerva and Annabelle endured. I shall *know* when I am in love with a gentleman.'

'Oh, *love.* You've been reading novels again. Love has little to do with a good, sensible marriage.'

'On the contrary,' said Deirdre firmly, 'it is everything. As a man of God, Papa, you would naturally never dream of forcing one of your daughters into a loveless marriage contract.'

'Minerva was prepared to,' pointed out the vicar crossly.

'She was fortunate she did nor have to do it,' said Deirdre. 'What did you wish to speak to me about?'

The vicar thought rapidly. No need to cross swords with Deirdre until he had seen this Lord Harry Desire. Perhaps nothing would come of it. And he could always wait until one or both his sons-in-law returned from Paris. But he had asked them for money before, and he knew that this time Lord Sylvester Comfrey might take over the management of the vicarage lands himself as he had threatened to do last time. And Lord Sylvester considered the vicar's private hunt an extravagance.

'I just wanted to tell you I am off to Town in the morning,' he said grumpily. 'So be a good girl and look after your mother and sisters.'

'Oh, Papa,' said Deirdre, her strange eyes shining in the firelight, 'take me with you. *Please.* It is so boring here. Daphne is no fun any longer. All she does now is droop in front of the looking-glass.'

'No. You've your duties. You've got to read to Lady Wentwater. Then you'd best take some cordial to Mrs Briggs what's poorly.'

'What about your sermon?'

'Let Pettifor handle it.' Mr Pettifor was the vicar's overworked curate. 'Time enough for you to be jauntering to London when Minerva gets home.'

When Deirdre reached the privacy of her room, she found her hands were shaking. She knew the vicarage finances were at low ebb. She knew her father probably planned to rescue them by marrying her off to some rich man who would provide a large marriage settlement. Then she smiled to herself and began to relax.

Although she had met many young men when she had visited her two sisters' homes, not one of them had shown more than a passing interest in her. She knew she was always damned as a blue-stocking but that suited her very well. Deirdre was an intense romantic and believed in the marriage of true minds. She was content to wait. And Minerva would not allow Papa to force her into any marriage she found distasteful.

12

'If she complains to Minerva, then Minerva will put a stop to it,' mused the vicar as he set out for London on the following morning. 'Well, I'll put a spoke in *that* wheel. I'll give a guinea to John-postboy to drop her letters to Paris down the nearest well until I give him leave to do otherwise.' His conscience gave a sudden, vicious stab. But he started to recite the names of his hounds like a litany to comfort himself. Not one would have to be sacrificed if his plans came out right. He had made a few mistakes in breeding, but now he was sure he was on his way to owning the best pack in England. Women were always bleating about love and marriage anyway. It was an attitude. The poor dears were supposed to think that way. Now he, Charles Armitage, had never loved his wife and if he could put up with her plaguey maunderings and moanings for all these years, then so could anyone else, he reasoned, rather incoherently. And women were the lesser breed. Definitely.

Like Lord Chesterfield, he considered women to be 'children of a larger growth', and 'a man of sense only trifles with them, plays with them, humours and flatters them as he does with a sprightly forward child.'

By the time he had reached Town and had made use of his daughter Minerva's town house, he was once more happy within himself.

Barbered and pomaded and laced into a pair of Cumberland corsets under a sky-blue coat of Bath superfine and the latest thing in canary-coloured pantaloons, the vicar creaked and swaggered his

13

way down St James's Street and turned in at the door of White's.

White's Club had changed little since the vicar's salad days, although the entrance had been moved lower down and the old doorway turned into a bow window. The subscription fee had been raised to eleven guineas and the entrance fee from ten to twenty guineas. Beau Brummell passed fashionable judgement on London from his seat in the bow window.

Swift had called White's 'the common rendezvous of infamous sharpers and noble cullies' but White's was, in fact, *the* club. Certainly it was the place to hunt down such an Exquisite as Lord Harry Desire.

The club was remarkably quiet although it was three in the afternoon. It transpired there had been a heavy gambling session the night before and no doubt everyone was still sleeping off the effects. He espied Colonel Brian, and, after some hesitation, approached him.

The elderly colonel had been the paramour of Lady Godolphin, a distant relative of the vicar's wife who had brought out Minerva. Lady Godolphin, that ancient Mrs Malaprop of society, had believed the colonel to be married, when in fact his wife was dead. The colonel had put all that right by asking her to marry him. He had been accepted. For a month afterwards, Lady Godolphin had talked of little else but the preparation of her torso—her word for trousseau—and then, quite suddenly, it had all fizzled out. The gossips would have it that the colonel had jilted her. But no one could find the truth of the matter since both parties refused to discuss the subject.

'I say, Colonel,' said the vicar breezily, 'I haven't seen you this age. You do not seem to be in plump currant.'

For the colonel looked sadly woebegone.

The colonel looked carefully at the painted and groomed vicar for several moments and then his face cleared. 'Charles Armitage!' he exclaimed. 'I would not have known you.'

'Course not,' said the vicar with awful vanity. 'I've growed fashionable.'

'Quite,' said the colonel nervously, taking a step back to escape from the overpowering smell of musk which hovered round Mr Armitage like a great yellow cloud. 'How are your girls? Well, I trust?'

'Minerva and Annabelle are in Paris.'

'The whole of society seems to be in Paris,' sighed the colonel. 'The town is remarkably thin of company. It will be a drab Little Season.'

'I plan to call on Lady Godolphin later,' said the vicar airily. 'Care to accompany me?'

The colonel shook his head sadly, and looked at the floor.

The vicar was longing to ask him the reason for his disaffection with Lady Godolphin, but the thought of his real reason for being in the club made him drop the question he had been about to ask, and demand instead, 'Know Harry Desire?'

'Slightly. I saw him a minute ago.'

'I would like an introduction,' said the vicar. 'I have a private and personal matter I wish to discuss with him.'

'Very well,' said Colonel Brian. 'He is in the coffee room. If you would do me a small favour in return ..?'

'By all means.'

'When you call on Lady Godolphin, tell her Arthur sends his warmest regards. No. Do nor ask me anything.'

'"Arthur sends his warmest regards,"' repeated the vicar impatiently. 'Now, lead me to Desire.'

Lord Harry Desire was sitting barricaded behind a newspaper in the coffee room. He looked up as the colonel stood behind him and cleared his throat. Colonel Brian then introduced the vicar and took his leave.

The vicar sat down opposite Lord Harry and studied him intently.

Lord Harry stared back, his gaze empty, blue and limpid.

He was not quite the fashionable rakish Exquisite the vicar had expected. The first thing that struck the vicar was the man's incredible beauty. Lord Harry had thick, black, glossy hair falling in artistic disarray over a broad white forehead. His blue eyes were clear and innocent like the eyes of a child. The lids were curved, giving him the lazy, sensual look of some classical statues. His mouth was firm, but there was a certain air of languid effeminacy about him caused by the girlish purity of his skin and by the slimness of his tall figure.

His clothes were beautifully tailored, reflected the vicar with a pang of envy. His bottle-green coat sat on his shoulders without a wrinkle and his buff-coloured pantaloons looked as if they had been painted on to his legs. His hessian boots shone like black glass. His cravat rose from above his striped waistcoat in intricately sculptured folds.

'You're younger than 'I thought,' said the vicar abruptly.

'I am remarkably well-preserved for my thirty years,' said Lord Harry earnestly.

'Aye well, just so,' said the vicar.

There was a long silence. Outside, someone was murdering Mozart on a barrel organ.

'Well, well,' said the vicar, rubbing his chubby hands together. 'Well, well, well,'

Lord Harry continued to survey him with a pleasant smiling look.

'You must wonder what it is I want to speak to you about,' said the vicar desperately.

'Oh, no,' said Lord Harry gently. 'I never wonder about anything. It is too fatiguing. And I am sure you will tell me in your own good time.'

The vicar looked at him in irritation. Then he thought instead of the nabob uncle's fortune and leaned forwards and patted Lord Harry's knee in an avuncular manner.

Lord Harry looked at the vicar, looked at the hand on his knee, and looked at the vicar again. His expression did not change, but the vicar's face reddened and he hurriedly withdrew his hand.

'See, it's like this here,' said the Reverend Charles Armitage, beginning to perspire, 'I heard you was in need of getting married so you could inherit your uncle's fortune.'

Lord Harry surveyed him blandly. The vicar felt himself becoming angry. Why didn't the young clod *say* something? This was worse than he had imagined it would be. Better get to the point.

'I have this daughter, see. Deirdre. Eighteen. Beautiful. I ain't got the blunt, you need the wife, what say we strike a bargain?'

17

A flicker of something glinted in his lordship's blue eyes and then was gone.

'Indeed!' he said politely.

'Well?' said the vicar impatiently. 'What about it?'

'Does she have red hair?' asked Lord Harry, looking vaguely in the direction of the chandelier. 'I can't abide red hair.'

'Dye,' decided the vicar to himself. He thought briefly of God the way one thinks of a nagging, bullying parent, slightly closed his eyes, took a deep breath and said, 'No.'

'And she is in Town?'

'No,' said the vicar. 'But she will be. In four days' time.'

'I met your eldest daughter,' mused Lord Harry. 'Lady Sylvester Comfrey. Very beautiful and very wise. She told me how she despised men who put pride in dress before pride in leading a virtuous life.'

'Oh, Minerva will have her little joke,' said the vicar jovially, privately cursing his eldest for her priggish moralizing.

'Is your daughter—Deirdre—vastly clever?'

The vicar looked at Lord Harry from out of the corner of his little shoe-button eyes and wondered whether Lord Harry wanted a clever wife. Lord Harry looked back with an expression of absolute vacancy on his beautiful face.

'Oh, no,' said the vicar. 'Very womanly. Pretty little thing. Domesticated. Been well-trained. See here,' he went on, improvizing rapidly, 'she will be staying with Lady Godolphin next Monday and we shall be having a little *musicale*. Perhaps you would like to attend?'

There was a long silence. A bluebottle, brave survivor of summer, buzzed against the glass. A log shifted on the fire and several clocks began to chime the half hour.

'Yes,' said Lord Harry at last. 'I will be there.'

'Good, good, send you a card,' gabbled the vicar, now desperate to escape.

Lord Harry raised one long, slim, white hand as the vicar rose to his feet.

'You are sure your daughter's affections are not otherwise engaged?'

'No,' said the vicar, glad to be able to tell the truth at last. 'Deirdre's never even looked at a man, if you know what I mean.'

'No, I don't,' said Lord Harry pleasantly.

'Well, don't trouble your brain with it,' said the vicar, patting him on the shoulder. 'We look forward to the pleasure of your company on Monday.'

'What an idiot!' muttered the vicar to himself as he left the club. 'Never mind. He's a manageable idiot and Deirdre will be quite happy with a complacent husband.'

He set off at a brisk pace in the direction of Lady Godolphin's house.

He needed all the help he could get!

TWO

Deirdre Armitage sat reading a novel she did not like to Lady Wentwater whom she did not like either.

The drawing room was dark and musty. Lady

Wentwater was white and doughy and musty. As she read, Deirdre wondered about Lady Wentwater's nephew, Guy. No one had seen him in the county since the time it had seemed he was enamoured of Annabelle.

Rumour had it that the vicar had frightened him away. Guy Wentwater had said he was a slave trader, and although he had long quit that ghastly means of earning money, the Armitage family were happy that he chose to stay away.

Then Deirdre's thoughts turned to the story she was reading. It was called *Ludovic's Revenge* by A Lady of Quality and Deirdre judged it quite the silliest tale she had ever read. Everyone seemed either to turn scarlet or go 'ashen pale'. Men and women fainted with amazing regularity and there wasn't even a decent ghost.

Deirdre took a quick glance at the clock. Then she closed the book firmly.

'It is late, Lady Wentwater,' she said. 'I must return home.'

'Then come tomorrow.'

'Daphne will come tomorrow,' said Deirdre, privately vowing to give her sister's hair a good yank if she did not.

'Oh, *Daphne*. I will need to shroud every looking glass in the house or I won't hear a word out of her,' snorted Lady Wentwater. 'Too taken up with herself, she is.'

'She has reason to be,' said Deirdre, who, though she privately agreed with Lady Wentwater, did not like criticism of any of her sisters. 'She has become even more beautiful than Minerva or Annabelle.'

'Aye, and she knows it. Why, Guy! When did you arrive?' Deirdre gave a little gasp and leapt to her feet, turning to face the monster slave trader.

Guy Wentworth stood smiling at her, looking so handsome, so normal, and so, yes, *ordinary* that Deirdre lost her fears and was able to drop him a curtsey with an air of composure.

'Permit me to escort you home, Miss ... Deirdre. It is Miss Deirdre, is it not?' smiled Guy.

Deirdre nodded, but added that she was perfectly capable of seeing herself home.

To her annoyance, he walked with her to the door.

'We have not seen you in some time, Mr Wentwater,' said Deirdre, praying that he would leave her at the main door.

'No, I have just returned from Paris. I finally sold out.'

'Sold out? Then you were in the military, sir?'

'Yes,' he sighed, looking grave. 'I know what you and your family think of me, Miss Deirdre. Have you ever considered the disgust I feel for myself? The barbarous trade I briefly engaged in was the senseless folly of a young man. I fought for my country at Waterloo. It was one way to prove to myself that I am not quite so evil.'

'Oh, tell me about Waterloo,' pleaded Deirdre, quite forgetting that she had wished only a moment before to be quit of him. 'Everyone says such subjects are not fit for female ears. But it was a wonderful victory.'

He gently took her arm in his and walked with her down the drive. His tale of glory and bravery and courage and death fascinated Deirdre, who hung rapt on his every word.

She could not help admiring his tall, slender figure, the quiet elegance of his dress, and the hard

21

lines about his mouth, 'put there by suffering,' she told herself.

They reached the vicarage all too soon.

He seemed to recollect his surroundings with a start. 'Forgive me,' he said in a low voice, 'if I do not come any further. I do not wish to embarrass your family. In fact, I would be grateful if you would not mention that I am in Hopeworth. It will be *our* secret.'

'Yes,' said Deirdre breathlessly, for he had taken her hand and was holding it in a tight clasp. 'But if I told them how brave you are, how you have made your amends ... well, they would see things differently *now*. As I do.'

'I cannot risk losing a friendship so new and so precious to me,' he said. 'Other people might not have your generosity of spirit.

'*I have* changed, Miss Deirdre. I have put away the shallow affections and affectations of my youth. The friendships I now crave are the friendships of the mind. Do you understand?'

'Oh, yes,' breathed Deirdre.

'Then I shall see you again. Perhaps you would care to walk with me tomorrow afternoon?'

Deirdre hesitated only for a moment. Guy Wentwater was straight out of her private fantasies, a reformed villain, a man of the world, an equal companion, a soul-mate. She felt full of an aching, heady, suffocating exhilaration.

'I will meet you in the churchyard,' she smiled. 'At two.'

He raised her hand to his lips.

'Until tomorrow,' he whispered.

He turned away and strode off down the road. Deirdre watched him for a few moments and then rushed indoors, up to her room, and threw herself face down on the bed, feeling her whole body throb in an aching turmoil of excitement and yearning. All the loneliness and boredom of her days had fled. Had she not known that if she waited there would be one special man? He had been a slave trader, yes. But so long ago. And he had made his amends and paid his debt.

Nothing could spoil her idyll. Papa needed money and Guy Wentwater had money.

Papa would come about. All he wanted was money to breed more and better hounds.

*   *   *

The Reverend Charles Armitage sat in the Green Saloon in Lady Godolphin's mansion in Hanover Square and poured out his tale of financial woe and the necessity of arranging a marriage between Deirdre and Lord Harry Desire.

'There, there,' admonished her ladyship when he had finished. 'There's no need to become historical. I can understand the practicality of an arranged marriage. We *all* need money,' she added firmly, in case the reverend had any hopes of asking her for any.

'So you'll do it?' asked the vicar. 'You'll house Deirdre and arrange this *musicale?*'

'Yes, provided you repay me when you can,' pointed out Lady Godolphin. 'You still look worried. What is the matter?'

'It's her hair,' said the vicar gloomily. 'She'll need to dye it. Desire can't abide red-heads.'

'No need to dye,' said Lady Godolphin. 'Wear a wig. I always do.'

23

She patted her flaxen wig complacently. Like the vicar, she battled the increasing years with a great deal of paint.

Lady Godolphin was in her late fifties, squat, with a bulldog face buried under a layer of blanc and rouge.

'He don't like clever misses either,' went on the vicar.

'Deirdre's a bit of a chatterbox,' said Lady Godolphin. 'Can't understand half what she says. Last time she was here, she was prosing on about bacon and I thought she meant pigs but it turned out she was talking about some Elizabethan philanderer.'

The vicar recollected his message. 'Saw Colonel Brian at White's today,' he remarked casually. 'Sends his warmest regards. Said, "Arthur sends his warmest regards."'

'Oh, he did, did he,' said Lady Godolphin airily. 'Trouble with Arthur is, he's too old for me.'

'Oh,' said the vicar hopefully, waiting for more.

But Lady Godolphin returned to the subject of Deirdre. 'Deirdre always was a bit wild, she and Daphne. Is Daphne still a hoyden?'

'No, she's grown vain. Looks at herself in the glass and does little else.'

'Ah, a narcotic,' said Lady Godolphin, nodding her great head wisely.

'A what?'

'A narcotic. Really, Charles, did they teach you nothing at Oxford? He was one of them Greeks what was so beautiful he wouldn't even have anything to do with echoes and he fell in love with his reflection in a pool, and since he couldn't marry his reflection, he pined away and turned into a

24

narcotic. It's that yellow and white flower.'

'I don't have anything to do with echoes either,' said the vicar in bewilderment.

'Oh, *stoopid,* echoes was not a them but a *her.'*

'It's all heathen talk,' said the vicar righteously. 'And a far lot o' good it did them Greeks either. Where are they now? Hey? Slavin' for a lot o' Turks.'

'In any case,' said Lady Godolphin firmly, 'you bring Deirdre to me and I'll have her married off in no time. Why, only think what ...'

The door opened and Lady Godolphin broke off and simpered girlishly and played with the sticks of her fan.

A young man entered. He was thin and gawky but dressed in the height of fashion, from his frizzed and pomaded hair to his boots with their high heels and fixed spurs. He walked forwards with that peculiarly rolling gait forced on anyone who wears fixed spurs. He wore more scent than the vicar and the vicar's musk met a strong aroma of 'Youth in Springtime'. It was as if two great fog banks of scent had merged, blotting out every other scent in the world.

'My ... er ... friend, Mr Anstey,' said Lady Godolphin, simpering quite horribly.

The vicar left as soon as he could. 'Poor Colonel Brian,' he thought. 'So *that's the* reason.'

The vicar of God told himself that perhaps he ought not to introduce his daughter to such a household. The huntsman dreamed of a pack which would outclass the Quorn, scented the wet, rotten bracken of damp November days when the wind blew from the east, saw his hounds bunched together 'so close you could cover them with a table

25

cloth.' The huntsman won.

* * *

The vicar had expected Deirdre to treat the news of her forthcoming visit to London and the glowing description of the superior qualities of one Lord Harry Desire with suspicion and with her usual impertinent questions. Never had he expected outright rebellion.

'No, Papa,' said Deirdre firmly. 'I wish to remain here.'

'Why?' demanded the vicar, almost pawing the ground.

'Because my duty is to stay home and care for my sisters,' said Deirdre with a saintly expression on her face reminiscent of her sister, Minerva, at her worst.

'Piffle,' said the vicar. 'That's your best gown you got on. It's a fellow. Who've you been fiddling about with as soon as my back is turned?'

'There is no one, Papa,' said Deirdre. How could she explain to this father of hers, who appeared to have harboured not one spiritual thought in the whole of his life, the purity of her friendship with Guy Wentwater? How could she explain the excitement of shared ideas, the tender sweet awakening of love so far above the petty lusts of men?

She thought of the meeting in the churchyard, of his serious grave voice, of the way his blue eyes met hers in a direct and open look.

'It's no use bamming me,' she went on. 'You've got a marriage arranged for me and all because you have squandered good money on a silly pack

26

of dogs.'

'WHAT!' Never had the vicar dreamed of hearing such a piece of blasphemy from one of his own daughters.

They were standing in the vicarage garden, facing each other across a flowerbed, their breath hanging in the frosty air like smoke.

'I'll get my whip,' said the vicar grimly. He turned on his heel and strode into the vicarage.

Deirdre stood frozen to the spot. He would not *dare!*

The vicar emerged brandishing his whip.

Deirdre turned and ran.

After her, hallooing and shouting came her father. Attired in a ridiculously thin muslin gown and thin silk slippers—for Deirdre had been loitering in the garden in the hope that Guy Wentwater would stroll past and see her—she picked up her skirts and fled off down the road with the vicar in hot pursuit.

Deirdre scrambled over a stile beside the road and set off over a ploughed field, feeling like a hunted fox.

The vicar's cries died away behind her, but she was still too shocked at the violence of her father's behaviour to slacken her pace.

Her dress was torn and muddy and her slippers were ruined. Her red hair flew about her face as she stumbled over the frost-hard earth of the fields behind the village, heading for the grounds of the Hall where her uncle, Sir Edwin, lived, knowing instinctively that that would be the last place the vicar would think of looking for her.

She scaled the mossy wall which bordered the grounds, hoping that one of her uncle's gamekeepers would not shoot her in mistake for a poacher.

The woods on either side of her were quiet and dark and still. Deirdre listened hard but could no longer hear any sound of her father's noisy pursuit. She stood still, her heart beating hard. What would happen when she returned to the vicarage, as return she must? There was no Minerva to intercede for her.

She was filled with a sudden, suffocating hatred for her father. Why couldn't he behave like the clergyman he was supposed to be? The vicar of St Ann's in Hopeminster was a quiet, scholarly, aesthetic man, quite unlike her father. When the vicar wasn't reeking of musk he smelled of the stables and seemed to be perpetually covered in dog hair.

The whole vicarage smelled of damp dog, thought Deirdre savagely. Here she was with a whole new love; trembling, innocent and fragile. And there was the vicar, scouring the lanes of Hopeworth for her with his whip in his hands.

'No one understands me except Guy,' whispered Deirdre to the uncaring trees.

In desperation, she sank to her knees and prayed to God for aid. She prayed long and feverishly while a pair of squirrels chattered above her head and a curious rabbit stared at her with unblinking eyes.

And then, all at once, He spoke to her. She could hear a voice in her head telling her exactly what to do.

She must return to the vicarage and apologize to her father and say she would go with him to London. While there, she would make sure this

Lord Harry Desire took her in such dislike, he would never want to see her again. Then when she returned in respectable disgrace to Hopeworth, she would seek out Guy and ask him to elope with her.

A great calmness descended on Deirdre. It is quite amazing how the Almighty can occasionally tell people to go ahead and do exactly what they want to do anyway. Only very devout people manage to muddle along as best they can without hearing voices or the whirr of wings.

Feeling exalted and noble, Deirdre brushed down her skirts and made her way back home.

The vicar was already feeling ashamed of his outburst of anger. By the time he had cooled himself off with several glasses of shrub at The Six Jolly Beggarmen, he had decided to return home and wait for Deirdre. When she returned, he would simply order her very calmly and quietly to see to the packing of her trunks. His cool dignity would overawe her.

But to his relief—for this calm and dignified picture of himself was beginning to fade by the time he reached the vicarage—Deirdre was waiting to give him a very pretty apology.

The vicar's normal shrewdness deserted him before the pleasure at having got his own way so easily.

Diana and Frederica accepted the news of Deirdre's forthcoming trip to London with all the aplomb of two little girls who were used to their elder sisters jauntering about in the great world. Both still attended the seminary at Hopeminster, the vicar's plans for hiring a governess having never come to anything. Daphne alone seemed shaken out of her narcissistic calm, and started to write out a long shopping list for Deirdre which contained, it appeared, the name of every beauty cosmetic to be had in London.

Mellowed by several glasses of port, the vicar leaned back in his chair after supper and surveyed his family indulgently.

He caught Deirdre looking at him with the sort of blazing green gaze he had seen in the eyes of cornered animals. But as soon as she noticed his suddenly sharpened expression, Deirdre immediately cast her eyes meekly down and presented a demure picture of a dutiful daughter.

Deirdre felt she was seeing her father for the first time. Her acid eye took in the glory of his too-tight coat, his flushed face, the creak of his corsets. Her very biting contempt was armour to her bruised soul. Such a father *deserved* to be deceived. And her mother had never been any help, wrapped up as she was in her various ailments.

All at once, she became aware he was talking about Guy. 'I hear young Wentwater's back,' said the vicar. 'Strange thing about the Wentwaters. Lady Wentwater came to live here nigh on twenty years ago. No one's ever heard of a Lord Wentwater and she don't figure in the peerage. I've asked her time and again about her late husband, but she always goes deaf. But she's a harmless old lady. Pity the same can't be said about her nephew.'

'Hardly, Papa,' said Deirdre sweetly. 'Since no one in their right mind could call Mr Wentwater an old lady.'

The vicar looked at her sharply but she had cast her eyes down again.

'Hey, well,' he said. 'So long as he don't come nosing around here like a fox after the hens. How

30

Bella could have been so stupid as to even look at the man ...'

'We all thought him well enough,' pointed out Mrs Armitage languidly, 'until he told us the nature of his trade. You yourself could find no fault with him up until then, Mr Armitage.'

'That's fustian. 'I ...' The vicar broke off and stared at the ceiling in a puzzled way. 'How can it be leakin' in here. Better run upstairs and see if the bedrooms are flooded.'

'It's not the rain,' said Deirdre. 'It's Betty. She's crying,' she added as the maid whipped herself out of the dining room.

'What's she got to cry about?'

'Crying is quite benefacial to the eyes,' said Mrs Armitage, with sudden enthusiasm. 'It exercises the retina.'

'Betty is crying,' said Deirdre, loudly and clearly, 'because she was promised two years ago that she could leave our employ and marry John Summer.' John Summer was the vicarage coachman. He also acted as groom, whipper-in and kennel master.

'Well, she'll just need to wait,' said the vicar testily. 'Can't have servants marrying. Never heard of such a thing. We can't afford another maid at the moment, and we can't afford to pay John Summer enough to set up a household. So there!'

Deirdre thought bitterly of the vast amount of money that had gone to buy new hounds and new hunters and opened her mouth to make an acid retort. But then she remembered her plan and kept silent.

At last the evening meal was over and the girls collected their bed candles from the table in the hall and mounted the stairs to their rooms.

31

With the departure of Minerva and Annabelle from the family nest, Daphne and Deirdre each had a room to themselves, while Diana and Frederica still shared their old room.

The storm had died down. Deirdre opened the window and leaned out. The chill fresh air smelled of damp, rotting leaves and evergreen.

The figure of a man appeared beyond the high hedge which bordered the vicarage garden, his stock gleaming whitely in the darkness.

'Guy,' murmured Deirdre, her heart beginning to hammer against her ribs.

She threw a cloak over her shoulders and crept out of her room and slowly down the stairs, walking on the edge of each foot so as not to make a sound.

The rumble of her father's voice, and her mother's faint high-pitched replies filtered through the parlour door.

She stood very still in the hall. Betty and cook would still be in the kitchen. The hall door was not yet locked and bolted for the night. She would have to try to get out that way and pray that she did not make a noise or that her father would not choose to look out the parlour window as she made her way down the drive.

The hall door opened with a snap of its hinges like a pistol shot. Deirdre froze, already thinking up excuses. But the voices in the parlour went on, and the clatter of dishes sounded from the kitchen.

She slipped quietly out, forcing herself to rake time to close the door slowly and carefully behind her. She made her way down the drive, keeping to the black shadow of the yew trees, for a treacherous moon was bathing everything in a silvery glow.

The iron gate wailed like a banshee, but Deirdre

could no longer school herself to wait for possible repercussions. She let it swing behind her with a clang and ran out into the road, looking this way and that.

No one.

She gave a little gasp of disappointment, and then a gasp of fear as an arm came from behind and slid round her waist. She whirled about.

'Guy!'

'I thought you might see me and come looking for me,' he whispered. 'Walk with me a little way. Will they miss you?'

Deirdre shook her head, thinking how handsome he looked in the moonlight with his teeth gleaming white and his eyes glinting in an exciting way.

Her father's remark about a fox after the hens came into her mind, and she said nervously, 'I *hate* this furtive meeting. Oh, how I wish you could call at the vicarage and that papa would be *sensible.*'

'I came because someone told me your father was chasing you with a whip,' he said in a low serious voice. 'I could not sleep. I was worried about you. Believe me, I do not like these clandestine meetings either.'

'Is it not amazing?' said Deirdre softly, 'we should become such friends? It is as if our minds were twins.'

'I think it is because I am tired of simpering, giggling females,' said Guy. 'I admire a woman with a *brain*. Oh, I confess your sister, Annabelle, dazzled me with her beauty, but that was before I learned some sense.'

'Yes,' said Deirdre in tepid agreement. She would have liked Mr Wentwater to say he was dazzled with *her* beauty as well as her brain.

33

'Oh, Mr Wentwater,' said Deirdre, stopping in the moonlit lane, and clutching hold of both his hands, 'I must tell you. The most dreadful thing has happened.'

The wind sighed over their heads and a shower of damp leaves blew about them.

'Tell me. Why was your father chasing you? If there is anything I can do to help?' said Guy, pressing her hands and holding them to his chest.

'Papa has a marriage *arranged* for me. I am to go to London tomorrow and stay with Lady Godolphin so that some creature called Lord Harry Desire can look me over, check my teeth, and say whether he will have me or nay.'

'This is outrageous! Your father already has two rich marriages in the family. What does he need with another?'

Deirdre sighed and the wind over the high hedges on either side of the road seemed to pick up the sigh and send it blowing across the bare autumn fields. 'We are in low funds again,' she said.

'Papa spends a great deal of money on the hunt. This Lord Desire must marry in order to inherit his uncle's fortune, he needs a wife, Papa needs the money, I am to be the sacrifice.'

He released her hands and turned a little away from her so that his face was in the shadows. Deirdre waited, straining to hear him say that he would marry her himself.

'I had hoped,' he said at last, 'that we might come to know each other better ... that I might establish myself with the county and come to be on calling terms with your family. We have really only just met.'

He gave an awkward laugh. Deirdre shivered

34

and pulled her cloak tightly about her shoulders.

'But,' he brightened. 'There is no guarantee this Lord Harry will want to marry you. Then you may return home and we can all be comfortable again.' He chuckled. 'I am sure you will know precisely just how to give him a disgust of you. An intelligent woman like yourself ...'

'Oh, Guy, how our minds do run together,' said Deirdre, forgetting her disappointment in him. 'Thar is *exactly* what I plan to do.'

'You must return,' he said, tucking her arm in his and leading her back towards the vicarage. 'I do not want your father to get out his pack and hunt me out of the county again.'

'What!' Deirdre stood still, and Guy cursed himself for the temporary slip. She obviously had not heard of his humiliation at the hands of the vicar. She must never know how much he hated her father for that day when he had been hounded, literally, down the summer roads with the vicar's pack in full cry behind him. She must never guess how he had dreamed and plotted revenge. She must never guess that her one attraction for him was that he saw her as an instrument of revenge.

'Papa did *what?*' pursued Deirdre.

He laughed and tugged at her arm so that she had, perforce, to fall into step beside him. 'You misunderstood me. I meant, I *hope* Mr Armitage doesn't hunt me down. A joke, you see.'

The parlour lamps were out and the house was in darkness. It would be even more difficult getting back, thought Deirdre. For this time, she did not know where her father was.

But the magic of Guy's presence gave her courage. She glanced up at the firm line of his jaw, the whiteness of his clean linen, his handsome profile, and felt almost unworthy of such an escort. He was worlds removed from her ranting, vulgar father and his petty machinations.

'Goodnight,' he said softly, holding open the gate, and pulling it gently closed behind her.

She turned and faced him through the bars of the tall gate, feeling the cold bite of the iron on her ungloved hands.

'Goodnight,' she echoed softly.

He leaned forwards, and she leaned towards him as well. He kissed her very gently through the bars; a fleeting, chaste kiss.

Deirdre's face blazed with naked love and adoration and Guy watched her intently, feeling a surge of power.

Deirdre floated into the house, not even noticing that the hall door was still unlocked, not even trying to creep quietly up the stairs.

Had her father confronted her at that moment, then Deirdre would have confessed her love, and her idyll with Guy Wentwater would definitely have been over.

But no one met her on the stairs and she reached her bedroom without seeing a soul.

For a long time she sat beside the window, lost in dreams.

Tomorrow, she would go to London. On Monday, she would meet Lord Harry Desire.

And if she played her cards aright, she would be back home very shortly after that, unengaged, and free to pursue her romance with Guy.

After such a failure, her father would surely be glad to marry her off to *anyone*.

THREE

'If you do not help me, Betty,' said Deirdre Armitage severely, 'I will make sure you slave at the vicarage until the end of your days and die a spinster.'

'If you don't do as vicar says,' sniffed the maid, Betty, 'then you won't be getting married to anyone neither, what with Mr Armitage not having any money and Miss Minerva and Miss Bella being gone to heathen parts.'

'Lady Sylvester and Lady Peter to you, miss,' said Deirdre tartly. 'Don't be a grouch, Betty,' she went on in a wheedling tone. 'Everything will be all right when Minerva and Bella come back from Paris— Paris isn't heathenish, Betty. Think of the hats!— and I will *make* papa let you marry your John. But if you aid Papa in forcing me to wear that terrible wig, then I shall do all in my power to encourage him in the idea that we cannot afford to pay John Summer any more money.'

'But I'll get the blame o' it!' wailed Betty.

Deirdre was about to make her curtsey to Lord Harry Desire.

She had told Lady Godolphin that Betty would manage very well as lady's maid. Betty had been told to curl and arrange one of Lady Godolphin's second-best, nutty-brown wigs and to make sure not one offending red curl escaped from beneath it.

The gown which had been chosen for Deirdre by her father and Lady Godolphin was of white muslin embroidered with rosebuds, a dressmaking masterpiece which combined innocence with decadence to a nice degree. The bodice was cunningly boned at the back and fitted at the front to push up Deirdre's breasts into two mounds over the low neckline. The skirt was short enough to show almost the whole of her ankles.

'I know what to do,' said Deirdre. 'I will drop this wig in the basin of water and say it fell off my head when I was washing my face. *I* will take the blame. Come now. I will wear this scandalous dress.'

Betty had not been told of his lordship's aversion to red hair.

So after scowling doubtfully at Deirdre's hair and then at the wig, she suddenly smiled and said she was sure Lady Godolphin had 'been in her altitudes' when she gave the instructions. Anybody could see Miss Deirdre would look much better with her own hair, although it was a pity the rosebuds on her dress were so *pink,* not to mention the broad pink sash which tied under her bosom.

In other circumstances, Deirdre would have been terrified because, in a way, she was to be guest of honour. The *musicale* was simply a piece of stage management. But her aching, tender, delicate love for Guy Wentwater made her feel she could endure anything.

Instead of chiding herself for the speed with which she had fallen in love with a man of doubtful reputation, like many dazzled lovers before, she only prided herself on 'falling in love at first sight'. And like many another love-blinded girl, she was convinced that the rapport of her mind and Guy's was a rare and precious phenomenon.

She stood patiently while Betty dressed her and arranged her hair in an elaborate Grecian style, taught her by Annabelle's lady's maid.

Satisfied that the combination of pink and white muslin with her flaming red hair was sufficiently repellent, Deirdre completed the effect by putting a pink silk stole about her shoulders.

'I look quite dreadful, Betty,' said Deirdre gleefully, as she pirouetted in front of the long glass.

Betty surveyed her young mistress. The maid thought privately that Deirdre had never looked better. The pomade she had added to Deirdre's hair had darkened it to a deeper red, and the pink and white gown showed her excellent bosom and delicate ankles to perfection. The odd combination of pink and white with her red hair and green eyes made Deirdre look oddly and excitingly exotic. Betty decided it would not be wise to praise Miss Deirdre Armitage. Too much vanity had nearly ruined Miss Annabelle and was well on the way to ruining Miss Daphne.

'You'll do,' was all Betty said, and Deirdre went downstairs satisfied that her appearance was quite horrible.

Lord Harry Desire was lounging in quite the latest manner on a sofa in the drawing-room. It was hard to tell from the beautiful blankness of his expression what he was thinking.

At one point, he did put up his glass and stared about the room in a dazed sort of way.

With the exception of the still-not-present Deirdre Armitage and Mr Anstey, Lady Godolphin's simpering cicisbeo, there was no one else present under the age of fifty.

Lady Godolphin had not wanted his lordship's eye, or Deirdre's for that matter, to be attracted by anyone else. Even the soprano who was to star at the *musicale* was fat, florid and fifty and her accompanist turned the pages of the music with a shaking, liver-spotted hand.

Lord Harry recognized old Lady Chester who looked and smelled as if she had been brought out of moth balls for the occasion.

High cracked voices discussed humours and agues and spleen. Lady Godolphin looked the youngest present. She was enjoying herself because all this creaking old age about her made her feel rejuvenated.

But she joined in the conversational illness competition with relish by saying her doctor had told her she had rheumatism but she herself was convinced it was Arthur's Eitis.

She had moved onto a lively dissertation on her Haricot Veins when the door opened and Miss Deirdre Armitage came in.

Lady Godolphin sprang from her chair with amazing alacrity. The vicar uttered a loud oath which caused a shocked murmur of old voices and a fluttering of feathers.

'I'll pretend she's someone else,' thought Lady Godolphin, speeding across the room, 'and get her upstairs and into her wig as soon as possible.'

But right behind Deirdre, Colonel Arthur Brian made his appearance.

Lady Godolphin blushed like a schoolgirl under her paint. She opened and shut her mouth but no sound emerged.

Deirdre smiled benignly on the company, made her curtsey, and walked in the direction of a single chair placed in the farthest corner of the room.

'Hey!' said the vicar, blocking her way. His little shoe-button eyes gleamed as hard as jet but he forced a jovial smile on his face. 'Come along, my girl. There's a handsome gentleman dying to make your acquaintance.'

'Delighted, Papa,' said Deirdre demurely, deliberately sinking in a low obeisance in front of an antediluvian gentleman by the name of Mr Sothers.

'Not him, you buffle-headed jade,' howled her father. There was a stunned silence and the vicar looked around wildly. 'Ha, ha, ha,' he said, baring his teeth in an awful grin. 'We will have our little family jokes. My Deirdre is a naughty puss.' He took his daughter firmly by the upper arm as if he were arresting her, and marched her over to Lord Harry.

Lord Harry Desire uncoiled himself from the depths of the sofa and stood up and made a magnificent bow.

Deirdre studied him from under her lashes with great amusement. This was going to be *much* easier than she had thought. He was a very handsome man, she reflected, but the sheer stupidity of his expression robbed him of any attraction he might otherwise have had.

He stood smiling down at her in a vacant, amiable manner.

'Sit down, sit down!' said the vicar heartily.

He gave his infuriating daughter a mighty push and she collapsed on to the sofa. Lord Harry sat down gracefully next to her and looked at her with a polite, social expression.

Deirdre played with the sticks of her fan.

'I went to the play the other night,' began Lord Harry amiably. 'Saw Mrs Siddons as Queen Catherine.'

There was a silence.

The vicar, hovering on Deirdre's other side, hissed, 'Well, *stoopid,* ask him how he liked it!'

'How did you like the play, my lord?' asked Deirdre dutifully.

'Very much,' said his lordship after a great deal of serious thought. 'I was wearing my cravat in a new style, entirely my own. Petersham said it looked like a frozen waterfall. But although I confess I was pleased at the compliment, I did not find it very apt. Sculptured snow would have been better, don't you think?'

'No,' said Deirdre. 'I have no interest in fashions whatsoever. My mind would have been on the play.'

A look of almost hellish glee lit up Lord Harry's lovely features but when Deirdre looked up to study the effect of her rudeness, his face was once more a correct and social blank.

'Do you know why you are here?' asked Lord Harry, as the vicar gave a great shrug and moved out of earshot.

'Yes,' said Deirdre. 'I am here to meet you.'

'Do you know *why* it is important you should meet me?'

'I believe my father has marriage in mind,' said Deirdre forthrightly. 'But, of course, as you can see, we should not suit at all.'

'Why, pray?'

Well, the answer to that one was, 'Because you are a stupid lummox and I am not,' but Deirdre felt she had already been rude enough.

She gave a little laugh. 'For a start, you may have noticed I have red hair. My father tells me you can't abide red hair.'

'Did I say that?' exclaimed Lord Harry. 'By Jove,

42

that's right, I did. You see, red hair in a lady has a terrible effect on me. I fall in love with ladies with red hair ... well, almost on sight.'

'Then it is as well that I am reputed to be something of a bluestocking,' said Deirdre quickly. 'For that will surely give you a disgust of me.'

'It certainly would if it were true,' said Lord Harry earnestly. 'But you may be easy on that score, Miss Deirdre, for I do not find you intelligent *at all.*'

Deirdre let out an outraged gasp but the angry retort died on her lips, for the soprano had commenced to sing.

Her name was Madame Vallini. She was possessed of a loud and piercing voice, the delight of the back rows of the gallery who could proudly claim to hear every note.

In a private drawing-room the effect was quite horrendous.

Under Deirdre's fascinated gaze, Lord Harry produced a snuff box from the tails of his morning coat. He flicked it open and took out a small white ball of wax. Then he produced a penknife from another pocket, neatly cut the wax in two, rolled each half in his fingers, and then solemnly popped the resultant wax plugs in each ear. He leaned back at his ease, half closed his eyes, and, it appeared, sent his mind off on a holiday.

'How Guy will laugh when I tell him about this coxcomb,' thought Deirdre with amusement.

Then a great wave of sadness engulfed her.

Guy.

Oh, to be back in Hopeworth, walking along the country lanes under the clean, windy country sky, listening to the sound of his voice.

43

Papa would *not* understand, she realized. How could someone as earthy as her father grasp the spirituality of the meeting and joining of two souls. Guy had talked to her of the army, of the great Battle of Waterloo. He had treated her as an equal.

Two large tears trembled on the edge of Deirdre's long lashes.

Through a hazy blur, she saw with surprise that her indolent companion was holding out a large serviceable pocket handkerchief.

She flushed, but took it, and dabbed at her eyes. He would presume she was affected by the music, thought Deirdre.

She knew that at some period when the singing was over, the vicar and Lady Godolphin would contrive to leave her alone with Lord Harry.

She must try to impress on him the downright unsuitability of this proposed alliance.

Then all at once Deirdre suddenly felt as if Guy were with her in the room, as if he were communicating with her in some way.

She smiled to herself. She knew, in a flash, where he was. He was sitting in the old little-used library in Lady Wentwater's dark mansion. He was leaning his chin on his hand, looking out over the shabby lawns, thinking of her.

All her loneliness and distress fled and she felt loved and comforted and sustained.

*   *   *

Not very far away, right at that moment, Guy Wentwater stretched his booted feet in the sawdust of Humbold's Coffee House and smiled at his companion, Silas Dubois.

44

He was nor paying much attention to Mr Dubois. The only reason he was enduring his company was because it had been thrust upon him and Mr Dubois had paid for the wine. Guy's thoughts were firmly focused on the black curls and white bosom of a girl who was strolling up and down the pavement outside.

He was just considering whether to leave abruptly and try his luck with her when a gentleman came up and bowed to the saucy girl and they walked off arm in arm.

Guy sighed regretfully. He would have liked to warm his bed with something like that.

He became aware that Mr Dubois was asking him a question. 'Ever see anything of the Armitage family?' Dubois was asking, his small eyes squinting over the promontory of his large nose.

'No,' said Guy Wentwater. 'The vicar and I had a certain argument once. I am not on calling terms. Not that it matters. A very provincial family.'

'And yet one that has done remarkably well in the marriage mart,' said Mr Dubois slowly.

'So I gather,' yawned Mr Wentwater. 'I hear he is going to marry Miss Deirdre off to Lord Desire.'

'So I hear in the clubs,' said Mr Dubois. 'That must mean the dear vicar is in low funds again.'

'Yes, the reverend has a good number of daughters in the bank, however.'

'Is this Deirdre as fair as Minerva and Annabelle Armitage?'

'Not really,' shrugged Guy. 'Foxy little thing with terribly red hair.'

'I wonder,' mused Mr Dubois, rubbing his one hand with the other. 'Would you say Minerva is particularly fond of this sister, Deirdre?'

45

'What a fascination the Armitage family does have for you,' sneered Guy. 'Minerva The Good is devoted to the whole pack o' them.'

'And she would be monstrous upset should anything go wrong?'

Guy looked at Silas Dubois narrowly.

'Oho!' he said. 'Now I begin to remember. Rumour had it that you fought Lord Sylvester in a duel over the fair Minerva and that Lord Sylvester shot the pistol clean out of your hand.'

'A trick, a fluke,' said Mr Dubois. 'He ruined my aim. I was the best shot in England before then.' He nursed his right hand.

'And you want revenge?'

'Why not?'

Guy Wentwater grinned. 'Then perhaps you might be interested in a little proposition which would serve both our ends. I, too, wish revenge on the Armitage family. Lean forwards and listen very carefully, very carefully indeed ...'

*   *   *

The soprano hit her last high note. There was an arthritic spattering of applause, and then the company began to rise, preparatory to moving to the dining-room.

'What is Arthur doing here?' demanded Lady Godolphin of the vicar.

Mr Armitage threw her a distracted look. 'I talked him into coming,' he said. 'You can't really be interested in that popinjay, Anstey.'

'I don't need to stand here and listen to your muddleactions,' said Lady Godolphin. 'I'll speak to you about it later. What we've got to do at the

46

moment is to get the guests into the dining-room and make sure Deirdre and Desire stay in this one. See?'

'Yes, yes, yes,' growled the vicar. 'Better leave it to me. I'll do it tactfully.'

Lady Godolphin looked at him doubtfully, but dutifully waddled off and soon her voice could be heard urging her guests to take a glass of 'Cannery of My-dearer.'

The vicar advanced on Deirdre and Lord Harry, who had risen to their feet.

'If you two are going to make up your minds about anything,' he said, 'you'd better start now.'

And with that, he turned round and shooed the remaining guests in front of him. Lord Harry tried to follow but the vicar stopped that by firmly closing the doors of the drawing-room right in his face, and firmly locking them on the other side.

'Oh, dear,' sighed Lord Harry. 'I am so very hungry.'

'You had better propose to me and be refused and that way we can get the whole silly business over with,' said Deirdre.

He took out his quizzing glass, polished it carefully, raised it to one eye and studied Deirdre carefully from head to foot.

'I *do* apologize,' said Deirdre, becoming flustered. 'I am very embarrassed, you see. I do not want to be married.'

'To me? Or to anyone?'

He had dropped the quizzing glass and his gaze was very level and kind.

'It is not that,' said Deirdre desperately. 'It's just ... oh well, it's just that I would like to become wed to a man of my choice.'

47

'That's natural,' he said equably. 'Now, I hare being forced to do anything. My nurse used to tell me to eat boiled cabbage because it was good for me and I've detested it ever since. You've been told this marriage is a good thing and so you detest the whole idea. You look on me and you see boiled cabbage.'

'Not quite,' giggled Deirdre nervously. He was standing very close to her. There was a disturbing, almost decadent aura of sensuality about him. She was all too aware of the firmness of his mouth and the breadth of his shoulders.

She wondered idiotically if they were padded. The rest of him was so slim. Except his legs, of course. One could not help noticing his legs since his trousers were so extremely close fitting. Perhaps he wore false calves. But when he moved, one could distinctly observe the hard ripple of muscle under the cloth ...

Deirdre blushed so violently, she turned almost as red as her hair.

'I have to get married, you know,' sighed Lord Harry. 'Well, I do not really *have* to, but I'm an expensive creature, you see, and uncle has bags and bags of money. Trouble is, I'm too lazy to run about the salons of London courting females. I thought this arrangement of your father's would save me a great deal of unnecessary effort.'

There was a gentle click from the door.

'The vicar has decided we have had time enough.'

'What shall I do?' asked Deirdre. 'I do so want to go home. I *hate* London. There is nothing for me here. If I say to Papa that we shall not suit, he will make me stay in London in the hope that

48

something will eventually come of it.'

'And you would love me more were I able to persuade the vicar to take you away to Hopeworth, say, tomorrow?'

'Oh, I would be most grateful.'

'Then it shall be arranged,' said Lord Harry comfortably. 'Let us go and join the other guests.'

Deirdre was only too glad to escape from him.

The elderly guests were piling plates high with delicacies from a buffet which had been set up in the dining-room. Lady Godolphin was having a bitter row in the corner with Colonel Brian and seemed unaware that Mr Anstey was paying assiduous court to Lady Chester.

Lord Harry began talking to the soprano. He seemed to have forgotten Deirdre Armitage's very existence. Deirdre saw her father bearing down on her and hurriedly engaged in conversation with the aged Earl of Derham.

Foiled of his prey, the vicar turned his beady gaze on Lord Harry who had just turned away from the *diva*.

While chatting to Lord Derham about the efficacy of vinegar and water to clean the spleen, Deirdre saw Lord Harry put his handsome head slightly on one side as he listened to whatever her father was saying. Then Lord Harry smiled and said a few words. The vicar looked delighted, clapped him on the shoulder and wrung his hand.

'Heavens!' thought Deirdre in dismay. 'That great fool has probably told Papa we are to be married. Nothing else would make Papa look so delighted.'

She hurriedly ended the conversation with the earl and edged cautiously in her father's direction.

He saw her coming and beamed on her.

'You're a sensible girl,' he said fondly. 'I always knew you had a shrewd head on your shoulders. When Desire told me this idea of yours that he should travel with us to Hopeworth on the morrow and stay with us until you both get better acquainted, I was fair flummoxed. I didn't expect you to be so sensible about the whole thing and that's a fact.

'"Soul, thou hast much goods laid up for many years; take thine ease, eat, drink, and be merry,"' quoted the vicar gleefully, reaching past Deirdre to grab a plate. 'I was that worrit, I been fair starving myself. But today I shall break my fast.'

Deirdre turned away to hide the blind fury of her face. 'The great fool!' she raged inwardly, cursing Lord Harry.

'But at least I shall be back home, and Guy will only need to see this idiot once to know that he must rescue me.

'Why, this Lord Harry is such a great ox, such a lumpkin, that he doesn't even realize I *don't* want to become better acquainted!

'Was there *ever* such a fool!'

FOUR

The vicarage had never seemed so small before. The arrival of Lord Harry seemed to reduce it, although it was a pleasant building with dining-room, drawing-room, parlour and study on the ground floor, six bedrooms on the first and the attics on the top. Deirdre and Daphne once more

50

had to share a room to allow bedroom space for Lord Harry since the dressing-room which had been the boys' bedroom was allocated to him for his personal use. The servants had to double up in the attics to make room for his Swiss.

Then there was the supremely elegant Lord Harry in residence. It was rather like buying a splendid new piece of furniture and noticing that the curtains were faded and the carpet worn.

To Deirdre, he made her home seem shabby and dark and poky.

She had carefully avoided being alone with him. Sir Edwin and his wife, learning of his presence, and, ever-anxious to secure a suitable *parti* for one of their daughters, and hearing that there had, as yet, been no mention of any official engagement to Miss Deirdre Armitage, had asked the whole family to a garden party by way of securing the attendance of Lord Harry. Deirdre had been praying for rain. She did nor like her uncle or his cold wife, or their silly, malicious daughters.

But then she overheard her father grumbling to his curate, Mr Pettifor, that Mr Wentwater was to be one of the guests, and, from that moment on, Deirdre could hardly wait for the Saturday of the garden party to arrive.

They had arrived from London on Wednesday morning. Already, it was Friday evening, and so far Deirdre had heard or seen nothing of Guy Wentwater.

She had sat Wednesday and Thursday evening by the window, looking out over the vicarage garden in the hope of seeing him walking in the lane.

She did not know he had been in London at the same time as she, for that vision of him sitting in the library, dreaming of her, was fixed in her mind. Besides, she had prayed to God for guidance, and although He had dealt her an unexpected blow by allowing Lord Harry to come on a visit, she was still sure He meant her to elope with Guy.

The vicarage was in a great bustle with preparations for the garden party. It was difficult to know what to wear. The Almanac promised a fine day. Should one freeze fashionably in muslin? Or be comfortable in wool?

Daphne would, of course, freeze. No sacrifice was too great. Fashion was all.

Had Minerva still been substitute mother, then they would all have had to dress sensibly. But Minerva was married. Minerva was in Paris, and Mrs Armitage had discovered a new and delicate complaint and had as little interest in what her daughters did, or did not do, as she always had evinced.

Deirdre heartily wished the elegant Lord Harry in hell.

He was too much of a favourite with her family for her comfort and they all seemed to see the marriage as good as arranged. In the parlour that evening, after supper, Lord Harry had been playing a noisy game of spillikins with Deirdre and Diana, recklessly gambling away his whole fortune and threatening to go out in the garden and shoot himself, much to Frederica's delight.

'This is worse than Waterloo,' he laughed, tugging Frederica's hair.

'How would *you* know?' asked Deirdre rudely.

There was a shocked silence.

'Deirdre!' said her father. 'I would see you in my study.'

Deirdre folded her lips in a mutinous line. Lord Harry's light husky voice was describing the typhoon which would surely strike the garden party tomorrow and even Daphne was giggling helplessly at the mad descriptions he was drawing.

The whole vicarage seemed too full of Lord Harry Desire, thought Deirdre crossly, as she followed her father across the hall to his study.

She had secretly hoped her family would take a dislike to this indolent, silly lord.

'Shut the door,' snapped her father, breaking into her thoughts. 'What was the meaning of that remark, miss?'

'What remark, Papa?' asked Deirdre sweetly.

'About Lord Harry not knowin' anything about Waterloo?'

'I thought it a just observation, Papa. There are many fine and brave men who fought at Waterloo. He should not dare even to suggest in a joke that he was one of them.'

'And why not? When he most certainly was.'

'You must be ...'

'See here, my girl, I had it from Lord Brothers that Harry Desire was one of the most courageous officers on the field. Just because the man don't preen and brag, don't mean he ain't brave.'

'I'm sorry, Papa,' said Deirdre meekly, although privately she hated Lord Harry the more for having made her look like a fool.

'I don't know what you've got in that brain-box of yourn,' went on the vicar. 'If there was another fellow in your life, I could understand it. Desire is an amiable chap. He's not too bright, I'll grant you that. He seems nearer Frederica's age than your own half the time. He listened to the belling of my

53

hounds and he said, "The bass is a trifle flat. You should have that animal tuned, don't you think?"

'But intelligence ain't fashionable and never was. He's a gentleman, and your true gentleman is stupid.'

'Would you describe yourself so?' asked Deirdre maliciously.

'Oh, I ain't stupid,' said the vicar seriously, 'but I've got the wit to hide the fact. Now, I've had letters from Minerva and Annabelle. Seems they think your come-out is to be next year. But we can't afford to wait.'

Deirdre clasped her hands and looked at her father with her strange green eyes. 'Papa, if I were to wed a man who had a great deal of money, you would surely not care what type of man he was?'

She looked at her father anxiously, Guy's name trembling on her lips.

'Course I would,' said the vicar stoutly. 'Imagine if our Bella were to have married that Guy Wentwater. He's to be at Edwin's garden party. I told Edwin, I did, "you ain't got any standards". Edwin says Wentwater ain't slave trading and has a mort o' money and he's thinking of him for Josephine or Emily, but I says to him, I'd rather we all starved than let that beast near the vicarage.'

All her new-found hate for her father burned twice as fiercely in Deirdre's bosom.

'I must write to Minerva and tell her of your plans, Papa,' she said.

The vicar looked at her narrowly, then he realized he had remembered to bribe the postboy. 'Very well,' he said with deceptive mildness. 'She's a sensible girl and would approve of my choice. I've been trying to leave you and Lord Harry alone together, but you always seem to make some excuse.

'Now he was brought here, I was told, so that the pair of you should get better acquainted. And you *are* going to get better acquainted, Deirdre Armitage.

'And that's an order!'

'Yes, Papa,' sighed Deirdre.

'It's a stupid idea of Edwin's, this here garden party. Whoever heard of a garden party nearly at the end of October? But the grounds of the Hall are pretty enough, and you make sure you and Lord Harry wander off somewhere.'

'Common, disgusting, *vulgar* man,' thought Deirdre, meaning the vicar.

Aloud she said, 'Yes,' now only wanting to escape.

'So go back in there,' said the vicar, 'and let's have no more rudeness from you, miss.'

There was no more rudeness from Deirdre because she did not address one remark to Lord Harry for the rest of the evening. At last, it was time for bed.

Once again, Deirdre sat by the window, watching to see if Guy would walk in the lane, waiting impatiently for Daphne to complete her lengthy bedtime toilet and go to sleep.

Daphne was fortunately too self-absorbed to wonder why her sister spent so much time sitting by the window instead of preparing for bed.

At last Daphne fell asleep, her head full of curl papers gleaming in the darkness.

And then the faint red glow of a cheroot stabbed the darkness of the lane. Deirdre stifled a gasp as she rubbed the pane of the window and peered out.

There was the tall figure, there was the familiar gleam of his white stock in the darkness.

She pulled on her cloak and scampered out of the vicarage, too excited even to try to be quiet.

White frost was gleaming on the grass and bushes of the garden. From the kennels, a hound sent up a melancholy howl to the moon. Stars burned in the black night sky.

Deirdre tugged open the gate and darted our into the lane.

At first she thought he had gone, and then she saw that red firefly of the lit end of the cheroot dancing at the turn in the road.

She scampered breathlessly along the lane and turned the corner. Nothing in front of her except the moon shining on the frost-white pebbles of the road.

Beyond the stile to the right, the little, tantalizing firefly of light danced across the fields.

Frightened to call out in case anyone heard her, Deirdre hitched up her skirt and climbed over the stile and then sped across the frost-hard rutted earth of the field until the tall, dark figure of a man loomed large at the edge of the woods. A cloud had crossed the moon, and she could only make out his silhouette.

'Wait!' she called breathlessly. 'Oh, please wait.'

He threw away the cheroot and turned to face her.

Filled with love and longing, she hurtled towards him and cannoned against his chest.

Strong arms went about her and she sighed and closed her eyes and turned up her face.

The kiss was all she had dreamed it would be, searing, burning, passionate, leaving her shaking and breathless. He loved her!

When he finally drew back, she gazed adoringly up at him. The fickle moon swam out from behind a cloud. The handsome features of Lord Harry Desire looked down at her.

'You!' said Deirdre, putting a hand to her mouth.

'Who else?' he replied, a note of laughter in his voice.

His arms were still tightly about her. Deirdre struggled to escape. She could not tell him about Guy. For he might tell her father.

'You have a pleasant way of furthering our acquaintance, Miss Deirdre,' said Lord Harry.

'I did not mean ... I was sleep-walking,' said Deirdre desperately. 'And I did not know who ... what I was doing.'

'Are you in the habit of kissing men when you sleep-walk? When we are married, I will need to keep you chained to the bedroom.'

'No. I have never done such a thing before. My lord, you are a gentleman. Pray let us return to the vicarage and say no more on the matter.'

'As you will,' he replied carelessly.

'But I cannot go *anywhere,*' pointed out Deirdre crossly. 'You are holding me so tightly.'

'So I am.' His eyes glinted down at her in the moonlight. 'I am cold, you see, and you are keeping me very warm.'

'Please let me go,' begged Deirdre. She looked wildly about. Mad fears of rape chased through her head. He no longer seemed the silly, indolent lord of the previous days. His masculinity was almost overwhelming and the hard strength of his arms about her made her feel helpless. He had all at once joined that mysterious world of men who told warm jokes, despised women, but undressed them with their eyes. That world of men she now realized she had always feared.

'Of course I will let you go,' he said soothingly. 'You must kiss me again, of course, for I cannot rest quietly tonight knowing I have been kissed by a beautiful young lady who was merely walking in her sleep.'

No, I will *not* kiss you again!'

'But you see I fear for your health. I feel sure your mother and father should be told of this dangerous malady of yours.'

'No, you must not. They would worry. It happens very rarely. Do not tease me.'

'Then kiss me.'

Deirdre's fears fled before a burst of sheer irritation. Only a *very* stupid man would keep boring on and on about a kiss when the girl in his arms so obviously wanted to escape.

'Very well,' she said testily. 'One kiss.'

She primped up her mouth and screwed her eyes shut. The next moment they flew open in surprise. For he had lifted her off her feet as if she weighed nothing at all. He had one arm behind her shoulders and the other under her knees. The moon sailed behind a cloud again, plunging them into darkness as his mouth descended on her own.

Just before his lips met hers, Deirdre thought savagely, 'Aha, *now* this coxcomb will see the difference ... now I know he is not Guy.'

His mouth seemed to cling to her own, moving gently against it while she waited listlessly for him to be done.

Then her treacherous body began to shake and

58

ache with all sorts of languorous pains. Her hand stole behind his neck, seemingly of its own volition, and buried itself in his thick curls.

He abruptly released her, swinging her lightly down to her feet, and steadying her with an arm about her shoulders.

She stood very still, looking down at the ground, sick, and shaken and frightened. This rampant lust that had briefly consumed her was terrifying. Love should not be like this. It should be sweet and pure: a delicate communing of minds, a meeting and merging of ideas.

Deirdre felt she had been unfaithful to Guy.

She glanced up at Lord Harry under her lashes. He had taken a flat case out of his pocket and was extracting another cheroot.

'What a beautiful night,' he said happily.

'You ... you will not tell my parents about ... about me sleep-walking?' said Deirdre in an odd harsh voice unlike her own.

'No,' he said gently, beginning to walk across the field. 'No, I think not. They might not believe me, you see. Your good father—who sometimes, if you will forgive me, Miss Deirdre, does seem to have evil thoughts for a man of the cloth, might jump to the conclusion that you had mistaken me for someone else.'

Deirdre stumbled and he caught her arm. She looked up at him anxiously and he smiled back, his eyes reflecting nothing more than a rather bovine good humour.

'Which would be very silly of him,' said Deirdre in a low voice.

'Which would be very silly,' agreed Lord Harry, 'since you kissed me back with the same warmth the second time as you did the first.'

'We will not discuss the matter any longer,' said Deirdre. 'Pray talk of something else. I learn from my father that you fought bravely at Waterloo.'

'I fought, yes.'

'Tell me about it,' demanded Deirdre.

'I don't want to talk about it,' he said lazily. 'I want to talk about your eyes. Do you ever wear jade earrings? I wish we were engaged so that I might buy you a pair.'

'I suppose you consider females too silly to hear stories about war.'

'The only people who want to hear stories about Waterloo are people who either were not there themselves or who have never fought in such a battle. It was not as the others, you know. It was slogging carnage and bloodshed.'

'A battle you obviously think England should not have fought.'

'Now, why would I think that? My French is quite atrocious, you know. I think that's why I had no desire to live under Napoleon. Also, think of their coats! Quite hideous, I assure you.'

'There is one man who has fought bravely at Waterloo and is not ashamed to talk about it,' said Deirdre, her voice tinged with contempt.

'Indeed! Who, pray?'

'You will meet him tomorrow.'

'Ah, I am to be surprised.'

'I think before we reach home, Lord Harry, that I should make it plain we do not suit. Oh, I am grareful to you for telling Papa you were coming on a visit so that I could leave London. But it is time to end this farce.'

'But I am very comfortable,' he said. 'I like your

60

family. I have not had much in the way of family life of late.'

'Do you have brothers and sisters?' she asked curiously, realizing how little she knew of him.

'I have three brothers, all younger than I, and two little sisters.'

'Do you visit your parents very often?'

'As little as possible.'

'I know what it is to detest one's parents,' said Deirdre in a bitter voice, feeling a kinship with him for the first time.

'I did not say I detested them,' he said airily. 'In fact I'm fond of them, but I prefer to live in town.'

He jumped nimbly over the stile and stood on the other side to lift her down.

'I am quite able to get over by myself, sir,' said Deirdre. But he appeared not to have heard. He held out both arms.

She gingerly put both her hands in his and prepared to jump down. But he tugged her forwards so that she fell down into his embrace.

Oh, treacherous, disgusting body with its melting lusts and palpitating nerves!

Deirdre wrenched herself free and stalked off down the road in front of him as gingerly as a cat.

He caught up with her. She glanced up at him and started at the look of shrewd, calculating intelligence on his face. But it must have been a trick of the moonlight, for the next second his lovely features looked as bland, stupid and good-humoured as ever.

The vicar met them at the gate. 'Well, now,' he said, rubbing his hands. 'That's what I like to see.'

Deirdre pushed past him and ran into the house.

That night, she cried herself to sleep.

The day of the picnic dawned bright and sunny. Deirdre's excitement had affected the other girls who were in a thoroughly strung-up state by the time they were at last ready to leave for the Hall.

Lord Harry had his own carriage and everyone assumed he would drive Deirdre, but Deirdre did not want to appear in his company. She wanted Guy to see her, unescorted, unspoken for, unattached. And so she talked Daphne into taking her place in Lord Harry's dashing phaeton and Daphne was only too ready to oblige.

Deirdre was wearing a jade-green silk gown with a pelisse of the same colour. A charming straw hat *à la bergère* all but hid her red curls. Roman sandals adorned her feet. The frost had melted from the grass and the air still had a sharp nip in it despite the glory of the sun.

She began to wish she had settled for wool. Of what use was a becoming gown if one's nose was red with cold?

All Sir Edwin's tenants had been invited as well as all the notables of the country. Deirdre was surprised to see John Summer driving a farm cart behind the family carriage, piled high with wood and bunting.

The reason for this became all too evident shortly after they had arrived. The vicar, it transpired, felt that garden parties should be in aid of something or other, and what better charity could there be but to raise funds to restore the roof of the church?

A booth was quickly erected, a placard asking for donations propped in front of it, and the beautiful

Daphne thrust behind it

Never had Deirdre seen her younger sister look so enraged.

Sir Edwin and Lady Edwin sailed forwards and neatly cut off Lord Harry and edged him gently towards their giggling daughters, Josephine and Emily.

Josephine and Emily were dressed in identical gowns of violent tartan. They wore enormous poke bonnets from which their giggles echoed as if emerging from the end of a tunnel.

A whole ox was being roasted to one side of the main lawn and members of the peasantry were sulkily dancing around a maypole on the other side, wearing Elizabethan costumes thrust on them by Lady Edwin.

Sir Edwin prided himself on being a good landlord and also prided himself on the fact that not one of his tenants had been known to starve to death. Of course, some of them were quite painfully thin, but, as Sir Edwin liked to point out, that was due to heredity.

Deirdre kept away from the crowds as much as possible. She was watching and waiting for Guy to arrive so that she could tell him of her plight and ask him to elope with her.

Lord Harry appeared to be perfectly happy to entertain Josephine and Emily.

All at once, Deirdre saw Guy with Lady Wentwater on his arm, entering by the south lawn.

But there was a great bustle as Lady Edwin marshalled the guests to the long trestle tables which had been erected down the centre of the front lawn.

Mrs Armitage swam into view. 'You must

help me, Deirdre,' she said plaintively. 'All that disgusting smell of roast meat makes me feel quite faint. Be a dear girl and find our where we are to sit.'

'I have found out, ma'm,' said Lord Harry, appearing at their side, a vision in blue cloth morning coat, white waistcoat and biscuit-coloured pantaloons. 'Allow me to escort you.'

He held out both arms. Deirdre bit her lip, looking towards Guy who was bowing before Lady Edwin.

He did not look in her direction once.

Deirdre longed to speak to him, to feel the reassuring touch of his hand, to see him smile.

He certainly paled before the glory of Lord Harry, but that made Guy Wentwater more attractive in her eyes than ever. In truth, Miss Deirdre Armitage was beginning to find Lord Harry Desire somewhat terrifying.

Only see the possessive way he helped her to sickening mounds of that disgusting meat and great horrible mountains of sausages and vegetables.

No, she did not want any game pie, she snapped, close to tears.

Josephine was seated on Lord Harry's other side and determined to make the most of it.

Guy was seated a little way down the table next to Emily. He was laughing and teasing her. Deirdre could not see Emily's face because of the long poke of the girl's bonnet, but the giggles and screams that were emerging from under the straw seemed to show she was well pleased with the attention she was getting.

And so the interminable meal went on, and on, and on.

64

Clouds covered the sun, the grass under Deirdre's sandalled feet, still wet from melted frost, seeped moisture through the thin soles of her sandals.

She kept squinting down her nose anxiously to see whether it was turning red with the cold, and Lord Harry smiled beautifully upon her and asked her if she were suffering from a fit of indigestion.

At long last, the steward rose to his feet and proposed a toast to the master, and the dutiful peasantry set up a ragged cheer. Many of them were secreting as much food about their person as they could.

Deirdre envied the squire who had his Indian servant standing behind him with armfuls of blankets, and, at a signal from his master, he would unwrap yet another one from the pile on his arm and deftly place it about the squire's thin shoulders.

Daphne was coughing and sneezing. She had arrived at the garden party in a vision of India muslin of the palest pink. Her forced inactivity on duty at the family fund-raising booth had brought her out in a rash of gooseflesh which seemed likely to become permanent, so blue and bumpy it looked. The low neckline of her gown revealed flesh above so blue and mottled, it looked as if she were wearing a blue gauze fichu.

At long last, the company was free to move about and inspect the gardens. Guy took Emily on his arm and headed off in the direction of the rose garden.

'Who is the fellow you said had been at Waterloo?' she realized Lord Harry was asking her.

'He has just gone towards the rose garden,' said Deirdre, coming to life at last. 'Oh, do let us go

65

there, my lord, and you may share reminiscences.'

'Very well,' he rejoined amiably, tucking her hand in his arm.

The rose garden boasted nothing more than a few frost-blackened, withered blooms but at least it was out of the chilly wind.

Guy was leaning nonchalantly against a sundial, whispering something to Emily, who was giggling and making patterns in the dust with the point of her parasol.

'Mr Wentwater!' cried Deirdre in a shrill voice.

'Oh, tish,' said Emily audibly. 'It's one of the pests from the vicarage.'

Deirdre marched forwards resolutely, almost pulling Lord Harry with her.

'Mr Wentwater,' repeated Deirdre when they had approached. 'Allow me to present Lord Harry Desire. Lord Harry, Mr Wentwater. Miss Emily Armitage, you have already met.'

Guy made his bow. A little silence fell. Lord Harry smiled blandly on the world, holding his curly-brimmed beaver and cane in one hand while the blustery breeze ruffled his glossy black curls. Emily darted a venomous look at Deirdre from the depths of her poke bonnet, like some small and vicious animal staring out of its hole.

'Well,' said Deirdre brightly, 'I felt I simply must bring you two gentlemen together. Lord Harry was at Waterloo as well, Mr Wentwater, and I am dying to hear your shared accounts of that great battle.'

'Good heavens!' cried Guy Wentwater. 'I hear my aunt calling me. She sounds in great distress.'

And he did look most flustered. He made an awkward bow and ran out of the rose garden.

Lord Harry took out his quizzing glass and gazed

66

through it at Guy Wentwater's rapidly retreating figure with interest.

'Marvellous ears that man has,' he murmured. 'Like a demned bat. Now, *I* couldn't hear a thing.'

'We had better go immediately,' said Deirdre. 'Lady Wentwater may be in need of help.'

She ran off in the direction Guy had taken without pausing to see whether the other two had any intention of following her.

But when she returned to the party, she could see no sign of Guy. The only loud noise was being made by her father and Sir Edwin. Sir Edwin was coldly stating that the introduction of a fund-raising booth to his fête was vulgar in the extreme, and the vicar was hurling biblical quotations at him, like so many stones.

Deirdre searched frantically, running hither and thither until she at last came on the squat figure of Lady Wentwater, sitting under an elm tree with Squire Radford, and sharing his blankets.

'Where is Mr Wentwater?' panted Deirdre, while the squire's kind eyes looked uncomfortably shrewd.

'Blessed if I know,' said Lady Wentwater. 'Why don't you look for him?'

'But I've looked and looked,' said Deirdre, clenching her hands into fists at her sides.

'What's amiss, then?' asked Lady Wentwater curiously. Her little currant eyes turned suddenly sly. 'Why do you *long* to see my nephew?'

'I don't long to see him at all,' said Deirdre, blushing red. 'And he said he heard you calling out in distress.'

'Not I. Keep on looking,' said her ladyship airily.

And Deirdre did.

She not only searched the grounds but the Hall as well. But of Guy Wentwater, she saw not the slightest sign.

Her misery was aggravated by the fact that when she left the Hall to enter the grounds again a thin, cold rain was falling.

The tenants were hurriedly leaving, taking as much food with them as they could discreetly carry, and the more illustrious guests were congregating in the drawing-room where tea was to be served. The Armitage family had already left, leaving Lord Harry with instructions to bring Deirdre home, or so Lady Edwin told her in glacial tones.

Deirdre did not want to go home with Lord Harry, did not want to be alone with his suffocating presence.

Using her parasol as an umbrella, she fled down the long drive and let herself out through the tall gates to begin the long, weary walk back to the vicarage.

The rain grew heavier and the village pond had developed smallpox as heavy drops pitted its smooth surface. The burning need to see Guy was like an ache. Suddenly she swung about and headed as fast as she could in the opposite direction, going towards Lady Wentwater's mansion.

She was a sorry mess by the time she reached the old ivy-covered house.

Sending up a fervent prayer that he would be at home, she gave the knocker a resounding bang.

The grim-faced maid evinced no surprise at the wet and bedraggled figure on the step. She led Deirdre into the dark and chilly drawing-room and said she would inform Mr Wentwater of Miss Armitage's call.

Deirdre paced up and down, shivering. Would he never come? If he did not hurry up, Lady Wentwater would be back and all pleas for an elopement impossible.

She had quite given up hope when the door opened and Guy walked in. He strode forwards and took her hands in his.

'What is this?' he exclaimed, standing back to survey her. 'You are soaked to the skin.'

'I *had* to see you,' said Deirdre. 'I am in the most awful trouble.'

'I thought you had decided to accept the marriage to Desire when I saw him return with you,' said Guy.

'But I haven't,' wailed Deirdre. 'It's you I love.'

There, it was out. She had said it. She waited anxiously for him to say he loved her as well, but he dropped her hands and stood very still, staring into the blackness of the empty fireplace.

'What do you want me to do?' he asked at last.

'Elope with me,' whispered Deirdre.

She was now afraid to look at him, terrified of his rejection.

The wind moaned in the trees outside and a spatter of rain hit the windows.

'Why not?' he said with a sudden laugh.

'Oh, Guy!' cried Deirdre thankfully. She waited eagerly for him to take her in his arms, but he only stood a little away from her, looking at her with a sort of brooding, calculating expression she could not understand.

'I have it!' he said at last. 'Meet me tomorrow at the Hopeminster crossroads. I am afraid you will have to walk. Bring very little with you. I will buy you any clothes you need.'

Deirdre wanted to run into his arms, to be held, to have all her worries and doubts soothed away. If only he would say he loved her.

There came the rattle of carriage wheels on the drive outside.

'My aunt!' exclaimed Guy. 'She must not find you here. I'll tell the maid to say nothing. Come with me and I will show you how to leave by the back way.'

He hustled her out of the drawing-room and through the house to where French windows opened from a little-used morning-room into the gardens at the back.

Guy wrenched at the rusty catch and all but pushed her out into the garden.

'Until tomorrow,' he said urgently. 'Meet me at the crossroads at two in the afternoon. Now *go!*'

'Guy,' pleaded Deirdre, hanging on to his arm. 'I do not want to force you to do this. Do you love me?'

'Of course,' he said, with a little laugh. He leaned forwards and kissed her on the lips, then gave her a little shove. 'Be off with you! We can talk tomorrow,' he added, firmly shutting the window on her.

Well, that was that, thought Deirdre, as she scurried through the wet gardens and slipped out by a small gate leading into a narrow lane which skirted the estate. All the long way home, she was worried and anxious. She had dreamed and fantasized that things would miraculously be splendid and beautiful if he said he loved her and said he would elope with her.

And he had!

But the worry and dread would not go away.

She could only be glad that no one saw her creep into the vicarage. She went up to her room and changed quickly into a comfortable old wool gown and towelled her hair dry, pinning it back from her face in a severe style.

How on earth was she to pack a couple of bandboxes—for she could not take any more—and escape from the vicarage unseen?

A way suggested itself at supper. Lord Harry was cheerfully planning a visit to Hopeminster the following day. Even Mrs Armitage had roused herself from her customary lethargy to express enthusiasm. The family decided to leave directly after morning service.

'I shall pretend to be sick,' thought Deirdre. 'And when they have all left for Hopeminster, I will make my escape. It would take her a full hour to walk to the crossing. The vicar kept eyeing his daughter throughout supper, noticing the feverish light in her green eyes and the pallor of her face.

His conscience smote him, and finally he listened to its harsh voice. It was a pity Deirdre showed no signs of forming a *tendre* for Lord Harry. But if the very idea was going to make her ill, then he would need to cancel the whole thing and write to Lord Sylvester and wheedle some money out of him.

The vicar's heart sank at this thought for he stood very much in awe of his elegant son-in-law; his other one, the Marquess of Brabington, could, on occasion, be even more formidable.

Lord Harry seemed in an unusually sombre mood. Knows she doesn't want him, thought the vicar gloomily.

He left the table as soon as he could and fled to the kennels to sit and tell his troubles to his hounds, which sometimes seemed to understand better than any human.

Deirdre was glad to escape to bed. She thought she would not possibly be able to sleep, but she fell asleep as soon as her head touched the pillow, worn out with worry and exhaustion.

The day dawned bright, glittering and cold. Ice had formed in the cans of washing water. While Daphne still slept, Deirdre sat chewing her nails and planning how to pretend to be ill.

But as it turned out, she did not have to pretend very much. The vicar had gone ahead to the church and the rest of the family and Lord Harry were all assembled in the parlour waiting for her when Deirdre walked in. She opened her mouth to tell her very well-rehearsed lies, closed it, and burst into tears instead, crying and crying as if her heart would break.

Daphne hustled her from the room and led her back upstairs.

'What is it Deirdre?' she asked in her soft voice, forgetting about her own appearance for once.

'I-I'm not well,' hiccupped Deirdre. 'I w-walked h-home in the rain yesterday, and ... and ... I must have caught a chill. My poor head aches so much. All I want is to be left alone. Please go to Hopeminster after the service without me.'

'I know what it's like,' said Daphne, stroking Deirdre's red curls. 'I get blinding headaches sometimes and all I want is to be left in peace. I am really very fond of you, Deirdre. Don't cry. I will not let Papa bully you into coming with us to Hopeminster and I shall tell Mrs Hammer to leave a cold collation for you in the dining-room so you may eat if you feel like it.'

'Thank you,' mumbled Deirdre miserably. She longed to confide in Daphne, but she knew instinctively that Daphne would go straight to their father.

So Deirdre lay down on top of the bed and turned her face into her pillow.

Daphne picked up a quilt, tucked it around her and with a soft 'goodbye' left the room.

Deirdre fully expected her mother to pay her a visit, for Mrs Armitage could be very firm when it came to family outings although she was remarkably lax in everything else. But Daphne turned out to show a vein of steel that no one had hitherto guessed at, and said decisively that Deirdre must on no account be disturbed.

Daphne had the honour of being escorted to church by Lord Harry. As they walked sedately along the narrow lane behind the rest of the Armitage party, Lord Harry reflected Daphne was a dazzlingly beautiful young girl when she managed to get her mind off her own appearance.

'Tell me,' he said lightly, 'all about Mr Guy Wentwater.'

'Oh, you don't want to know about him,' exclaimed Daphne. 'He is most disreputable, and not a gentleman.'

'And yet he seems to be on calling terms with your uncle, and Miss Deirdre was furthermore most anxious to introduce me to him.'

'How odd,' said Daphne softly. 'Sir Edwin would invite Mr Wentwater because Mr Wentwater is very rich. But for Deirdre even to go near him!'

'What is so bad about Mr Wentwater?'

'Oh, at one time it seemed as if he would marry Annabelle, but we found out just in time that he

73

was a slave trader. So that was that. He does not trade any more but Papa says once you do that sort of thing, you're apt to go ahead and replace it with something just as nasty.'

'How true,' said Lord Harry. He could almost feel the fair Daphne becoming self-absorbed again. She had paused to glance down at her reflection in a puddle.

'But Miss Deirdre did not seem to hold him in aversion,' he pursued.

'Do you think so?' asked Daphne vaguely. 'Well, maybe she is sorry for him if she found out what Papa did to him.'

'Which was?'

'You mustn't tell anyone, for I am not supposed to know, but I overheard John Summer, our coachman, telling the maid, Betty. They tell each other things because they have an understanding and hope to be married.'

'Yes, yes, and what *was* it that you heard John Summer tell Betty?' asked his lordship with a rare touch of impatience in his voice.

'Only that Papa had taken out his pack and hunted down Mr Wentwater, right in the middle of summer!'

'I cannot see how he could manage to set a pack of fox-hounds on a man.'

Daphne giggled. 'John Summer hid an old fox in the box of Mr Wentwater's carriage. So *that* is what the hounds were chasing although Mr Wentwater was sure it was himself. That was over three years ago and Mr Wentwater has not been seen up until now.'

'How could Miss Deirdre have an opportunity of meeting him then, if he is not allowed to call at the vicarage?'

'Oh, I suppose she might meet him at Lady Wentwater's. Deirdre often reads to her, you see.'

They turned in at the church gate. Daphne realized that in her worry over Deirdre she had quite forgotten to put on her new bonnet and this fact drove all other thoughts from her mind.

Deirdre was packing feverishly, half unable to believe she was about to take such a drastic step. No longer did the vicarage look shabby and poky; instead it seemed a safe, warm haven filled with happy memories. She longed for Minerva. Somehow, had Minerva still been at the vicarage, Deirdre felt that things would have taken a different turn.

Her heart was beating hard and her fingers were trembling. What would the twins, Perry and James, think of her when they heard the news?

They would be home at Christmas, and she would not be there. She was sure the vicar would not allow her to set foot in the vicarage again.

At least the family and Lord Harry were going to leave the church and go straight to Hopeminster without returning home. She would need to keep away from the main road and make her way the long way round by the back lanes.

She put on a serviceable pair of walking boots and pulled a thick cloak about her shoulders.

She put a poke bonnet on her head, one she had never worn, considering the long poke ugly. But it hid her face, and if the Armitage family should see her, by ill chance, from a distance, they would surely not recognize her.

Finally, she made her way slowly down the stairs, starting at every creak, trying not to bump the two bandboxes against the bannister.

She had reached the bottom step when the door to the kitchen opened and Betty came into the hall.

'What are you doing here?' demanded Deirdre, fighting for composure. 'You were supposed to be at church.'

'I was told by Miss Daphne to wait behind in case you wanted anything,' said Betty, her black eyes snapping with curiosity. 'Where are you going and why have you got them bandboxes?'

'I am taking these things up to the Hall,' said Deirdre. 'Lady Edwin is collecting old clothes for the poor. I feel much better. Don't make a fuss, Betty.'

Deirdre thought of the tear-stained letter she had left on her pincushion. What if Betty saw it too soon and alerted everyone?

'Well, if that's the case, Miss Deirdre, I'd best be fetching my bonnet and come with you,' said Betty cheerfully.

'There is no need for that,' replied Deirdre, forcing herself to be calm, although she felt like screaming at the waste of time. 'A walk in the fresh air is just what I need to clear my head. I shall go back round by the church and join the others.'

Betty hesitated, and then gave a reluctant nod.

Deirdre took great gulps of air as she escaped from the vicarage and hurried off down the lane. Any moment, she expected to hear Betty running after her.

She swung away from the Hopeminster road, keeping to little lanes and footpaths which would lead her to her destination by a circuitous route—and also add several miles to the length of her journey.

Lord Harry's phaeton and the vicar's antique travelling carriage had been brought round in front of the church by the servants.

Daphne once again had the honour of being driven by his lordship, torn between worry at the damage the wind would do to her complexion and the thrill of sporting a dash in such a handsome equipage.

But Lord Harry seemed strangely reluctant to set his usual spanking pace and was content to amble along after the vicar's carriage.

Gradually, the woods on either side thinned out. Across the bare fields Lord Harry saw a figure dart behind a tree. He kept glancing in that direction, but only caught a glimpse of a head peering round the trunk.

A frown settled on his forehead. He suddenly urged his team forward so that they passed the vicarage carriage and then, once in front of it, he slowed his team to a halt and waved his arm to signal to the vicarage carriage to stop also. He jumped lightly down and stood, holding his horses, while the vicar ambled up to him.

'I'm afraid you will have to take Miss Daphne. One of my traces is in danger of breaking,' he said. 'I can fix it given some time and I will follow you into Hopeminster.'

Normally, the vicar would have demanded to see the trace and would have offered all sorts of suggestions but Deirdre and his money problems were weighing heavy on his mind. Daphne was only too glad to get into the closed carriage so that she could study her face in her pocket glass and repair the damage done to her hair by the wind.

Promising to see them all at the inn at Hopeminster, Lord Harry waved them all a cheerful goodbye. He stood in the middle of the road until the lumbering carriage had turned a bend and was hidden from view.

Then he led his team back to the crossroads and looked about. Over the fields and far away, a little figure with two bandboxes was climbing over a stile. A gust of wind whipped the figure's hat off and sent it bowling across the fields. Sunlight shone on a flash of red hair.

He looked from the distant figure to the Hopeworth–Hopeminster crossroads and quietly led his team a little away and into a field. He unhitched his horses, setting them free to graze before he left the field, carefully shutting the gate behind him.

There was a stand of alders a short way from the crossroads, set on a mound. He strolled into it. It afforded an excellent view of the crossroads and the surrounding fields.

He leaned his back against the sun-warmed trunk of a tree and studied the little figure, laboriously crossing the fields. The figure grew larger and finally resolved itself into that of a dusty and dishevelled Deirdre Armitage.

She had lost her hat and the wind was whipping her red hair about her face and she kept impatiently setting down the bandboxes and trying to pin it up.

Deirdre finally reached the crossroads and sat wearily down on a milestone.

Gradually the wind died and the sun grew warmer, and Deirdre Armitage waited patiently; hidden in his stand of alder trees, Lord Harry

78

Desire waited patiently as well.

The minutes grew into quarter-hours, half-hours, and then hours. As the sun sank lower on the horizon the little figure on the milestone grew more and more hunched and forlorn.

Lord Harry straightened up and walked back to where his horses were quietly grazing. He hitched his team up to the phaeton again and led them out of the field towards where Deirdre sat patiently on the milestone.

She did not even look up as he approached, but she must have sensed his presence for all she said in a dull voice was, 'Oh, it's you.'

'I had a minor accident to my phaeton,' said Lord Harry cheerfully. 'Are you waiting for anyone? Or can I take you anywhere?'

'No, I'm not waiting for anyone. That is, I'm waiting to see if my father will return from Hopeminster and take me home. I am so very tired, you see.' Tears started to her eyes and she brushed them away with an impatient hand.

'You would have a long wait,' he said gently. 'Your father spoke of taking supper at the Cock and Feathers before returning. Come and I will take you to join them.'

'Only if I can return to the vicarage first,' said Deirdre, thinking of that incriminating letter pinned to the pincushion. 'I am such a mess. I was feeling so much better and decided to walk. I had these clothes, you see, to take to the poor of Hopeminster. But perhaps I should show them to my mother first.'

Of course,' he said soothingly. 'We will go to the vicarage first, and then we will go to Hopeminster.'

Deirdre was too tired and miserable and

79

humiliated to protest. He drove at a spanking pace, and, in no time at all, she was back home.

Betty looked relieved to see her, and Deirdre dully wondered if the maid had begun to suspect anything. But Betty had obviously not been in her bedroom. Deirdre tore up the letter addressed to her mother, bathed her face, burst into tears, bathed her face again, changed her gown, and found a smart bonnet, and went wearily down the stairs to join Lord Harry.

To her relief, he did not seem inclined to talk, his horses eating up the miles to Hopeworth and then to Hopeminster at a tremendous pace.

The Armitage family was just sitting down to supper in a private parlour.

Deirdre sent up a prayer that somehow Lord Harry would not mention finding her sitting on the milestone at the crossroads with two bandboxes. *He* was so stupid, he had easily accepted her story. But her father, she was sure, would not believe such a tale. Desperately she wished she had cautioned Lord Harry not to say anything. And what if Betty talked? But that wouldn't be so bad. She could simply add on yet another lie and say she was sure Lady Edwin wanted old clothes. 'But what old clothes have you got that would fill two whole bandboxes?' her mother was sure to ask.

So busy was she in forming lies and excuses, and so subsequently relieved was she when Lord Harry let everyone assume he had collected her from the vicarage that it was some time before the whole weight of depression and humiliation returned.

The vicar saw the look of pain on Deirdre's face and became more than ever resolved to take Lord Harry aside and tell him there was no hope.

He felt quite virtuous at having come at last to this very definite resolve instead of the half-hearted promise he had made to himself the night before. He would tell Jimmy Radford all about it, and impress his old friend with his, the vicar's, nobility of soul.

But every time the vicar looked at Lord Harry's handsome profile, he was reminded of all the couples of hounds he could have bought if the deal had only worked.

The vicar of Chalton St Ann's, six miles on the other side of Hopeworth, was selling his hounds, or about to sell them in order to retrench. Now, they would need to go to some other lucky huntsman.

The vicar heaved a great sigh. God moved in mischievous ways, as Lady Godolphin would put it, his wonders to perform.

Deirdre let out a dry sob which she tried ineffectually to change to a sneeze. The vicar sighed again. The sooner he told her not to worry about the engagement, the better.

'The town's full of Armitages,' said the vicar, realizing he had been sitting silent for some time, and feeling obliged to add his mite of conversation to the company.

'Edwin and those poxy daughters of his were walking past when we arrived. 'I mentioned earlier we were going so they probably set out to hunt us down.'

'Why?' asked Lord Harry.

The vicar took a pinch of snuff while he debated his reply. The truth, as he knew very well, was that his pesky brother was still trying to capture Lord Harry for one of his daughters. But if Deirdre would not have the Desire fortune—or rather the

81

fortune he would gain when his uncle kicked the bucket—then the vicar was damned if Josephine or Emily were going to get their claws on it. What a repulsive pair of antidotes they were, thought the vicar. And what truly dreadful fashions they always wore. It was amazing their mother did not know how to guide them since she was a bit of a fashion plate herself, if you didn't notice her pale cold eyes and her pursed up mouth and...

'Why?' asked Lord Harry again.

'Oh, ah,' said the vicar. 'Er ... well, because I'm such a fashionable fellow, and Edwin's a bit of an old stick. He likes to imitate me, don't you see.'

'Not quite,' replied Lord Harry in a puzzled way. His gaze was kind and bland but somehow the vicar felt uncomfortable under that childlike stare and tugged at the points of his waistcoat which had ridden up over his middle to expose several bulging inches of shirt.

'Never mind,' said the vicar hurriedly.

Meanwhile, Deirdre had found she was surprisingly hungry. Despite the fact she had had nothing to eat since breakfast, she was quite sure tragedy had robbed her of her appetite. But by the time she had discussed a generous helping of grouse pie, several slices of ham, some smelts and the inevitable potatoes which accompanied every dish, she began to feel as if she might live through the night to come after all. Several glasses of strong wine brought a little spark of hope which gradually grew to a flame.

How could she have been so disloyal in her thoughts of Guy? Of course, something really serious must have prevented him from coming. What if he were ill?

Her colour returned as her fatigue and despair fled.

With the resilience of youth, she shot from hopelessness to the heights of dizzy optimism. Poor Guy. How worried he must be. How his heart must be aching for her.

The ladies were invited to join the gentlemen for port and nuts, the little girls taking theirs with hot water.

Deirdre began to feel sleepy and content. The world had miraculously righted itself.

By the time they were ready to leave, Deirdre accepted the suggestion she should travel home with Lord Desire without demur, although this time the suggestion came from Mrs Armitage, not the vicar.

Deirdre was being helped up into Lord Harry's phaeton by her father when she suddenly stopped short and nearly fell backwards. Two spots of colour burned on her cheeks.

For out of the inn behind them came Sir Edwin, Lady Edwin and their two daughters—and Guy Wentwater. They had obviously just eaten supper as well.

Guy was holding Emily's hand and whispering in her ear and she was giggling and wriggling while her parents looked on with indulgent smiles, and Josephine pouted.

Then Sir Edwin's party saw the vicarage party. The vicar walked forward.

Deirdre took her seat next to Lord Harry and stared straight ahead. Her father said some words to Sir Edwin, Sir Edwin waved a hand to indicate the presence of Guy Wentwater. The little vicar puffed out his chest and raked Mr Wentwater with a beady look from head to foot, then, ignoring his outstretched hand, turned on his heel and walked back to his own carriage.

'Dear me,' murmured Lord Harry. 'The cut direct.'

'Drive on, my lord,' said Deirdre in a harsh voice.

How *could* he, she thought with anguish. What *was* Guy doing, fit and well, and paying court to that awful Emily?

Her thoughts churned and burned all the way to the vicarage. From time to time Lord Harry essayed a few remarks but Deirdre was deaf to everything but the voices clamouring in her own head.

She gave Lord Harry a curt goodnight and escaped to her room.

When Daphne arrived, Deirdre was lying fully dressed on the bed, staring sightlessly up at the canopy.

'We sat and talked downstairs for *hours,*' said Daphne sleepily. 'I wanted to fetch you but Papa told me to leave you alone which is most odd since he has been throwing you at Lord Harry these past few days.'

Deirdre twisted her head and looked at the clock on the mantel. Midnight! And she had arrived home at ten. So absorbed had she been in trying to find a loophole out of her humiliation that she had not noticed the time passing.

'Are you feeling better?' asked Daphne solicitously.

Deirdre nodded.

'Papa is in a high rage,' went on Daphne, sitting down at the dimity flounced toilet table and picking up a hairbrush. 'He says that Wentwater is a vulgar adventurer and that no man would be attracted to

84

Emily unless he had a mercenary motive.'

'That's rich,' said Deirdre, twisting on to her side. 'When has marriage meant anything to Papa other than a means to get more money for those smelly hounds of his?'

Daphne at last focused on her pretty reflection in the glass. She thought she saw a pimple and leaned forward, holding the candle so close to her face she almost set her dark hair on fire.

Deirdre lay and thought and thought. Daphne eventually appeared on the other side of the bed in her nightgown and begged Deirdre to move so that she could get under the covers.

Rising as jerkily as a marionette, Deirdre moved to her favourite seat by the window and looked out. A small snore from the bed behind her told her Daphne had fallen immediately asleep.

All at once, Deirdre was sure Guy was calling her. She heard his voice inside her brain.

The pain at her heart lessened. This magical communion between their minds was an incredible and beautiful thing. He seemed to be telling her that he had been unable to get away, but had joined Sir Edwin's party to Hopeminster in the hopes of seeing her.

Tired as she was, Deirdre knew all at once she must go to him.

FIVE

Squire Radford was unable to sleep. A particularly painful twinge of rheumatism stabbed down his left leg. At last, he gave up the battle and climbed out of bed, wrapping himself up in a greatcoat with a blanket over his shoulders.

A breath of air in the garden was just what he needed.

He shuffled out in his slippers across the lawn and stood by the tall hedge, looking through a small gap in it to where the moonlight turned the village pond to a sheet of silver.

It was then his sharp old eyes saw a girl carrying two bandboxes walking quickly along the road on the other side of the pond. He watched until she had disappeared from view, wondering who on earth she could be, abroad at this time of night.

Deirdre half walked, half ran in the direction of Lady Wentwater's.

Over the River Blyne she went, by way of the hump-backed bridge. The river chattered and gurgled underneath, restless and busy like the thoughts in her head.

She now felt disloyal. A gentleman such as Guy Wentwater would not say he loved her or make a firm arrangement to elope with her and just forget about it.

No. Some unforeseen circumstance must have prevented him.

And that is why she was on her road to join him, complete with bandboxes and newly written letter to mother back on the pincushion at home.

Deirdre planned to make her way round to the back of the house and see if Guy had left the window of the morning-room open. She must try to find his bedroom.

How delighted he would be to see her, she told herself firmly. For had not God himself spoken to her, giving her permission to elope with Guy, and was he not yearning for her at this very moment? Every fibre of her being told her it was so.

To her relief, the window had been left unlocked. She gently opened it and crept inside.

Opening the door from the morning-room which led into the hall, she stood very still, listening intently. The sound of laughter and masculine voices was coming from the drawing-room. Then she heard Guy's voice. 'By Jove, it's good to see you fellows. Of course you are welcome to stay. Aunt has bags of room.'

Still clutching the two bandboxes, Deirdre crept across the hall. The drawing-room door was open and a yellow oblong of light sliced across the darkness.

Deirdre looked in.

Guy was lounging at his ease with a bumper of brandy in his hand. Two friends were seated facing him around the fire. They seemed uncouth, they did not seem like gentlemen, but, strangely, Deirdre did not feel alarmed. Their unexpected arrival must have been the reason for Guy abandoning her.

They were so merry and at ease together. They all belonged to that fascinating world of men—a world which Deirdre envied as much as she feared.

At times she chafed at being a woman and having to listen to silly women's prattle. She longed to discuss philosophy and world events and politics. Guy had accepted her as an equal. Therefore it followed his friends would do so too.

She took a deep breath and entered the room, still carrying the two bandboxes.

Guy was facing the door. He looked straight at her in dawning surprise and then his blue eyes sparkled with drink and malice.

87

His friends followed his gaze.

One of them, thickset and burly, with greasy, pomaded locks plastered to his low brow, twisted round.

'The deuce!' he said. 'What's this?'

'A drama from Astley's Amphitheatre,' drawled Guy. 'The Maiden From the Vicarage Leaves Home. Allow me to present Miss Deirdre Armitage.'

Both men arose and made their bows. The thickset one was introduced as Mr Benjamin Rowse and his thin companion as Mr Bill Wilson. Both were obviously well to go.

'There's a story here,' crowed the one called Bill. 'Do tell, Guy. What wickedness have you been up to?'

Guy rose to his feet and walked to where Deirdre stood. He reached forward and for one blissful moment Deirdre's world righted as she thought he was about to take her in his arms. But, instead, he seized her by the upper arm and dragged her towards the mantel.

'Look in the glass, Miss Deirdre,' he laughed. He moved his grip to her shoulders and thrust her face forwards. Deirdre stared at her reflection. Her bonnet was awry, there was a smudge on her nose, and great purple shadows under her eyes.

'Yes, hardly a fashion plate are you?' he jeered.

'Guy!' cried Deirdre, wrenching herself free. 'What has come over you? What happened? I do not understand the cruelty of your manner. You said you loved me. You promised to elope with me.'

Her eyes grew soft and pleading. 'I-I am here, Guy, and I have brought my belongings with me.'

'Oooh, how touching!' said Guy, mincing about

the room with one hand on his hip while his friends roared with laughter.

Deirdre's face turned hard and set.

'Good evening, gentlemen,' she said, walking to the door, her back very straight.

'Wait a bit!' called Bill Wilson. 'Guy may be too nice in his taste but Benjie and me ain't above a bit o' fun with a redhead.'

He clipped her round the waist with one beefy arm and thrust his great red face towards her own.

Guy Wentwater smiled lazily and closed the drawing-room door. 'I agree she is not to my taste, my friends,' he said lazily, 'but don't let me stop your sport.'

Appalled, Deirdre tore herself free from Bill's grasp. Benjie rushed to guard the door. Guy sat down in his chair again and picked up his glass and settled back with the air of a connoisseur about to watch a good play.

Now Deirdre looked like the fox of her father's imaginings. Green eyes blazing, she backed away from them towards the fire.

A canterbury filled with old newspapers stood beside the hearth.

She picked one up in one lightning movement, set it alight, and threw the blazing pages full at Guy who jerked back violently in his chair so that he overbalanced and fell on the floor, tearing at the blazing paper which covered his chest.

'Back!' hissed Deirdre as the other two closed in. Why didn't the servants come? Should she scream? No! One thing burned in Deirdre's mind. No one must know she had been here.

Bill and Benjie began to move nearer. Deirdre edged closer to a brass stand on the other side of the fireplace which held a selection of riding whips, polo sticks, umbrellas, and sword sticks.

She seized a sword stick and managed to jerk the blade out of its sheath before Bill found the courage to try to seize her hand.

Slicing the blade through the air in great sweeps, she held them off until she had reached the door.

Then she wrenched it open and ran instinctively to the morning-room. It was as well she did. For the great door at the other end of the hall was barred and bolted for the night and by the time she had unlatched and unlocked everything, they would have been upon her.

She fled down the Hopeminster road which led from Lady Wentwater's estate into the village of Hopeworth. She did not stop running until she had reached the gates of the Hall, determined to rouse the lodge keeper should she hear sounds of pursuit. For Deirdre now felt there was no way her humiliation and stupidity could escape detection.

But no sounds of chase came to her ears. The night was cold and quiet and still. Deirdre sank down on to a tussock of grass beside the gates of the Hall and buried her face in her hands.

Never again would she believe in God. He had tricked her, she thought illogically, following quite a common line of reasoning—'He did not help me, therefore I won't believe in Him.'

And as for the marriage of true minds! Piffle! And men? Worse. Some were better mannered and better dressed than others, but *au fond* they were all the same; great, hairy, selfish, hot-handed, slavering satyrs.

Out of the whole pack of them, she hated her father the most. If he had behaved like a true father, then all this would never have happened.

There is nothing more comforting than finding someone else to blame and so Deirdre lashed her rage up against the vicar.

'You do seem to make a habit of sitting around by the roadside,' came a plaintive voice from somewhere above her head.

Deirdre started and looked up. Impeccable and urbane as ever, Lord Harry Desire stood smiling down at her in the moonlight.

Deirdre looked up at him sullenly. 'Have you come to jeer and torment me?' she asked.

'No,' he said amiably, 'only to find you. Daphne awoke and found your bed empty and raised the alarm. Betty said you had been running around earlier with two bandboxes. The good vicar decided you had run away from home.'

If only, thought Deirdre wildly, she could keep her stupidity over Guy a secret!

'I left a letter,' she said.

'Well, I don't think anyone has found it yet,' he said.

'I must get back and tear it up,' thought Deirdre.

'Thank you,' she said, rising and brushing down her skirts. 'I am ready to go home now. I couldn't sleep. The letter explained all that, you see.'

'The bandboxes!' cried a voice in her head. 'You left the bandboxes!'

'No bandboxes this time?' went on Lord Harry as if reading her thoughts.

Deirdre began to walk down the road with him. She felt very, very tired. She never wanted to see her father again.

There was only one way in which a gently brought up young girl could free herself from

91

home.

Marriage.

'I will marry you,' she said abruptly.

Lord Harry strolled along in silence. Oh, God, thought Deirdre, even this fool does not want me.

Dark figures were scurrying here and there through the village.

'What is the matter?' asked Deirdre.

'You,' smiled Lord Harry. 'Mr Armitage has sounded the alarm.'

He called out to one of the figures. One of the village boys came running up.

Lord Harry fished in his pocked and handed the boy a shilling.

'Go and tell everyone Miss Deirdre has been found,' he said. The boy grabbed the coin and ran off, moving from one figure to the other.

The vicar met them half way down the lane leading to the vicarage.

Even in the moonlight, it was possible to see his face was dark with rage.

Lord Harry put his arm round Deirdre's waist as she braced herself for the tirade to come.

Before the vicar could open his mouth, Lord Harry said quickly, 'Congratulate me, Mr Armitage. Your daughter has done me the great honour to accept my hand in marriage.'

The vicar opened and shut his mouth like a landed cod. Rage was replaced by joy which was promptly replaced by worry.

Did Deirdre want this marriage? Or had she simply broken down under pressure?

'Wonderful,' he said. 'But where on earth did you go in the middle of the night, girl? I have been worried to death.'

Another lie coming up, thought Deirdre wearily.

'I decided to go out for a walk so that I could make up my mind,' she said, not looking at her father. 'Lord Harry found me and I told him of my decision.'

The vicar looked at her narrowly. He did not believe a word of it. Deirdre did not look like a girl who had just been proposed to by an eligible man. She looked ... numb.

Mrs Armitage had been having one of her famous Spasms, but rallied remarkably on hearing the news. The girls were all delighted, clustering shyly round Lord Harry in their nightgowns and curl papers.

Deirdre accepted hugs and kisses and champagne, wishing all the time she could go to bed.

Somehow, she was sure, the real reason for her journey out into the night would soon be revealed.

She had left those wretched bandboxes. If Guy had not hidden them, Lady Wentwater's servants would find them, and she could not explain that they were clothes meant for the poor when they contained all her best gowns.

Only someone as stupid as Lord Harry would have believed her.

'I'll have a word with you in the morning, Deirdre,' said the vicar, and Deirdre nodded dully.

As she finally went up the stairs to bed, the remembrance of that letter on the pincushion made her teeth begin to chatter. She quickened her steps and burst into her bedroom, her candle held high.

And there was the letter. Just where she had left it.

She snatched it up and tore it into shreds and

hurled it into the embers of the fire.

'I didn't read it,' came a soft voice from the doorway. Daphne was standing there, watching.

'Just as well,' said Deirdre, forcing a laugh. 'It was nothing but a series of household notes I meant to give Mama in the morning.'

'I'm glad,' said Daphne, moving into the room. 'When you were missing and after I had sounded the alarm, I saw the letter and I thought you had run away from home. But letters are so final. I thought if they could find you and bring you back, then no harm would have been done.'

'What an imagination you have, Daphne,' said Deirdre with a laugh that ended as a sob. 'Only see how tired I am? I am nearly in tears over nothing at all!'

*   *   *

Guy Wentwater tossed and turned, trying to get to sleep. But despite the amount of brandy he had drunk, sleep persisted in eluding him.

His glee over the humiliation of Deirdre Armitage was beginning to turn sour but he would not yet admit to himself that he was heartily afraid of the Reverend Charles Armitage.

There had been his own ignominious hounding out of the county by the vicar. And then there had been that fellow who had tried to break up Annabelle's marriage. He had heard the stories about that. The vicar had whipped him out of the church and the local boys had debagged him and thrown him in the village pond.

Perhaps it would be best to say nothing about it, except perhaps to Silas Dubois, who would enjoy the story. He would leave out the bit about how Deirdre had battled her way free from three grown men. Best tell it that she had left in tears.

Benjie Rowse and Bill Wilson would not remember the name of the girl in the morning. He would make them keep their mouths shut anyway.

But those bandboxes! Burn them. No, that wouldn't do. He would need to wait and see what happened.

If Deirdre didn't talk, then he was safe.

He should have planned some sort of revenge that the vicar would never know about. Even now Mr Armitage could be riding up the road with that dreadful pack of hounds howling before him.

And then the door of his bedroom opened and a tall figure walked in.

'Who's there?' cried Guy, struggling up against the pillows.

'Desire,' said a polite, social voice.

Guy swore under his breath and lit the candle beside the bed.

Lord Harry Desire ambled forward and sat down elegantly on the end of the bed.

'How did you get in?' blustered Guy. 'I locked all the doors and windows.'

'I picked the lock,' said Lord Harry pleasantly.

'Why?'

'To see you, my friend.'

Guy reached out to the bell rope which hung beside the bed. With one graceful, fluid movement, Lord Harry raised his cane and struck Guy across the wrist, a sharp stinging blow.

'Now, now,' said Lord Harry soothingly as Guy cursed and rubbed his wrist. 'We do not want to wake the whole household, now do we?'

'What do you want?' demanded Guy.

'I came to find out about a visit Miss Deirdre Armitage made to this house earlier tonight.'

'That little redhead!' sneered Guy. 'Never saw her.'

Lord Harry's fist flew out and struck Guy full and hard on the mouth.

He yelped with pain and tried to leap from the bed, only to find his shoulders held down by two powerful hands.

Lord Harry's face looked as beautiful and pleasant as ever. Guy looked wildly this way and that, searching for another assailant, for this graceful lord who was smiling at him so disarmingly could surely not have dealt him such a ferocious blow.

So Deirdre hadn't talked. And this idiot was in love with her.

'Very well,' said Guy, leaning back against the pillows and trying to affect a world-weary air. 'I would have told you had I not been trying to protect the poor girl's name. She got it into her head I was going to elope with her because she didn't want to be pressured into marrying you.'

He looked quickly and eagerly into Lord Harry's blue eyes for signs of hurt but Lord Harry smiled blandly down on him and begged him to go on.

'She said she loved me and she would be waiting for me at the crossroads at two in the afternoon,' said Guy. 'She came to see me on the day of the garden party. I heard my aunt returning, and fearing for Deirdre's reputation, I just said, "Yes, yes," and pushed her out of the back way, thinking when she heard no more from me that would be an end of it.'

96

'But the silly chit ...' Lord Harry's hand moved and Guy quickly changed it to '... I mean, Miss Deirdre arrived in the middle of the night with those wretched bandboxes and started begging and pleading which was most embarrassing because I had two friends with me at the time.'

'Are they still here?'

'Yes, but you don't want to bother with them.'

'We'll see. Go on.'

'Well, that's all there is to it. When Miss Deirdre found out I wasn't going to marry her, she fled out the back way. And that's that.'

There was a silence. Guy eyed the bell rope, wondering if he could reach it. This lord could throw him from one end of the room to the other, and the servants would not come. They had once interrupted one of his noisier revels and he had commanded them never to appear unless called for. And his aunt slept like the dead.

Lord Harry gave a little sigh, and stretched out his legs, and studied the glistening leather of his hessian boots. Then he raised his eyes to Guy's.

'Now this time,' said Lord Harry in the same easy social tones, 'you will tell me the truth. Begin at the beginning.'

Guy twisted this way and that and fiddled with the bedclothes. 'Let me get up and put on some clothes, and then we can talk,' he pleaded.

'No,' said Lord Harry equably, 'begin at the beginning.'

Guy thought furiously. Obviously this wretched lord must be madly in love with the girl. Therefore, if he told another story saying he, Guy, had been in love with Deirdre but stopped himself from eloping with her out of the purest motives, *that* might perhaps be accepted.

So he began with much of the truth; the stolen moments in the churchyard and in the lane. Then he proceeded to lie. He said that much as he loved Deirdre, he knew her father would cast the girl off if she married him, and Deirdre would eventually regret the estrangement from her family, and so he had turned her away.

There was another long silence when he finished. Again Lord Harry sighed.

'Again,' said Lord Harry. 'Start at the beginning and get it right this time.'

'Look here!' blustered Guy. 'You force your way in here and...'

He broke off and gazed in horror down the length of a couple of yards of cold steel. Lord Harry had drawn his swordstick and was holding the point of the blade to Guy's throat.

Guy had never felt more terrified in his life. There was something horrible and monstrous about the placidity of the beautiful face looking at him.

'Well, you can't blame me,' he babbled. 'You see, it was all like this ...'

Two hours later, Lord Harry Desire, carrying two bandboxes, softly let himself out of Lady Wentwater's mansion. His knuckles were sore and bleeding, but he was sure that neither Benjie Rowse nor Bill Wilson would dare say a word. All three men would be gone from Hopeworth in the morning.

He whistled jauntily as he walked back in the direction of the village.

Squire Radford heard the whistling and swung his stick-like legs over the edge of his bed and felt for his slippers. He walked to the window and

98

looked out.

In the pale grey light of dawn Lord Harry Desire was walking on the other side of the village pond, carrying two bandboxes. His elegant reflection was mirrored in the cold glassy waters of the pond until a bustling duck cut across it and sent little pieces of Lord Harry's reflection shimmering across the surface.

How odd, thought the squire. Some young girl goes out in the middle of the night with two bandboxes, and now here is Lord Harry Desire walking back with them. Perhaps they are different bandboxes. Perhaps it was a wager.

He sighed and turned back to the warmth of his bed. He would dearly have loved to meet this Lord Harry. But for the first time ever no invitation had come from the vicarage, nor had the vicar called.

'Charles must be up to something bad,' mourned the squire. 'I only wish I knew what it was.'

Deirdre awoke in the morning with a pounding headache. The day was all hard and glittery with bright sunlight splintering off the glass bottles on the toilet table.

Betty had already been in and made up the fire and opened the curtains.

Daphne had already awakened and gone downstairs.

Deirdre turned over and buried her face in the pillows as the memory of terrible yesterday flooded over her.

But she could not hide in her room forever. Her father wanted to see her. She twisted round and looked at the clock. Eleven! How could she have slept so deeply and so late with all this trouble awaiting her?

99

Well, by now the news would be out. Guy and his coarse friends would have made her the laughing stock of the village. Lord Harry would be disgusted because even such a fool as he must have some sort of pride.

As for her father ...

Deirdre shuddered and climbed from the bed to make a hasty toilet. She was half way down the stairs wearing one of her best ensembles, a round gown of fine cambric under a pelisse of emerald green rep sarsnet with a rich silk cordon with full tassels about her slim waist, when she realised with a shock that this very gown was one she had packed and left in the bandboxes.

With faltering steps she made her way back into her room and pulled at the doors of the tall marquetry wardrobe as if she were opening Pandora's box.

Her clothes hung in serried rows, gowns and mantles and cloaks and pelisses. Her shoes were neatly lined up like a regiment underneath. She ran to the clothes press and pulled open the drawers. Her underwear lay in neat folded piles of muslin and cambric, silk and lace.

She sat down on the bed, her heart beating hard. Someone had entered the bedroom while she slept and put away the contents of the bandboxes. And there were the wretched boxes themselves, neatly stacked on the top of the wardrobe!

Betty! Of course, it must have been Betty.

Some servant from Lady Wentwater's had delivered the bandboxes and Betty had put the contents away.

Now, her secret would be out. Well, better to get it over with.

Deirdre walked slowly downstairs and across the hall. Her father poked his head around the study door. 'A word with you, Deirdre,' he called.

This was it!

Deirdre squared her shoulders and walked in.

'Sit down,' said the vicar in a kindly voice.

Deirdre sat down, wondering at his manner.

The vicar sat behind his desk. He fiddled with a snuff box and then he fiddled with the quill of a pen.

At last he looked up. 'Want to marry Desire, do ye?'

'Yes, Papa,' said Deirdre faintly. 'I told you so last night.'

'Well, hey, that's all holiday with me but it's Clarence House to a charlie's shelter, you're only doin' this to please me.'

'When did I ever try to please you, Papa?' said Deirdre, shocked into honesty.

'Never,' said the vicar with a relieved grin. 'Well, that's all right and tight then. Set a date?'

'No, Papa.'

'Well, well, you'll want to wait until the girls get back from furrin parts.'

'Possibly, Papa. I will need to ask Lord Harry.'

'Oh.' The vicar's face fell again before this unusual display of meekness.

He studied her face anxiously. She was upset about something, and, yes, she was frightened too! Why should he feel so guilty? He had not forced her into anything. If only she would look happy.

His face cleared. She hadn't had her breakfast. An empty stomach, in the vicar's opinion, was responsible for most of the humours and sadness in the world.

'Run along then,' he said more cheerfully. 'Have your breakfast and we'll talk later.'

Still Deirdre hesitated, unable to believe her father had heard nothing about Guy Wentwater.

'Betty should have awakened me earlier,' said Deirdre. 'It is my duty to see the girls off to school.'

'They ain't going anywhere today,' said the vicar. 'We were all up and about half the night.'

Deirdre went slowly out into the hall where she nearly collided with Betty, the maid.

'Oh, Miss Deirdre!' said Betty. 'Them bandboxes arrived this morning but you were that tired, I put 'em all away whilst you were asleep. You must have been fair mazed to pack all your best stuff to give to the poor!'

'What?' said Deirdre, blanching. 'Bandboxes? What bandboxes?' she asked, while her thoughts raced this way and that.

'Well, that's what I said to Lord Harry. He was standing right where you are, ever so early, and looking down at these bandboxes. "What's this?" I asked, and he says they arrived from somewhere because you'd put good clothes in 'em by mistake. So I says they must be from the Hall, 'cos that's where you was takin' 'em.'

'And what did Lord Harry say to that?' asked Deirdre anxiously, remembering she had told him she was taking them to the poor of Hopeminster. So many lies!

'Well, miss, he just looked at me absent-minded like and then he says for me to hang them away and not be rousin' you on account of you being up last night. Ever so thoughtful, he is.'

'Yes,' said Deirdre, walking away to the dining-room. How fortunate Lord Harry was so ...

102

so *unaware* of things. But if he hadn't been there at those opportune moments, then her father would definitely have found out about Guy Wentwater.

Guy Wentwater.

The dining-room was empty, so Deirdre helped herself to some tea, hardly noticing it was stone cold, and sat down and thought about Guy Wentwater, and the more she thought about him, the more bitter about life and love she became.

He had tricked her, her mind had tricked her with fantasies of spiritual rapport, her God had tricked her, therefore He did not exist, she reminded herself fiercely.

But her love for Guy had been a powerful and heady drug, so suddenly cut off, that a great part of Deirdre's mind longed for reassurance.

If he had walked in the door at that moment and said he had been drunk and apologized humbly for his behaviour, then she would have forgiven him so that she could plunge back into that secure, rosy, exalted world again.

But the memories were dark and filled with humiliation. The malice in his eyes still haunted her.

She absent-mindedly ate two pieces of cold toast.

But he *had* been drunk, her mind nagged. Very. And gentlemen were strange when they were in their altitudes. Why, even her own father had become disgracefully drunk after a successful hunt last year and had ridden his horse right into the Hall and up the stairs.

Her brow darkened as she thought of the vicar. It was all his fault, him with his painted face, coarse manners, lack of breeding and awful, awful creaking corsets.

The door opened and Lord Harry Desire sauntered in.

'Ready?' he asked.

'For what?' demanded Deirdre wearily.

'To go driving with me. If you recall, we made the arrangement last night.'

Deirdre could remember no such arrangement but she was too overset to say so. She meekly remarked she would fetch her bonnet and hurried upstairs.

She pulled on the first bonnet that came to hand, which was, fortunately, the one designed to go with her gown. It was of green curled silk and vastly fetching. She remembered it had recently nestled in one of the bandboxes and that she had planned to wear it for Guy. Two large tears hung on her lashes. She brushed them angrily away and went down to join his lordship.

It was only when Deirdre realized they were turning in at the gates of Lady Wentwater's ivy-covered mansion that she burst into speech.

'We cannot call here!' she said desperately. 'We are not expected.'

'But we are,' he said, reining in his team in front of the house.

A groom came running from the stables to take the horses. Lord Harry jumped lightly down and then helped Deirdre to alight.

'I met Lady Wentwater at the garden party,' he said, 'and promised to call. Are you all right? You have gone very white.'

'Yes,' said Deirdre, feeling her knees beginning to tremble. 'Yes, let us go in.'

For she had decided her monumental luck could surely not hold out any longer. Better get it over

104

with.

Lady Wentwater received them in the drawing-room. There were no signs of the fracas of the night before. All was dark and gloomy and quiet. Sunlight filtered through the fluttering ivy leaves which cloaked most of the windows, creating a subterranean effect.

'I'm glad you've called,' wheezed Lady Wentwater, her small currant eyes the only thing alive in the doughy mass of her face. 'It's gone so quiet since Guy left, although I should be glad of that. Why, the noise he and his friends made carousing till all hours! Not that I heard them, I sleep so sound, but my maid told me the servants thought an army had invaded, it got so bad, and at one point she thought she heard a woman's voice, but that can't be the case since there are no lightskirts around here, except Maggie Trumper, who everyone knows is no better than she should be. But Guy had told them all, the servants that is, not to interfere when he was entertaining, but my maid said at one point they heard one of the guests crying blue murder for help and it was as much as they could do to stop themselves from running in to see what the matter was.'

'Mr Wentwater has gone?' asked Deirdre, her lips feeling numb and stiff.

'Yes. Off he went this morning. I'll miss the lad bur I wish he'd keep better company. Those friends of his! Such a mess. Faces all beaten up. But they will fight among themselves when they're in their cups.'

'Did he say anything about ... about me?' asked Deirdre in such a soft voice that Lady Wentwater had to strain to hear her.

'Nary a word,' said Lady Wentwater maliciously. 'But he sent his regards to Miss Emily up at the Hall.'

She turned and engaged Lord Harry in conversation while Deirdre sat in a daze.

She was free! Free from public humiliation. By a series of strange coincidences, she had escaped. One of Lady Wentwater's servants must have found the bandboxes and sent them to the vicarage without saying a word.

What a miracle!

She sat on in a daze of relief until it was time to go, barely noticing when Lady Wentwater offered her congratulations on their engagement.

When they were driving sedately along the road again, Lord Harry's first words hit her with the effect of a bucket of cold water.

'I would like to be married very soon,' he said.

'Oh,' faltered Deirdre. 'I am afraid I rushed you into things. Perhaps you don't want to marry me at all.'

'Indeed I do,' he laughed. 'So much so that if you were to go back on your word, I would sue you for breach of promise.'

'Nonsense,' said Deirdre, forcing a laugh. 'Only ladies do that. Only a lady is allowed to sue.'

'Then I shall make legal history,' he said with great good humour.

'We can at least wait until my sisters return from Paris,' said Deirdre.

'Oh, why?'

'I would like them to be there when I am married.'

'Very well,' he said. 'So long as you promise to marry me as soon as they return.'

'Oh, yes,' said Deirdre. Something would arise to save her before then. For had not Minerva said they would not be returning until the following spring?

'In that case, my love,' he said easily, 'I will take myself off to Town today. I have trespassed on your family's good nature long enough.'

He reined in his horses at a quiet bend in the road and kissed her gently and passionlessly. 'You will not break your promise?' he said, his voice unusually serious.

She looked up into his clear blue eyes, childlike, innocent, candid eyes, and realized there was no escape.

'No, I will not break my promise,' she said.

'Remember,' he said lightly as he set his team in motion again, 'should I not be wed when my uncle dies, then I inherit nothing.'

'Where does the money go? I mean who inherits it?' asked Deirdre, although she barely heard the answer since she was still hoping that some miracle would happen so that she need not be kept to her promise.

'Oh, some distant relative. Very unpleasant. Silas Dubois.'

They drove on in silence.

'Hey, what's this?' asked Lord Harry cheerfully. 'Your home is all a-bustle.'

The short driveway was blocked by two magnificent travelling carriages. Liveried servants were bustling here and there.

The door of the vicarage flew open.

Minerva and Annabelle stood on the step, their arms held out in welcome. Deirdre's older sisters had come home.

So she would need to marry Lord Harry Desire.

She *despised* the man. Oh, he was pleasant enough. But she, Deirdre Armitage, who had prided herself on being the most intelligent of the sisters, was to be tied for life to a handsome fool.

Minerva must do something. Minerva had always been able to solve any problem.

But two minutes of her sisters' company shattered her hopes. They were delighted with her choice of husband. They thought Lord Harry was the finest young man on the London scene. Her elegant brothers-in-law, the Marquess of Brabington and Lord Sylvester Comfrey, had also emerged from the vicarage and were thumping Lord Harry on the back and welcoming him to the family.

The vicar stood behind a curtain in the study, watching Deirdre's face.

She looked miserable. She looked trapped.

He cursed himself. Despite his fears, Lord Sylvester had come across with a hefty sum of money and without even one mumble of reproach.

So there had been no need to sacrifice his daughter. But she had promised to marry the man.

So what was he to do?

SIX

The Armitage girls were becoming famous for good marriages and short engagements.

In the months preceding her wedding, Deirdre saw much of her two elder sisters and had ample opportunity to unburden herself.

But Annabelle and Minerva had become so

fashionable, so *mondaine,* that to confide her infatuation for Guy seemed impossible. The six sisters were all rivals in a way. Annabelle had grown fonder of Minerva than she had ever been, but the old rivalry was still there. Minerva had produced a son, a lusty, adorable baby boy, while Annabelle, as yet, showed no signs of blessing her husband with an heir. And so she envied Minerva and was apt to sympathize with Minerva overmuch about the sad existence of a mother being kept away from the joys of society by a small baby—carefully ignoring Minerva's advantages of having a nanny, a wet-nurse, and a large staff of adoring servants.

Deirdre in her turn had always been jealous of Annabelle's glorious golden beauty. She was also jealous of Minerva's stately manner. But she had always consoled herself with the fact that she, Deirdre, was the *brains* of the Armitage family. How could The Brains confess to such a piece of stupidity. How could she say, 'I fell in love with a villain, and only agreed to marry Lord Harry to get myself out of a humiliating mess?'

Then *not* marrying Lord Harry meant staying at home with Papa, and Deirdre still detested the vicar and considered him the worst of men; vulgar, posturing and bullying.

Deirdre was much in Town, as her two elder sisters threw themselves enthusiastically into the arrangements for the wedding.

But a visit to Lord Harry's family was impending and Deirdre knew she not put it off any longer. Lord Harry's father, the Earl of Carchester, had estates to the north of London.

Perhaps Lord Harry, sensing her reluctance, had decided that more than an afternoon's visit would be too much for her, or perhaps it was because a longer visit would entail inviting the rest of the Armitages, but it transpired that he and Deirdre would call on the Earl of Carchester and family for tea, and return to London the same day.

Deirdre was dreading the visit. She imagined a whole family of Lord Harrys, stupid, amiable, dressed to perfection.

She had not been alone with him since Hopeworth. He had seemed amazingly content to see her in the company of others, and although there were occasions when he could have contrived to see her alone, he did not make use of them.

Deirdre had rehearsed a whole series of conversations with which to while away the time on the journey. Silence was too intimate a thing.

She dreaded him making any more of those warm advances. Sometimes, she imagined herself struggling to protect her virtue in some quiet lane, which showed the frantic state of Deirdre's mind that she could even consider such an elegant and languid man as Lord Harry Desire wishing to deflower her under the eyes of two footmen at a damp roadside when he could have her in a warm bed in only a few months' time.

So it was with great relief and surprise that Deirdre found out at the last moment that Lady Godolphin was to accompany them.

Deirdre was dressed in a gown of jaconet muslin made with a gored bodice finished with a tucker of fine embroidery. Over it, she wore a cambric pelisse with long sleeves falling over her hands. A bonnet of white sarsnet with raised spots, bound and trimmed with Danish blue satin, ornamented her head.

Lady Godolphin was also dressed in her finest—
or what she considered her finest. Because of
the youthful years of her lover, Mr Anstey, Lady
Godolphin had blossomed out in girlish fashions.

Her muslin gown was a miracle of pink and
white gores and tucks and flounces. Her flaxen wig
gleamed like the sun above, and rouge burnished
her withered cheeks like the autumn russet bloom
on fallen crab apples.

It was embarrassing to Deirdre to find out
that Lady Godolphin's search for youth did not
stop at her appearance. She tittered and giggled
and slapped Lord Harry's wrist with her fan and
referred to herself and Deirdre as 'we girls'.

Lord Harry smiled vaguely at all Lady
Godolphin's sallies and then fell asleep in a corner
of the carriage.

They were using his travelling carriage. The day
was cold and brisk but Deirdre longed to open one
of the windows since Lady Godolphin's perfume
was worse than the Reverend Armitage's, being a
mixture of musk, lavender water, rose water, Joppa
Soap, sweat, garlic, and Something That a Lady
Does Not Talk About.

'It's all very romantical,' sighed Lady Godolphin,
smiling on the sleeping Lord Harry. 'Such a
beautiful young man. Ain't got much in his
cock-loft, but then that's all to the good. He has got
good legs.'

Deirdre blushed and turned her head away.

'I said, his legs are good,' went on Lady
Godolphin cheerfully. 'Can't abide a man with
skinny legs. Now, Mr Anstey ain't well-endowed in
that direction. Arthur has lovely legs, but he's so
old.'

'Do you mean Colonel Brian?' asked Deirdre faintly.

'Yes. Him. I told him I didn't want to be calloused, but that we were obviously not meant for each other. Of course ... *well!*'

Lady Godolphin's eyes were bulging from her head as she stared out of the carriage window. The horses had slowed down as they negotiated the steep slope of Highgate Hill. Deirdre leaned forwards to see what had caught Lady Godolphin's attention.

Outside a hostelry on a rustic bench in the chilly sunlight sat Mr Anstey and Lady Chester—the octogenarian Lady Chester.

Lady Godolphin leaned back quickly, biting her lips. 'No, I won't go and ask him what he's doing,' she said aloud, although obviously talking to herself. 'It's a chance redervows. He's sorry for the poor old bat, that's all.'

She began to fan herself vigorously, looking the picture of misery.

Deirdre felt dreadfully embarrassed and wished Lord Harry would wake up. A large tear rolled down Lady Godolphin's cheek, turning red as it rolled down through a patch of rouge.

Picking up her parasol, Deirdre stabbed Lord Harry in one of his delicious legs.

'Ouch!' said his lordship, rubbing his leg. His summer-blue gaze came to rest on Lady Godolphin's distressed face.

'You should not become so exercised, ma'am,' he said gently. 'It quite ruins your unique beauty. What is wrong?'

'I am a trifle sick from the motion of the carriage,' said Lady Godolphin, looking

112

woebegone.

He pulled a silver vinaigrette from out of his pocket and handed it to her.

'So I am not the only one who is too cowardly to talk of my folly and humiliation,' thought Deirdre.

She gave Lady Godolphin's hand a squeeze, her own eyes filling with sympathetic tears. Did Guy really hate her so much? Oh, if only by some miracle he would appear again and tell her he had been insane with drink and that he was dying with love for her! Sometimes the weight of shame seemed too much to bear.

She often started from her dreams with the sound of his jeering voice in her ears. Lord Harry looked hopefully at Lady Godolphin as if waiting for something, but she soon sniffled herself into silence and then nodded off.

Deirdre looked out of the window, hoping he had not noticed her own distress.

To her relief, he went to sleep again.

She fell to wondering about his family. He had said he had three younger brothers and two little sisters. His brothers were called William, Paul and Jonathan. The girls, Amy and Elizabeth. The brothers were not married. That made it all very unnerving. Perhaps they would think Lord Harry had been trapped and would talk him out of marrying her—which would serve her ends but be a very uncomfortable operation all the same.

In her mind's eye, she could see them now, all lined up to meet her; all beautifully dressed, exquisitely mannered, and impenetrably stupid.

At last, the carriage turned into a driveway and began to bowl along a well-kept road through pretty parkland.

The name of the Earl of Carchester's residence was Archer Hall. Deirdre wondered whether Archer was an old family name.

Archer Hall turned out to be a fairly modern edifice, built only about sixty years before when aristocratic families had started moving their saloons and drawing-rooms from the first floor to the ground floor and putting in french windows, the better to enjoy the sylvan beauties of the countryside.

Clouds covered the sun as they swept around under the portico and an icy wind rattled the bare branches of the trees. A mournful, moulting peacock screamed harshly at them before it turned and walked away.

Lord Harry came as neatly and quickly awake as he had fallen asleep. Lady Godolphin rallied bravely as she was helped down from the carriage, although she looked as if she would like to have a good cry.

Some ten minutes later, Deirdre was studying the Carchester family and searching their faces in vain for some resemblance to Lord Harry.

They were all remarkably dark and squat and ugly. The Countess of Carchester, Lord Harry's mother, was a massive, brooding woman with a heavy moustache and a sallow complexion. Her rather wet brown eyes surveyed her eldest son and his fiancée with suspicion. Deirdre was to learn later that the Countess always looked like that.

His father, the earl, was also squat and sallow, but where his wife was generously endowed with hair in all the wrong places, he had none in the right places, being as bald as a coot.

Lord Harry's three brothers, and two 'little'

sisters—they were more or less the same age as Deirdre—were all squat and dark, like so many trolls.

What they lacked in looks, they made up for in exuberance, laughing loudly at family jokes which were unintelligible to the outsider.

They made no effort to engage Deirdre in conversation. The whole afternoon's conversation revolved around when Uncle Jeremy would die and leave his money bags to Harry. Lord Harry's sisters did seem, at one point, to become aware of Deirdre's presence by agreeing it was a shame poor Harry had to marry to get the money.

Deirdre, whose *amour propre* had been pretty much wrecked by Guy Wentwater, was now made to feel a positive dowd by the Carchesters. Without precisely saying so, Lord Harry's family all seemed to consider it a marriage of convenience. They seemed to quite hero worship this one Adonis in their ugly brood and perhaps would not have considered any female good enough for their beautiful brother.

But Deirdre felt herself growing smaller and uglier by the minute, and tried to console herself with a fantasy that a party of simply dashing young men would arrive, and each and every one of them would promptly fall head over heels in love with her.

Time is a strange thing. Sometimes it seems to race along and sometimes it seems to stand still. Deirdre was quite convinced a whole hour had passed and nearly burst into tears when she realized she had only been sitting enduring the company of her future in-laws for ten minutes.

Lady Godolphin was out of sorts. She refused

115

tea and demanded brandy. She insisted on giving Lady Carchester a recipe for a depilatory which used an incredible amount of slaked lime.

Lady Godolphin seemed fascinated by the Countess's moustache and kept returning to the subject. She told a story of how the Earl of Albemarle, ambassador extraordinary to Paris in 1752, had managed to persuade a 'celebrated artist' to cross over to England and pay a professional call on the Duchess of Newcastle, wife of the Secretary of State. This barber successfully shaved her Grace's upper lip. 'The performance lasted but one minute and three seconds.' The Duke was so pleased that he settled four hundred pounds a year on the Frenchman for life.

Then she went on to recommend another depilatory by Marcus Hyams—'a composition for shaving without the use of razor, soap or water.'

Most of this fell on stony ground since Lady Godolphin did not say 'depilatory' but 'debilatory' and confusion was added to confusion when the earl decided she was talking about aids to sexual potency and silenced her by saying it was not a fit subject for the drawing-room.

At last it was time to leave.

Lord Harry took casual but affectionate farewell of his doting and horrible family. Deirdre curtseyed low, hoping they had all taken her in such dislike that they would forbid the marriage.

But, on the other hand, if they did, she would have to return home. Impossible to suggest to Annabelle and Minerva that she come to live with one of them since she could not stand *père* Armitage. Minerva would be shocked to the depths of her Christian soul, and Annabelle would laugh

116

and tell her she was being ridiculous.

Lady Godolphin grumbled on about the strange and incalculable ways of men to an uncomprehending but sympathetic Lord Harry and Deirdre affected to fall asleep. Soon the act became reality and she dozed off.

*   *   *

Meanwhile, Guy Wentwater had almost forgotten about Silas Dubois. He had removed himself and his friends from Hopeworth as quickly as possible. His friends had cursed him roundly for having put them in a position where they were roused from their beds in the middle of the night by Lord Harry Desire who had threatened them into silence in no uncertain manner.

He strolled into Humbold's coffee house in St James's. The announcement of Deirdre's marriage had not surprised him; probably Lord Harry had clubbed her into submitting to the engagement and would drag her off to the altar by the hair.

A shadow fell across him and he looked up into the unlovely features of Silas Dubois.

Mr Dubois had been called a walking lampoon by his critics by virtue of his small, slight figure and very large nose.

He slid into a chair opposite Guy with his usual furtive, crab-like motion and fixed him with his beady eyes.

'I have been looking for you,' said Dubois. 'A fine mull you made of things. Desire is to marry that Armitage chit.'

'The arrangement was to humiliate the Armitages and I achieved just that,' said Guy

117

attempting an air of nonchalance.

'How?' demanded Silas Dubois eagerly.

And so Guy told him a carefully edited account of his promise to elope with Deirdre and his subsequent humiliation of her in front of his friends.

'And what did the good vicar say when he heard of this?' asked Silas drily.

'Well,' said Guy, flushing. 'He did not hear of it from her ... evidently. And I decided it would not be gentlemanly to speak of it. We agreed to humiliate her. I have done so. My part is played.'

'You cowardly fool,' hissed Silas. 'It was to humiliate the whole family. Had you played your part aright, then Desire would never have married the chit.'

'He is not yet married to her,' pointed out Guy huffily.

'Nor must he,' said Silas.

'Eh?'

'I have a distant relative, Jeremy Blewett, a nabob. By coincidence, he is Desire's uncle. He will leave his fortune to Desire if he marries. If he does not, the money comes to me. I learned all this from the cagey old fool a bare week ago. Evidently Desire has known of it for some time.'

'Everyone's known about it for some time,' sneered Guy. 'You heard in the clubs that Armitage was planning a marriage between Desire and his daughter. Did you not know the *reason* Desire wanted the marriage?'

Dubois bit his knuckles and stared at Guy over the large promontory of his nose.

'No, I did not know. But you told me you planned to *seduce* the Armitage girl. Not promise

118

to elope with her, tell her you couldn't because she was a dowdy doxy, and then keep the humiliation between yourselves. It seems from your account that she went straight back and told Desire to marry her.'

'No doubt the other way round. Desire's in love with her.'

'Love!' scoffed Silas Dubois.

'"Love is the *fart*
Of every heart;
It pains a man when 'tis kept close;
And others doth offend, when 'tis let loose."'

'Would you say Deirdre Armitage was in love with you?'

'Oh, yes, definitely,' said Guy smugly. 'Mad for me, she was. Not now, of course.'

'Then you must make her so,' said Silas.

Guy stood up. 'Who are you to give me orders, sirrah?' he said coldly.

'I gave you my time before because it amused me to plan a way to revenge myself on the Armitage family. Sooner or later the vicar will learn his precious daughter only became affianced to Desire on the rebound. That is enough.'

'Sit down,' said Silas coldly.

Guy half-turned to leave. 'Sit down, Mr Evans,' said Silas in a soft voice.

Guy whirled about, his face blanching. 'Oh, aye,' chuckled Silas. 'I know the history, you see. Learned it once down Bristol way. That so-called aunt of yours is really your mother. Made a mort o' money running a chain of bawdy houses in Bristol. Biggest abbess in the town. Had you out o' wedlock, brought you up and gave you enough money to start your life and turned you out of the nest. Took herself off to the depths of the country, adopted a fake title, and pleaded genteel poverty although she's as rich as Golden Ball.

'You took to slave trading and made your pile. You sold out because you wanted the rank and life of gentlemen. You play my game and you can keep it and earn money from me besides. You keep on walking and the whole of London and Hopeworth and Berham county will learn by nightfall that you're the bastard son of a brothel keeper.'

'I'll kill you first,' whispered Guy, sitting down again.

'You don't need to,' grinned Silas. 'Just do one little thing for me. Tell this Deirdre Armitage you cast her off because you knew her father would never recognize her again if she married you. Get her to fall in love with you so that Desire will have nothing to do with her. Stop the marriage. Blewett's on his last legs. He's not going to make out a new will until after the wedding. Even if you delay the wedding, that will be enough.'

Guy closed his eyes. He was terrified of Lord Harry punching him in the face again, he was terrified of the vicar and his pack of hellhounds, but now he was even more terrified of Silas Dubois.

'You knew of the will,' he accused Silas, 'when you listened to my plans to seduce Deirdre Armitage. Well, I did plan to seduce her, but marrying her cousin, Emily, seemed better game. Sir Edwin is very rich and his social standing is high. But you, you wanted me to make her shoddy goods so that Desire would not touch her. You knew about the will.'

'In faith, I did not,' said Silas with a shrug. 'But that is now beside the point. You have a month in which to reanimate the affections of Miss Armitage.'

'But what if 'I can't!' said Guy, perspiration dotting his brow.

'Then you must do it by other means,' said Silas Dubois, 'or your life in society will come to an end. Oh, it was bad enough you being a slave trader, but then so were a lot of respectable gentlemen and no one thinks the worse of them once their trading days are over. *Now,* you are respectable. See you do all in your power to keep it that way.'

He slid out from behind the table and made his way out of the coffee house, turning every so often to smile over his shoulder at the still, rigid figure of Guy Wentwater.

*   *   *

The Reverend Charles Armitage was pacing the hall of his daughter Minerva's town house, waiting for Deirdre to arrive back.

He was troubled in his conscience. Deirdre had become quieter and quieter and unhappier and unhappier since they had arrived in Town. Neither Minerva nor Annabelle had seemed to notice anything amiss with their younger sister and for a while this had eased the vicar's worries. But all at once he felt he must ascertain whether Deirdre really wanted this marriage or not.

Because he was nervous, he had dressed in his best. His corsets were lashed to suffocating point, his paint was artfully delicate, like the sunset on a watercolour painting, and his white waistcoat had

121

silver stripes.

He heard the rumble of the carriage wheels. Lord Harry did not enter the house with Deirdre but kissed her hand and went back to escort Lady Godolphin home.

The butler held open the door and Deirdre entered, looking weary and dejected.

'Come into the library,' said the vicar.

'Must I, Papa?' said Deirdre listlessly. But she pulled her bonnet from her head, and, dangling it by the ribbons, trailed after him.

The vicar held open the door and ushered her in. He held out his arms and pinned an affectionate, paternal smile on his face.

'My darling, little daughter,' he said, trying to take her in his arms.

Deirdre shrank back with such a look of naked disgust on her face that the vicar stood frozen to the spot. She walked past him and stood with her back to him.

'What is it, Papa?' she asked in a flat little voice.

'Hey, well, don't you see,' blustered the vicar, 'I am worried about you. Seems you are not happy about this here marriage.'

He struck an attitude. 'Well, I tell ye, there's no need for you to worry. I'll cancel the whole wedding. There!' He stood beaming.

Deirdre turned around, her green gaze raking him coldly from head to foot. She had an all-consuming desire to let him know just how much she despised him.

'It does not matter whom I marry, Papa,' she said. 'One man is much like t'other in my opinion. None fortunately disgust me as much as you.'

'What!' screamed the vicar, hardly able to

believe his ears.

'Oh, strike me if it makes you feel better,' said Deirdre, still in that horrible, little voice. 'You are a bag of wind, Papa; a selfish, painted, posturing boor. You! A vicar! You would sell your daughters on the slave market if you thought we would fetch a high enough price. I shall marry Lord Harry ... to escape from you and your repellent presence. How Mama put up with you all these years, I shall never know. You should be happy. Another rich husband tethered in the Armitage stable. Now, if you will excuse me, I must lie down.'

The vicar stood, puffing and panting, his eyes starting from his head, his hand on his heart.

Deirdre walked past him and quietly closed the door of the library behind her.

*　　　*　　　*

Squire Radford was a very unhappy and lonely man. The long days had passed without gossip or bustle or incident. He had a bad conscience. He had accused his friend, the vicar, of having no faith to lose, and, furthermore, he had insulted his personal appearance.

The sad fact was that life without even a puffed-up posturing vicar was deadly dull. Assailed with nervous boredom for almost the first time in his life and plagued with many of the irritating little pains and stiffnesses of old age, the squire began gloomily to wonder how much longer he could be expected to live. One thing was sure. He must make his peace with his old friend.

But the vicar was in London. The squire had been invited to the wedding, but all of a sudden, he decided he could not wait until then to present his humble apologies to Charles Armitage. He would leave for Town that very afternoon and seek him out.

The gates at the end of his drive creaked loudly on their hinges. He stood up and went to the window.

Muffled up against the cold in a many-caped greatcoat, the Reverend Charles Armitage was riding slowly up the drive.

Excitedly, the squire rang the bell and told his servant the vicar was to be ushered into the library immediately and one of the best bottles of port brought up from the cellar.

Then he scuttled quickly to answer the door himself. The stable boy was leading the vicar's horse away towards the back of the house.

The vicar stood on the doorstep, his shovel hat in his hand. He raised a pair of eyes swimming with tears to the squire's face, and blurted out, 'I need your help, Jimmy. I'm in sore pain.'

'Come in, Charles!' cried the squire, much alarmed.

He tugged his friend's heavy cloak from his shoulders, and with urgent murmurs of comfort and little pushes in the back propelled the vicar into his old seat in front of the fire.

The squire sat down opposite and leaned forward.

'I have missed you, Charles,' he said. 'But I have only myself to blame. I cannot forgive myself for my harsh words to you.'

'Oh, *don't!*' wailed the vicar, completely overset. He knuckled his eyes with his chubby hands and cried and cried. Finally, he took out a huge, red, belcher handkerchief and blew his nose with a sound like the last trump and then mopped his streaming eyes.

'Tsk! Tsk!' said the poor squire, now thoroughly alarmed, despite the comforting glow that was spreading through his old frame. Charles was in trouble and had come to him for advice as he had come so many times before.

'We have had our troubles in the past, Charles,' said the squire earnestly, 'and together we have managed to solve all problems.

'Ah, Ram. Leave the bottle and glasses on the little table and place it between us and then leave us. Now, Charles. Drink a glass of this and tell me your troubles.'

The vicar hiccuped dismally, but nonetheless managed to toss back a full glass of port without pausing for breath. His face lightened and he promptly helped himself to another.

'I'm that ashamed,' he said, his face puckering up like that of a hurt baby. ' "Woe, woe unto them that draw iniquity with cords of vanity, and sin as it were with a cart rope." Isaiah, Chapter Four, Verse 18.'

'Dear me!' exclaimed the squire, becoming more alarmed by the minute.

'Yes,' said the vicar, heaving a gusty sigh. 'Vanity. That was my downfall.'

The squire noticed that the vicar's face was free of paint and that his ample figure was no longer confined by a corset.

'Now my own daughter spits in my eye. I have nourished a viper in my bosom!' moaned the vicar, putting out a feeble hand for the bottle of port and helping himself to yet another glass.

125

'Deirdre?' asked the squire.

'Yes, her,' said the vicar. 'Not my fault. Told me she wanted to marry Desire. *I* didn't force her into it. But she says she's marrying him because all men are the same and I'm the most disgusting of the lot. She ... she called me "a selfish, painted, posturing boor." And, oh, it's true. After she said that I went upstairs and looked at myself in the long glass. The scales were dropped from mine eyes and I saw this awful little painted caper-merchant staring back at me.'

'Now, now,' said the squire soothingly. 'You see the problem is that when you are yourself, Charles, and attired in your usual country good taste, why, you look a very fine figure of a man. With your paint and ... er ... other embellishments, it was like meeting a stranger, and very upsetting it was, too. Only remember how cruel I was to you? It was very harsh and impudent of Deirdre to say such things, but I am sure they were prompted by love ... as my remarks were.'

'Aye, you're right,' said the vicar. 'But Deirdre is dreadfully unhappy about something. She's not the same girl, not by a long chalk.'

'I accused you quite wrongly of lack of faith,' said the squire tentatively. 'Have you thought of placing your daughter in God's hands?'

'Turn my will over to Him? Oh, I find that mortal hard. I tell 'ee, Jimmy, my prayers are like those coloured soap bubbles. I send 'em up to Heaven, saying, "Here it is, Thy will be done," but afore they can get very high, I say, "Hey, wait a bit. I'll do it my way," and I stick up my finger and pop the bubble before it rises any higher.'

There was a long silence.

A few tiny snowflakes began to spatter against the glass and bounce about the lawn outside. The wind gave a sudden howl in the chimney and great yellow and red flames shot up with a roar, and then died down, leaving a small heaven of red stars burning in the sooty back wall of the fireplace.

'There is a mystery here and I think it concerns Miss Deirdre,' said the squire.

'It was the night you put out the alarm she was missing. I was about to tell you what I knew but by the time I found my coat and boots, a village boy came rushing up to tell me she had been found.' He went on to relate how he had seen a young woman like Deirdre carrying two bandboxes, hurrying along the far side of the pond, and how later, at dawn, he had seen Lord Harry returning with two bandboxes.

The vicar sat up straight, his lips moving soundlessly as he tried to work something out.

'Wentwater,' he said at last, while the squire looked at him with bright eyes. 'By all that's unholy. She tried to go to Wentwater so as to escape the marriage and Desire found out. So why does Desire want to marry her, heh? What do I know of this Lord Harry? Heh? Seemed an amiable enough clod. Where's Wentwater?'

'Gone. He left the morning after Deirdre went missing.'

'Oho! I wonder if I can get anything out of Lady Wentwater. No. Waste of time.' He settled back comfortably in his chair, looking so much like his old self that the squire felt sentimental tears pricking at his eyes.

The wine sank lower in the bottle and the day darkened outside as the vicar sat and thought.

'Deirdre was always a strong-willed girl,' he said. 'She didn't want none of Lord Harry, not a bit of it. Then she suddenly changes her mind, and, while he's at the vicarage, although she's a bit rude with him and off-hand, like, she still has a glow about her. Then when she comes back with him that night, she's gone all hard and cold and bitter. Now she's even more bitter, and demme if I don't think she's frightened of Lord Harry. See here, Lord Harry found out something about her that night and is making her marry him.'

'Dear me,' said the squire. 'I wonder what it was? You do not think, do you, that there was any ... well ... foul play on the part of Wentwater?'

'No,' said the vicar slowly. 'He was chasing after Emily. But no one saw him near Deirdre. Lord Harry's the problem, mark you. It must be something awful bad for her not to have told Minerva and Annabelle. I asked both of 'em before I left Town but they seemed to find nothing amiss. O' course, Annabelle's so full of all them adventures she had at the wars, and Minerva's so taken up with Julian—my grandchild,' he explained unnecessarily and puffing out his chest, 'that they wouldn't notice anything.

'I'm going back to Town to find out all about it. I'll study them both and think of something to stop the wedding.

'For mark my words, Jimmy, that wedding is not going to take place or my name's not Charles Armitage.'

* * *

'Minerva!'

128

'My love?'

Lady Sylvester put down her sewing and smiled on her lord.

Lord Sylvester stretched his elegant legs in front of him and studied the gold tassels of his hessian boots.

'I am a trifle concerned over that sister of yours.'

'Deirdre? But why? She is to be married to a very suitable young man.'

'But I don't think she wants to get married,' said Lord Sylvester, his green eyes meeting those of his wife in an unblinking cat-like stare. 'I think your wretched Papa was groping around to find money while we were absent. Lady Godolphin confessed *he* proposed to Harry Desire.'

Minerva threw back her head. 'My sister shall not be constrained to marry *anyone*. I will talk to Papa.'

'No, my crusading love, there is no need to do that. See that Deirdre and Desire are kept apart as much as possible. If Deirdre seems glad to be kept away from him, then you will have the truth of the matter. It is all very simple. Weddings can always be cancelled, you know.'

*   *   *

Annabelle patted her sunny ringlets in front of the glass and blew a kiss in the direction of her husband. 'Why so solemn?' she laughed.

'Deirdre,' said the Marquess of Brabington, 'is scared to death of marrying Harry Desire.'

'Oh, *Deirdre,*' shrugged Annabelle. 'Fustian! She's always play-acting.'

'But, my sweeting, I can assure you ...'

129

'You can assure me of a kiss right this minute, Peter, or I shall scream.'

Half an hour later Annabelle murmured lazily, 'What were you saying about Deirdre?'

'What?' said the Marquess of Brabington, running a hand slowly over his wife's hip. 'Oh, nothing. 'Twas nothing at all.'

SEVEN

Deirdre let herself quietly out of her sister Minerva's town house in St James's Square and took a deep breath.

A light powdering of snow lay on the ground. The day was cold and damp with heavy, lowering clouds above, promising more snow to come.

She had passed a puzzling week. No longer did she have to plot to avoid Lord Harry's company. She had hardly had a chance to see him at all. Minerva took her everywhere, often on the flimsiest of excuses. And then the night before, Lord Sylvester and Minerva had taken her to the opera and Lord Harry was not of the party but two most eligible young men were. When Deirdre had asked the whereabouts of her fiancé, Minerva had replied, with uncharacteristic vagueness, that she had forgotten to invite him.

Then if it was not Minerva who was on hand to keep her out of her fiancé's way, it was her father and Squire Radford. The vicar, looking very much like his normal self, showed a sudden enthusiasm for seeing all the warehouses and shops in London, insisting that she must need extra ribbons and lace

130

for her trousseau. Deirdre found her father's new quiet demeanour more acceptable although she still disliked him, but the squire was, as usual, the complete gentleman, and Deirdre enjoyed his company immensely.

Once, when she was strolling along Bond Street with the squire and her father, Deirdre had seen Lord Harry approaching and had told her father. He and the squire had then behaved most oddly. They had seized her arms and hustled her quickly into the nearest shop.

Then there were the odd conversations. Minerva told of tragic marriages where the couples had been most unsuited; the vicar told her of instances where marriages had been called off at the last moment and the parties concerned had been grateful ever afterwards.

Obviously everyone concerned had gathered she did not really want to marry Lord Harry and was encouraging her with heavy-handed tact to break the engagement.

But if she told Lord Harry the wedding was off, then he would probably be absolutely furious and might even follow through his threat and sue her for breach of promise.

But yet, the prison gates seemed to be opening. Surely Lord Harry would not care to make a cake of himself in the courts by sueing her!

But now that she was kept away from her fiancé, Deirdre became filled with a paradoxical longing to see him, if just for a little.

At times, he had been very pleasant company indeed. He was not intelligent, but his manners were beautiful. Ladies seemed fascinated by his beauty, and Deirdre was feminine enough to enjoy their jealousy. And she had recently been introduced to a very intelligent member of the House of Lords who was supposed to be famous for his wit. But he had patronized Deirdre quite dreadfully, a thing Lord Harry would never dream of doing.

When she had been escorted by her tall and handsome fiancé, yes, she had to admit it was pleasurable to be looked on with envy. Now, with the Armitage family closing tightly about her again, Deirdre felt as if she were being driven slowly back to the nursery.

Minerva had even volunteered to read to her and kept giving her nasty little glasses of tonic because she 'needed building up'.

Deirdre would gladly have stayed at home at least one evening to play with baby Julian, but she was told that young misses like herself should be gadding about, and not sitting around the house like old, married ladies.

And so the more conspicuous Lord Harry became by his absence, the more Deirdre began to wonder about the strange and tumultuous reaction of her body to his kisses. Did lust have a place in love?

On that morning she had awoken with a craving to be left alone with her thoughts, and so she had escaped from the house, meaning to walk as far as Green Park. She did not have her maid with her or even a groom, but it was early and all the bucks and bloods who might annoy a solitary female could be guaranteed to be fast asleep for at least another five hours.

A small, slight man with a huge nose stared into her face intently, almost popping his own under the shadow of her bonnet to do so. Deirdre shrank back with a little cry and the man murmured some apology and scurried away.

The hour was nine in the morning. Nothing really came alive in the West End until ten. How still and white and deserted the streets seemed!

There was that strange little man again!

Deirdre was sure she saw him scuttling across the end of the street. She stood still. There was something eerie about it all.

There he was! But it turned out to be the shambling figure of the watch. He touched his hat as he passed. Deirdre half turned towards home. But the broad expanse of Piccadilly lay just ahead. And if she returned, Minerva would find her and immediately begin making plans for her day.

She bent her head and hurried into Piccadilly. There were a good few people about. Shopkeepers taking down shutters; shopkeepers who served the rich and therefore kept the same hours.

Crossing sweepers were busy with their brooms. A child rolled a large metal hoop this way and that, admiring the patterns it made in the snow. Another ran a stick backwards and forwards across the railings.

Deirdre entered Green Park, only walking a little way in so as not to be too isolated from the road. She brushed the light snow from a bench and sat down and tried to marshal her thoughts.

At last she came to the conclusion that she had treated Lord Harry unfairly. She was the one who had asked him to marry her. It was only fair to the man to tell him of her fears and doubts. In the depths of the country when he had said he would sue her for breach of promise, it seemed believable,

133

since, if he did not marry, he did not inherit his uncle's money.

But in Town, it was all too obvious that a great many ladies would be only too eager to marry Lord Harry if he dropped the handkerchief. And why was she afraid of him? He had been all that was kind and gentlemanly. His family was horrible, but then look at her own father!

Deirdre stood up at last feeling better than she had done for a long time. She *would* talk to Lord Harry. Getting him to understand simple things was often very hard, she thought, but she could try.

She began to walk towards the gates of the Park. A tall figure was standing right in her path.

Deirdre shied like a frightened horse and put her head down, ready to scuttle round him if he persisted in trying to block her way.

'Deirdre? Is it you?'

Deirdre looked up in amazement into Guy Wentwater's face.

'*You!*' she said in accents of loathing.

She gave him a great push and then hurried past him as fast as she could, the iron ring on the soles of her pattens striking sparks from the pebbles.

He hurried after her, caught her in a strong grasp and twisted her about to face him, his eyes pleading and anxious.

'You must listen to me,' he said intensely.

Guy had been rousted from his bed in his lodging only a short time before by Silas Dubois and ordered to 'go to it'.

He was frantic. He was tired of his shadowy wandering life and had a mind to settle down as a country gentleman. Marrying Emily Armitage would have made the vicar rage and would have

134

supplied him, Guy, with a respectable wife with a respectable dowry. Now he would need to find some other girl. For when his seduction of Deirdre Armitage became known, he would need to hide out in another part of the country and hope the vicar died of apoplexy. If he could, on the other hand, not seduce her but merely encourage her into some folly that would drive her to cancel the wedding, then there was still hope.

But he must re-engage her affections fast, or Silas would spread the awful secret of his birth all over the place.

'Leave me alone,' said Deirdre savagely, 'or I shall scream for the watch.'

'You must hear me,' said Guy, holding her fast. 'You will hear me. I am as much in love with you as I ever was. Yes, I treated you shamefully. But it was for your own good.'

'Indeed?' said Deirdre, standing very still now.

'Yes,' he went on eagerly. 'You must realize I was afraid our marriage would not work. Your family would never speak to you again. I was afraid you would grow tired of being estranged from them. I was frantic when you turned up at my aunt's. I had to be cruel. I felt I had to give you a disgust of me, to drive you away. I was drunk, yes. That I freely admit. But I have not known a night's sleep since then.

'Only look at me and say you forgive me.'

Deirdre kept her head bent.

'You were courting Emily as far as I could see,' she said at last.

'Ah, that was merely to throw sand in everyone's eyes. The minute I heard you were affianced to Desire, I felt ashamed. I felt responsible for you

135

throwing yourself away.'

Deirdre looked up at him at last, her eyes as green and cold as the North Sea. 'I am hardly throwing myself away by becoming affianced to a kind and handsome lord.'

'Of course you are angry with me,' he said in a coaxing voice. 'I deserve more, much more. How can I make you forgive me?'

Deirdre suddenly felt infinitely weary. It had all been too much. All her troubles churned round in her head; her fear of Lord Harry, her hatred of her father, her low self-esteem, all culminating in a great sickening wave of hot self-disgust. She wanted to punish the whole wide world—starting off with herself.

Deirdre took a deep breath. 'By eloping with me,' she said quietly.

Guy's mind raced. Gone were his hopes of Emily's hand in marriage. He need not marry Deirdre, of course. Perhaps he could hide her away somewhere and return her to her family unscathed. Perhaps she would be too ashamed of herself to tell them where she had been. She had obviously told no one of her last try at eloping with him.

But then there was Harry Desire. But he would not want to have anything to do with a girl who jilted him right before the wedding.

'Very well,' said Guy, feeling her penetrating gaze on his face. 'When?'

'Tomorrow,' said Deirdre. 'I mean tonight, but at two in the morning. Wait for me here.'

'You are sure you will be able to escape unnoticed?' asked Guy anxiously.

'Oh, yes,' said Deirdre simply. 'Now, let me go. I must return. It is cold.'

Guy tried to embrace her but she pushed him firmly away. 'Not here,' she said. 'It is too public.'

She broke free from him and hurried off over the snowy ground, moving so quickly that her cloak billowed out about her slight figure.

Guy watched her go, his heart beating hard. He must think where to take her. He must pray she told no one of what she planned to do.

Deirdre walked on, her mind filled with a savage elation. She had no longer any romantic thoughts about Guy Wentwater. She thought him shallow and common. And so, she was bent on marrying him.

We all have a little of the death wish in us ready to rear its ugly head when we fall out of love with ourselves. The depressed commit suicide. But that is not a genteel act. The polite gentleman either commits suicide by regular instalments of hard liquor or by journeying unarmed into the more squalid parts of the city. Young ladies find a rotter to ruin them.

By marrying Guy Wentwater, Deirdre could flagellate herself and make her father thoroughly miserable into the bargain.

Fate seemed determined to aid her in her proposed action, for the vicar had left for a brief visit to Hopeworth on urgent parish business (good hunting weather), leaving Squire Radford behind as a sop to his shaky conscience. The squire had been attacked by an acute attack of rheumatism and was confined to his bedchamber.

Minerva had suddenly become aware that she had spent a great deal of time away from her beloved child while looking after Deirdre and trying to keep her away from Lord Harry. But Lord

137

Harry was keeping himself away, and so Minerva was determined to spend the whole day at home, fussing over her baby to her heart's content.

Lord Harry Desire was paying a visit to his uncle, Mr Jeremy Blewett.

Mr Jeremy Blewett looked very old indeed. He was, in fact, fifty-two, but a life in India under a hot sun combined with a formidable capacity for strong spirits had aged him until he resembled a little dried-up mummy.

He had been talking about death for such a long time that it came as a surprise to everyone to find him still alive. Apart from his eyes which were very bright and twinkling, the rest of him looked dead, and quite often smelled it, since he had a horror of bathing.

'What brings you here ... as if I need to ask?' cackled Mr Blewett as Lord Harry strolled into his bedchamber. 'Come to see if I've written that will yet? Well, it won't be written till the wedding's over.'

'You don't need to worry your pretty little head one way or t'other about my bachelor state,' said Lord Harry amiably. 'I don't need your moneybags.'

''Course you do,' sneered Mr Blewett. 'Carchesters never knew how to keep money.'

'They never knew how to make it either,' responded Lord Harry cheerfully, 'until I came along.'

'Don't tell me you've started working for a living!' exclaimed Mr Blewett. 'No, nothing so horrible. Gambling is my salvation.'

'I should have known. White's and Brooks's have been the sepulchres of many a fortune.'

'Not them. The Stock Exchange. I have a

138

genius for speculation. I am possessor of quite a large fortune, uncle. Wealth has descended on me suddenly. So, you see, you will need to concern yourself with bullying Silas Dubois.'

Mr Blewett looked sulky. 'I never meant to leave him a penny anyway. He doesn't like me and hasn't the grace to hide it.'

'It serves you right for being such a miserable old sinner. Anyway, you don't need to leave me any money, and I don't need to get married.'

'Don't love the girl, eh?'

'I did not say that. I am merely pointing out that due to my exceptional talent for moving around stocks and shares, I am at liberty to marry anyone I please, and when I please. Nonetheless, you can trundle out your bath chair for the wedding and arrive like the bad fairy in time to bring down curses on my nuptials.

'But do, please put the horrible Silas out of his misery. He's perfectly capable of killing you just to get your money if you tease him too much.'

'That great walking nose! Never! Don't trip over the other relatives on the way out. They gather around me like vultures.'

'And don't you adore it. It's what keeps you alive, dear uncle, all this manipulating and string-pulling.'

Mr Blewett gave a harsh cackle of laughter. 'Perhaps you have the right of it, Harry. But I'll probably leave you the money anyway. You never cared a rap for my bullying and you don't creep around me in that fawning way Dubois has.'

'Oh, I am fond of you in my fashion,' said Lord Harry airily.

'Where are you off to?'

'To see my beloved. A thing I hardly do these days. By the time I meet her at the altar, I shall have quite forgot what she looks like.'

Lord Harry sailed out, and nearly collided with Silas Dubois who was standing outside.

'I wouldn't lurk there, dear boy,' said Lord Harry earnestly. 'The door is so thick, you can't hear a word through it, and you're only likely to get a terrible earache from pressing your ear to the keyhole.'

Lord Harry went off quickly down the stairs before Mr Dubois could think of a reply.

Mr Dubois went into the bedroom.

'Oh, it's you, is it?' snapped Mr Blewett huffily. 'Still waiting for me to die, Silas?'

'Of course not,' said Mr Dubois, his small mouth curving up under the shadow of his nose in what he hoped was an affectionate smile. 'I passed Desire on the stairs. There is a rumour he might not wed after all.'

'Nonsense,' said Mr Blewett, looking slyly out of the corner of his eyes at Mr Dubois. 'Needs to get married.'

'I hear he has been speculating on 'Change to some effect,' said Mr Dubois.

'All a hum,' said Jeremy gleefully. 'The terms of my will still stand. If Desire weds, he gets the money. If he don't, you do.'

Silas grinned. By tomorrow morning, everyone, including this horrible old carcase of a man, would know that Lord Harry's intended bride had eloped with Guy Wentwater.

'What you so happy about all of a sudden?' snapped Mr Blewett.

'Only happy to see you so well and in such good

spirits,' replied Silas Dubois, coming forwards and solicitously plumping up Mr Blewett's pillows.

His hands stilled for a moment. How easy it would be, he thought, to jerk out this silk and lace pillow and hold it down on the old man's face!

Silas became aware that Mr Blewett was staring up at him with a sort of unholy glee on his face, almost as if he could read his mind. He quickly finished plumping the pillows, and sidled to the foot of the bed.

Why commit murder? Tomorrow would see a change in the old man's thoughts. And he could not live much longer anyway.

*   *   *

Deirdre went into the morning room to find Minerva busy writing a letter to Mrs Armitage who had remained behind at Hopeworth with the younger girls.

'Where is His Lordship the baby?' asked Deirdre.

'Asleep,' smiled Minerva. 'Oh, it is so wonderful *not* to have any engagements! I shall lounge for the rest of the day. Oh, dear. Someone has arrived. I shall say we are not at home.'

'Lord Harry Desire,' announced the Comfreys' evil-looking butler.

'Tell his lordship we are not at home,' said Minerva quickly.

'Tell his lordship we *are* at home,' corrected Deirdre crossly. Now that she had set her mind on social ruin and personal degradation Lord Harry held no further fears for her. Besides, all Deirdre's old resentment at Minerva's bossy ways had come

141

rushing to the surface.

'Well, if you *really* want to see him ...?' began Minerva. But Deirdre had already left the room. Minerva hesitated, wanting to follow her. Then she relaxed. Sylvester had promised to have things out with Lord Harry some time soon and Deirdre would not have gone rushing to see a man of whom she was afraid.

'Have you come to take me driving?' asked Deirdre, as she met Lord Harry in the hall.

'No,' he smiled. 'I am come to talk to you, my love, about deep and serious things.'

'Oh,' said Deirdre anxiously. Then she rallied. It did not matter what he said; she would not be seeing him after today. It never crossed Deirdre's mind for a moment that Lord Harry might be hurt in the slightest by being jilted. Such a lummox could only have slow, bovine feelings. He was rather like an aristocratic peasant, she thought, briefly amused at her own wit.

'Well, where shall we go?' he asked, bringing Deirdre to the realization that they were both still standing in the hall.

She led the way into the library.

Lord Harry stood in front of the fireplace, and studied her face with his calm, blue gaze. She was strung up taut like a violin string, he thought. She looked just like someone about to jump off Westminster Bridge ... or elope with Guy Wentwater.

'Seen anything of that fellow who fought at Waterloo?' he asked. 'Whatshisname. Wentwater?'

'No,' said Deirdre breathlessly. 'Why do you ask?'

'I don't know. Making conversation, don't

you see.'

'What are the deep and serious things you want to talk to me about?' asked Deirdre.

'You shouldn't wear brown,' he said severely. 'Don't become you at all. It's a sort of mud colour. Not the thing.'

He put up his quizzing glass and stared at Deirdre's plain round gown with one horribly magnified eye.

'Is *that* one of the serious matters?' asked Deirdre acidly.

'No. Well, yes, it is in a way. Clothes are very important. Now, *I* look rather well in blue. It makes me appear more approachable.'

Deirdre looked at his faultless morning coat, the exquisite ruffles of his shirt, the wide innocence of his eyes, and her lip curled in contempt.

'Ah, but to come to the serious things,' he said. 'I say, can we sit down?'

'Of course.' Deirdre sat down primly on a small sofa in front of the fire and he arranged himself elegantly beside her.

He looked at her anxiously, his black curls tumbling over his forehead. Deirdre noticed for the first time that Lord Harry's lashes were extraordinarily long and thick.

'You see,' he said, 'I don't need to get married. I've made an awful lot of money on 'Change.'

'So you don't want to marry me?' asked Deirdre faintly.

'Well ... to put it bluntly ... no.'

'Oh.'

'You see, we should not suit. I am afraid I rather misled your father. I was teasing him, don't you see. I said I couldn't abide intelligent women, but I told a lie. I *adore* intelligent women.'

'Are you trying to tell me,' said Deirdre slowly and carefully, 'that *you* don't consider *me* intelligent?'

'You are beautiful and charming,' he said looking at her pleadingly, 'but an intelligent women has a mind of her own, and you ... well ... *"Tu nihil invita dices faciesve Minerva."*'

'I'm afraid I don't ...'

'No, of course, I forgot, you probably do not understand Latin.'

'On the contrary,' lied Deirdre, 'I *do* understand Latin ...'

'I was quoting from Horace ...'

'So there is no *need* to translate ...'

'And I said, "You will say nothing, do nothing, unless Minerva pleases."'

'I know very well what you said,' retorted Deirdre, her colour high. 'How *dare* you call *me* unintelligent. How would *you* know? You talk of trivialities the whole time. I *long* for someone to discuss politics with me, for example.'

'Certainly,' he said. 'I would like to hear your views on Parliamentary reform. I think Lord Liverpool and Lord Sidmouth are actually encouraging the radical faction so that an alarmed middle class will support all manner of repressive measures and the Tory supremacy will stand. What do you think?'

'I do not think you would understand my views,' said Deirdre, stalling for time. For she did not have the least idea what he was talking about.

'But an intelligent well-informed mind is capable of communicating his or her ideas. Pray, go on.'

'What is the point!' exclaimed Deirdre, jumping

up. 'You don't want to marry me anyway.' And overcome with a sudden realization of her own suicidal folly in rushing headlong into an elopement with a man who would probably abuse her, Deirdre burst into tears, and sat down again next to Lord Harry.

Guy had lounged back that terrible night and let his friends attempt to molest her. God only knew what he would do to her once they were married. Never had Deirdre felt so small or so silly.

A comforting arm stole about her shoulders and a large handkerchief was held out under her nose.

Deirdre took it gratefully and blew her nose and mopped her eyes.

'I thought I would please you,' said Lord Harry's voice at her ear, 'by telling you I didn't need to get married. You see, I could not help noticing you did not seem to favour my company. Also, I sustained a visit from your father before he left for the country. Poor man. He was torn with remorse over having forced you into an engagement you did not want, and the joys of hunting. John Summer, his whipper-in, had written to say the weather was excellent and that there was a wily fox sighted only a few miles from the vicarage. I put him out of his misery by saying I would not marry you. Then right on his heels came Lord Sylvester. *He* said you were frightened of me and he and his wife had done their best to keep you away from me, knowing that if you cared at all for me, you would become upset. But you didn't. Ergo, you don't like me. So I told *him* I wouldn't marry you.'

'Oh,' said Deirdre miserably, wondering why she didn't feel happy.

'I was worried about Mr Armitage. He said you

145

had come to loathe and hate him and it was all his own fault. He was so put about, like a sort of fox-hunting Shylock, running to the window to see if the carriage had arrived and wringing his hands and saying, "Oh, my daughter—oh, the hunt—oh, my daughter—oh, pray God Reynard gives us good chase."

'What misery I have caused you all! So all you need to do is nod your head and I will arrange for an announcement to be sent to the newspapers, terminating our engagement.'

He took both her hands in his.

'I know you wanted to elope with Guy Wentwater,' he said gently.

Deirdre had thought until then that she had tasted the dregs of humiliation, but this last statement proved her wrong.

'How did you know?' she whispered.

'Oh, little things all added up to the one big thing,' he said airily. 'So I went along and collected your bandboxes and had a most interesting talk with Mr Wentwater. After hearing how shockingly he had behaved, I was at least confident that you would never want to set eyes on him again. I thought, you see, that you might come to care for me a little.'

'And Mr Wentwater told you everything ... just like that?' mumbled Deirdre.

'Well, after a certain amount of ... er ... pressure. Do not worry. You will not be troubled by him again.'

Deirdre raised shaking hands to her hot face. The very idea of eloping with Guy seemed such a piece of madness now. A madwoman had made that arrangement.

'So,' he went on when she did not speak, 'I told your father I would escort you home to Hopeworth on the morrow, and then all your worries will be over. I know you hate it in Town. Perhaps I shall see you again during the Season.'

'I'm sorry ... for everything,' whispered Deirdre.

'You are not in any trouble?' he asked. 'Is there nothing you wish to tell me?'

Deirdre thought of her appointment with Guy Wentwater. She shuddered. Over and over again since he had walked into the library, this Lord Harry Desire, the man she had damned as a fool, had made *her* appear worse than an idiot. She could not tell him.

Deirdre dismally shook her head.

'Then I think you should tell Mr Radford the glad news of the termination of our engagement,' said Lord Harry. 'He only came to Town because your father begged him for help. I think it would be a great kindness if you could find it in your heart to forgive your father.'

'I must forgive myself first,' whispered Deirdre brokenly. 'I have caused all this distress. Now there are presents to be returned and ...'

'I am sure your sister, Lady Sylvester, will handle everything admirably. Now, I was to escort you to a ball at Lord and Lady Brothers' tonight. Lady Godolphin is to be of our party. If, however, you do not feel ...'

'I will go,' said Deirdre wretchedly. She knew all at once, if she stayed at home, then she would fret and worry about Mr Wentwater waiting for her in Green Park, and she would wait in dread in case he called at the house.

'Then I shall call for you this evening. I think

147

perhaps we might be friends, now that you do not need to fear marriage to me.'

'Yes,' said Deirdre in a low voice.

'Good,' he said smiling. 'Perhaps you might choose a bride for me.'

Deirdre looked at the sapphire and garnet ring on her fourth finger and twisted it off and mutely held it out to him. He took it and put it in his waistcoat pocket.

'You are still overset,' said Lord Harry. 'Allow me to tell your sister and brother-in-law and Squire Radford of the termination of our engagement.' He stood up and drew her to her feet.

She looked up into his face. He was looking down at her intently. He raised her hands to his lips and kissed them gently.

'Goodbye, Deirdre. We shall meet again, but as friends.'

He turned and walked from the room, leaving Deirdre shaken and buffeted by a series of emotions: humiliation, shame, and loss.

*   *   *

An hour later, Lord Harry entered his lodgings and looked thoughtfully at his Swiss.

'What is today's report, Bruno?' he asked, as he stripped off his driving gloves.

'Ah, milor,' sighed his servant, 'I regret I 'ave sad news. I had Miss Armitage followed as you requested. The man you 'ave watching the 'ouse in St James's Square who was to report if the lady went out alone, 'e come to me and say 'e follow 'er to the Green Park where she meet a man who ... who ... 'ug 'er, like thees,' he added, hugging

148

himself for emphasis.

'Our man keep behind the tree and 'e cannot 'ear everything but 'e 'ear mademoiselle say two in the morning in the Park.'

'Thank you, Bruno. You may call off the watchdog,' said Lord Harry, studying the pleats of his cravat in the glass.

'Milor,' said his servant apologetically, 'our man say mees was preparing, 'e tink, the elopement.'

'Just so. Pay him well.'

'Ver' good.'

Bruno bowed himself out, shaking his head over the peculiar ways of the English quality.

EIGHT

Minerva was not in the slightest pleased with her sister. She treated Deirdre to a long and severe lecture on the selfishness of allowing the wedding arrangements to proceed as far as they had. Deirdre had *deliberately,* said Minerva, turned poor Papa into some sort of ogre as an excuse for plunging deeper into the whole mess.

Feebly did Deirdre complain that Papa was not entirely blameless, and that a man who chased his daughter across the countryside with a whip could hardly be described as a loving and sensitive parent, but Minerva would not listen.

Lord Sylvester had had a *most* wretched time of it, talking to Lord Harry. Lord Harry was a perfect gentleman, and, in truth, probably too mature and polished for such a heartless hoyden as Deirdre.

The lecture would have gone on for much longer

149

if Lord Sylvester had not intervened by teasing his wife and saying all her prosing made his head ache.

Deirdre's only ally turned out to be the maid, Betty. Betty had learned that Sir Edwin had offered John Summer a job at the Hall. Had he taken it, then there would have been enough for them to get married. But John had proudly turned it down, saying, 'he would never desert the reverend.'

Men!

'You're not that bad, miss,' said Betty soothingly as she helped Deirdre to prepare for the ball. 'I heard what my lady said. But you are very young for your years and the vicar is a mortal hard man to cross. But all's well that ends well, for now you don't need to marry a man you don't want, and we can all be comfortable again.'

Deirdre sat miserably silent under Betty's ministrations. She had always believed that had she managed to be free of Lord Harry, then her relief and happiness would know no bounds. She never expected to feel as downcast and ... yes ... *silly* as this, for all the world like a spoilt child who boasts she does not care for a valuable toy, and yet cries bitterly when it is taken away from her.

Furthermore, Lord Harry had *tricked* her. Deirdre now knew he had gone out of his way to appear stupid. Not only that. He had quite deliberately shown her that she was singularly badly informed when it came to politics. Deirdre's idea of discussing politics and world affairs had been a hazy notion of listening to someone's views and promptly expressing those views to the next person she met. She realized she hardly ever read the newspapers.

All she really knew about the Battle of Waterloo was stories passed from one to the other. Guy's story of the battle she now discounted. He had probably never even been there.

Minerva was to blame, for Minerva had always laughed indulgently at Deirdre's opinions and said, 'Oh, little Deirdre is the *brains* of the family,' and what Minerva said other people came to accept and before you knew it, you had been presented with a whole lot of virtues you didn't really possess.

Minerva was apt to tuck people neatly into roles. Annabelle, beautiful and headstrong. Deirdre, intelligent. Daphne, the beauty of the family; modest and stylish. Diana, a wonderful way with animals. Frederica; dainty and funny, a whimsical little thing.

And yet Deirdre had longed for Minerva to interfere and rescue her from marriage to Lord Harry. And Minerva had. Or rather her husband had.

Deirdre's thoughts turned to her father. It seemed he had done his utmost to try to ensure her happiness, even though it meant he would be losing a rich son-in-law. Well, she forgave him, but she still did not think much of him.

And Guy Wentwater? What about Guy who would be waiting patiently in the snow of Green Park at two in the morning?

Let him wait, thought Deirdre savagely.

Yes, she had been mad to make the arrangement. But why should she spend one second worrying about a man who had left her waiting and then had jeered and humiliated her in front of his friends.

And yet, he *had* said he loved her.

How odd that Lord Harry should manage to wring the correct story from Guy, not knowing that

151

Guy had not confessed to his motives of revenge on the Armitages. Lord Harry had mentioned 'pressure' but she could not imagine that entailing any physical violence. He was much too elegant and indolent a creature to resort to that.

During all this hard thought, Deirdre had been standing and sitting and standing again, to allow Betty to dress her and arrange her hair.

'There!' said Betty at last, slamming down the lid of Minerva's jewel box. 'I've never seen you look so pretty. When you cry, Miss Deirdre, it makes your eyes even larger. Me, mine get all puffed up and red.'

Deirdre stood up and shook down her skirts, barely glancing in the looking glass.

She was wearing a slip of grass-green silk covered with a gauze overdress of a lighter green. A necklace of emeralds and dead gold was about her neck. One large gold silk rose had been cunningly embedded in a nest of curls on top of her head, its curling green silk leaves edged with tiny emeralds.

The bodice of her gown was lined and stiffened so that her bosom was pushed up into two swelling mounds. Dainty little grass-green slippers were on her feet and heavy emerald earrings blazed in her ears.

Betty, who considered the colour of Deirdre's hair too violent, had pomaded it so that it was now a rich dark red.

'You look like the fairy queen,' laughed Betty, admiring Deirdre's tilted green eyes and delicate bones. 'I'll fetch your fur-lined cloak for it's mortal cold. It's a good thing you put on them new drawers.'

Deirdre was wearing the latest in long, skin-tight

knitted wool drawers, an underwear fashion much in vogue to counteract the flimsiness of modish outer attire.

The semi-nudity of the last decade's fashions was beginning to go as men once more wanted something to be left to the imagination. But, during the evening, clothes were still almost transparent and some ladies still damped their muslin dresses, causing all sorts of lustful hopes in the masculine bosom.

Men often mistook all those hard and thrusting nipples as signs of hot passion, instead of cold, hard gooseflesh which is what they were.

Deirdre was to be escorted by Lord Sylvester to Lady Godolphin's home in Hanover Square. Lord Harry would meet her there.

Rather in awe of her tall and handsome brother-in-law, Deirdre sat very stiffly beside him in the carriage on the road to Lady Godolphin's.

'You look enchanting tonight,' said Lord Sylvester, studying the little fairy-like creature that was Deirdre. 'I am glad to see some colour in your cheeks. Lord Harry told me he had sent a notice of the termination of your engagement to the newspapers.'

'Yes,' said Deirdre in a small voice. 'Thank you, Lord Sylvester, for interceding on my behalf.'

'Think nothing of it. I was surprised to observe you seemed to be *afraid* of Lord Harry.'

'Oh, no,' said Deirdre quickly. Then all of a sudden, she became weary of lying. 'Well, as a matter of fact, I was. I do not know quite why,' she added.

'You certainly have nothing to fear from Lord Harry,' said Sylvester gently. 'He is one of the kindest men I know.'

'Yes,' said Deirdre in a suffocated voice.

Deirdre remembered why she was so frightened of Lord Harry. She was frightened of him because of what happened to her body when he touched her. But her silly dream-love with Guy was what had made that physical reaction seem so terrible.

But Lord Sylvester and Minerva were very much in love. There was a radiance about them when they were together. And yet, their love seemed to be of the purest. They never even held hands that Deirdre could see.

Perhaps there was a love which did not involve physical contact, thought Deirdre naively. The fact that her sister and brother-in-law had a son meant nothing to Deirdre since she did not know how babies were conceived.

She knew how the beasts of the fields went about it, but if anyone had ever told her that it was the same performance between humans, well, she simply would not have believed them.

And so Deirdre was sure her emotions when Lord Harry held her had nothing whatsoever to do with love. Lust, yes. Even Papa on his rare appearance in the pulpit pointed out lust was a dangerous and disgraceful thing and one of the worst of the seven deadly sins.

The carriage stopped and Lord Sylvester helped her to alight and saw her safely to the door. He made his apologies for not entering to see Lady Godolphin but explained he was anxious to return to his wife.

Deirdre heaved a sentimental sigh. A little hope came back to her. Perhaps one day, some man would love her as Lord Sylvester loved Minerva; a pure and precious love, free from the hot, heaving, sweating emotions of lust.

Lord Harry had not yet arrived so Deirdre took it upon herself to explain to Lady Godolphin that their engagement was at an end.

'Oh, lor',' said Lady Godolphin. 'Your nipples is off!'

Deirdre glanced down at the bosom of her dress, and then realized Lady Godolphin meant 'nuptials'.

'Didn't he want you?' asked Lady Godolphin sadly.

'We decided we should not suit.'

'Ah, love.' Lady Godolphin sighed gustily. 'I try to forget it but all the poems remind me. Never read poetry, Deirdre. It's too sad. Listen to this one,

' "When Love with incontinent wings
Havers around the gates;
And my divine Algae brings
To whimper in the grate;
When I lie mangled in her hair,
And frittered in her eye;
The Gods, that want not in the air,
Know no such livery." '

There was a little silence.

'I do not think I have heard that one,' ventured Deirdre cautiously.

'It's by Lovelace,' said Lady Godolphin in surprise. 'You know, the man who wrote the thing about, "I could not love thee dear so much, loved I not horrors more." '

'Oh, *that* one,' said Deirdre, realizing that if one sorted out Lady Godolphin's malapropisms,

155

it might take all day, but at least one could understand what she was talking about.

'Will Mr Anstey be joining us this evening?' asked Deirdre, hoping he would not for she had taken him in dislike and thought it disgusting for a woman of Lady Godolphin's great age to have such a young, if unprepossessing, lover.

'No,' sighed Lady Godolphin. 'He has made a fool of me. He has held me up to Reticule. He went off to live with Lady Chester who must be a hundred if she's a day. So now society thinks he was only hanging around my skirts for my money.'

'Is there no one else?' asked Deirdre, hating to see the normally robust and cheerful Lady Godolphin look so woebegone.

'No, said Lady Godolphin. 'I'm too old.'

'Not you!' Deirdre wanted to scream. It was horrifying hearing Lady Godolphin admit to being old. Although Deirdre had often longed for the reprehensible old sinner to settle down and act her age, there was something appalling in the fact that she was obviously now trying to do just that. Even her gown was subdued, being of brown silk shot with gold. A turban of modest proportions covered her head, and, wonder upon wonders, she was wearing *no paint at all.*

At that moment, Lord Harry was announced.

Apart from casting a look of gloomy lechery at his legs, Lady Godolphin behaved like a sad and respectable dowager.

Lord Harry kissed Deirdre's hand.

Deirdre looked at him with something like awe, seeing him for the first time as many women saw him.

He was wearing a dark blue evening coat with

156

pearl-coloured kerseymere breeches with strings to the knees, white silk stockings and thin pumps.

His only jewel was one enormous diamond pin in his cravat, which might have looked vulgar on another man, but only added to Lord Harry's air of magnificence.

His thick glossy black curls, Grecian profile, clear blue eyes and tall slim figure were enough to seduce the eyes of any lady with a clear brain and normal digestion.

Deirdre held on to her idea of that pure and celestial love as a barrier to all those nasty, gurgling churnings around her insides, and the prickling nervous feeling in the palms of her hands.

'So you are not to be married?' asked Lady Godolphin after they had all been helped to glasses of wine.

'No,' said Lord Harry equably.

'Then you had better return my present,' said Lady Godolphin. 'Cost me a mort of money.'

'Yes, of course,' said Lord Harry and Deirdre in chorus, and then they looked at each other and laughed.

Lady Godolphin's present to them had been an enormous oil painting of a singularly well-endowed Roman matron stabbing herself in a half-hearted way while she rolled her eyes upwards to a stormy sky. She was wearing only a thin wisp of gauze about her massive thighs which seemed to stay up by magical means since she was stabbing herself with one hand and pointing up to heaven with the other. Various hirsute and swarthy Romans rampaged about the background, avenging her, or something-or-other. Lord Sylvester had said it was probably meant to be Lucrece, since Lady

157

Godolphin had proudly presented it as a French picture, called Le Crease.

Lady Godolphin gloomily shook her head at them both, muttering something about the folly of youth, and said it was time to leave.

It was with some surprise that they discovered Lord Harry's high-perch phaeton drawn up outside with his Swiss manservant, Bruno, hovering on the backstrap instead of a groom.

'My dear Desire,' said Lady Godolphin. 'An open carriage! In *this* weather!'

It had not snowed very hard during the day so there was only a thin coating on the ground. Snowflakes were falling through the foggy air; large, light, lace snowflakes drifting slowly down under the flickering lights of the parish lamps.

'We are only going a step,' said Lord Harry cheerfully. 'I have plenty of rugs and hot bricks.'

'But there is barely room for three,' wailed Lady Godolphin.

'What! A sylph like yourself? Come along, Lady Godolphin.'

Grumbling awfully, Lady Godolphin was pushed from the back and pulled at the front until she reached the high perch of the seat. Lord Harry sat on one side of her and Deirdre on the other.

Deirdre gazed about her dreamily, thinking it was wonderful to be perched so high above the London streets, watching the hypnotic dance of the light snowflakes.

She had the beginnings of a sort of excited, suffocating feeling, such as she used to have at Christmas.

Christmas past had been rather disappointing. The boys had come home from Eton and had become very grand, strutting around like Bond Street beaux, and affecting languid airs which sat comically on their cheerful schoolboy faces.

Lord and Lady Brothers' mansion was a blaze of light. Thin strains of music drifted out into the foggy air. After all the worry and self-hate and tension of the past months, Deirdre felt her whole body and mind begin to relax. She would enjoy this one evening. She would imagine she was a respectable young miss with her handsome fiancé and not a disgraceful widgeon who had only such a short time ago been hell-bent on ruining herself.

As they mounted the staircase to the ballroom, Lord Harry slipped her engagement ring into her hand. 'Put it on,' he whispered. 'All the world will know tomorrow we are not to be married but tonight we do not wish to be badgered by questions.'

Deirdre nodded and slipped on the ring.

More than ever before she was conscious of admiring eyes, envious eyes, jealous eyes as the ladies of the ballroom watched her enter on Lord Harry's arm.

Lord Harry danced beautifully. Deirdre found it very hard to pay attention to her steps or listen to her partners when Lord Harry always seemed to be in her direct line of vision, flirting outrageously with one female after another.

She had had the pleasure of performing one country dance with him and was wondering whether he meant to ignore her for the rest of the evening when he came up and led her into the steps of the waltz. The feel of his hand on the small of her back sent fireworks shooting up her spine, the pressure

159

of his other gloved hand in her own made her go numb down one side. He held her the regulation twelve inches away, but she was conscious of every movement of his body. When the dance ended, she promenaded with him as was the custom, but dreading the moment when he would leave her and dance off with someone else.

But he said, 'Let us sit down for a little.'

He led her to a sofa in the corner, behind a bank of hothouse flowers. Deirdre fanned herself languidly because she was once again locked in that dreamy state, and the ballroom was hot. He went to find her a glass of lemonade and immediately she became anxious and worried in case someone would ask her to dance before he returned.

But he was soon back, handing her a glass, and settling himself comfortably beside her on the sofa.

'Here's to liberty,' he said raising his own glass.

'Liberty,' echoed Deirdre, sipping at her lemonade and wishing he had brought her something stronger to ensure that this relaxed dreamy feeling she had in his company did not go away.

'Lady Godolphin is not in plump currant,' he said. 'The horrible Mr Anstey left her for richer, if more withered, pastures.'

'Yes, she is very sad,' agreed Deirdre. 'She was quoting poetry, and getting all the words wrong. Something about love with incontinent wings.'

'Oh, that one,' he grinned. Then he began to quote softly,

' "When Love with unconfined wings
Hovers within my gates;

160

And my divine Althea brings
To whisper at the grates;
When I lie tangled in her hair,
And fettered to her eye;
The Gods, that wanton in the air,
Know no such liberty." '

'Quite,' said Deirdre huskily, staring into her glass. Then she essayed a laugh. 'I wish I could remember how Lady Godolphin put it, but it was vastly different, I assure you.'

'She should have married Colonel Brian,' said Lord Harry. 'Trouble is, he's always hanging about her, quite obviously dying of love. Now if *he* were to start paying attention to some other female, no doubt she would come about. Which reminds me, I am promised to dance with Lady Coombes, and I think you probably have an anxious partner looking for you.'

'Yes,' said Deirdre reluctantly, wishing they could sit together like this and not have to dance with anyone at all.

A niggling thought entered her mind, a nasty little voice whispering that she had had ample opportunity to enjoy Lord Harry's company these past few months but all she had done was run away from him.

From then on Deirdre danced and danced. Soon it would be two in the morning and soon it would be time for Guy to wait for her in Green Park.

But at one-thirty Lord Harry appeared at her side, yawning, and said he really must go home. Lady Godolphin would not be returning with them since she did not want to 'freeze to death' and had sent for her own carriage.

161

The night outside was cold and clear. Snow sparkled and shone in broad pools under the street lamps, and, far above the huddled black houses of London a small winter moon rose high in the starry sky.

'It is a beautiful night for a walk, Bruno,' said Lord Harry over his shoulder to his shivering servant on the backstrap. 'I suggest you make the most of it.'

'Ver' good, milo',' said Bruno gloomily. He climbed down and strode off into the night.

Lord Harry drew on his York tan driving gloves and set his team in motion.

'Come and sit beside me, Deirdre,' he said. 'You will get cold sitting all the way over there.'

Deirdre slid along until she was next to him. He put an arm around her shoulders, holding the reins bunched in one hand, the horses ambling very slowly over the diamonded cobbles of the snow-covered streets.

Deirdre was all too conscious of his hip against her own although they were both bundled up in cloaks and blankets.

His arm tightened about her and she gave a submissive sigh and leaned her head against his shoulder.

After they had been moving along in this dreamlike state for some time, he slowed his team to a halt and looked down at her.

'Keep the ring, Deirdre,' he said softly. 'You need not wear it on your fourth finger.'

She looked up at him, puzzled and bewildered by all the things she felt for him and could not yet analyze.

'And since we are to become friends,' he went

162

on, 'you might at least kiss the lover goodbye.'

Her lips trembled and she put up a timid hand to his cheek.

He took it in his own, and then bent his lips to hers.

This time, because it was all over, she did not feel afraid of him. He would never kiss her again, so there was no harm in kissing him back ... no harm at all.

And so she gave herself gladly, if innocently, up to hot, dizzy, heady passion, totally absorbed in the contours and feel of his mouth, the faint smell of cheroots, wine and cologne from his body, and the feel of his long fingers cradling her face.

They sat on the high-perch phaeton, right outside the gates of Green Park at two in the morning, totally absorbed in each other, oblivious to everything else.

Deirdre did not even know where she was.

Guy Wentwater stood frozen to the spot and stared in mounting savage fury at the two locked lovers, so brightly illuminated by the light of a lamp.

The carriage he had hired for the elopement was waiting out on the street. The driver kept rising up on the box and staring into the darkness of the park as if wondering what on earth this strange Mr Wentwater was doing.

At last, the phaeton moved off.

Guy Wentwater marched out and got into the black stuffiness of the closed carriage, biting his nails and sweating from every pore.

He hated the whole Armitage family more than he had ever hated them before, but this time, he hated Deirdre Armitage much, much more than he had ever hated the vicar. He felt she had deliberately stage-managed the whole thing to humiliate him.

And now Silas Dubois would learn there had been no elopement and Silas would ruin him.

*   *   *

Deirdre, Squire Radford, the maid, Betty, and Lord Harry Desire set out for Hopeworth the following day.

They were to break their journey that night at a posting house.

Deirdre was glad to escape from London before curious callers started to arrive, eager for gossip about the broken engagement. Squire Radford was puzzled. Paradoxically, Deirdre and Desire seemed closer than they had ever been before.

The snow had melted and a squally wind was hurtling grey clouds across the sky.

Weary with thought and confused emotion, Deirdre was glad to be going home. She wondered what Guy Wentwater had thought when she did not appear. Deirdre had been so wrapped up in and by Lord Harry's embrace that she did not even know they had been parked outside the gates of Green Park in full view of Mr Wentwater.

Guy, she thought, would assume she was getting her revenge—which she was, in a way.

'Good hunting weather,' observed Lord Harry. 'I wonder if the vicar has run his fox to earth.'

'I hope he has,' said Squire Radford in his dry precise voice. 'It will take his mind off his troubles. He has had many of late. Besides, he hopes to cut a dash. He took back with him a new coat of hunting pink.'

'Why is it called *pink*?' asked Deirdre idly. 'I assume you mean a scarlet coat.'

'It is named after Mr Pink,' said Lord Harry. 'He was a tailor who was left with a vast amount of red military material when the American war came to an end sooner than expected. So he turned to making hunting coats. Hence pink.'

'Perhaps this fox does not exist,' said the squire, pulling a bearskin rug more closely about his knees. 'There is a legendary animal which had been plaguing Mr Armitage for some time. It is seen first here and then there, and certainly hounds pick up the scent but they always end up wandering around in baffled circles. Mr Armitage is sure this fox can climb trees.'

Deirdre giggled. 'Papa often sees foxes which don't exist, particularly when he is in his cups.'

There was a reproving silence, and Deirdre felt she had just behaved like a bad child.

'When I get home,' she vowed to herself, 'I will read the newspapers every day and ... and ... I will learn Latin, and all sorts of things.' She wondered how long Lord Harry would stay with them this time. She had never really got to know him. She put a hand up to her lips, remembering his kisses. How strange that he was able to be so polite and formal with her now!

She chattered on to him about this and that, but he replied to all her questions and commented on her topics with a lazy smile, like a father indulging a favourite daughter.

Perhaps he will seek me out when we break our journey, thought Deirdre.

But Lord Harry appeared content to spend most of the evening talking to Squire Radford.

The squire had travelled a great deal, and it transpired Lord Harry had been to many of the countries the squire had visited.

To her disappointment, both men took up the conversation where they had left off at breakfast and continued all the way to Hopeworth.

On the outskirts of Hopeworth they heard the belling of hounds, the winding of the horn, and then streaking across the road behind his pack came the Reverend Charles Armitage with John Summer close behind him. He cleared the hedge beside the road and set off hell-for-leather over a ploughed field.

They had a momentary glimpse of his flushed and excited face and then he was gone.

He did not seem to have seen them.

Squire Radford was deposited at his home, and Lord Harry's carriage swung round the pond, heading for the vicarage.

'How long will you be staying with us?' asked Deirdre.

'I shall not be staying at all,' said Lord Harry, looking surprised. 'I shall return to Town just as soon as I have paid my respects to Mrs Armitage.'

Deirdre's heart plummeted.

But what else could he be expected to do? She had made it all too clear she did not want him.

But she hung around anxiously while he chatted with her mother after their arrival, tactfully explaining he was the most desolate of men for he and Deirdre had decided they would not suit. Then he teased Daphne, saying she grew more beautiful by the minute, to which Daphne answered with a surprised, 'I know.'

Hearing that the little girls were at school, he

166

decided to take his leave.

Naturally neither Mrs Armitage nor Daphne dreamed of leaving Lord Harry and Deirdre alone to say their goodbyes.

Mrs Armitage and Daphne were self-absorbed in different ways, Mrs Armitage with her imaginary illnesses and Daphne with her own beauty, but they had enough sensitivity to feel it would be monstrous awkward for poor Deirdre to be left alone to say goodbye to a man she had decided would not make a suitable husband.

He bowed very formally before her, looking more serious than Deirdre had ever seen him look before.

'I am to have my Season,' said Deirdre. 'I shall see you then, perhaps?'

'I don't know,' he replied. 'Squire Radford has given me a mind to travel. 'Tis a pity, perhaps, we are not to be married. We could have seen all those wonderful places together—Paris, Rome, Naples, Venice ...'

He bowed again and entered the carriage. The coachman cracked his whip, Lord Harry raised a white hand in salute, the carriage rumbled down the short drive, out into the lane.

He was gone.

Only dimly did Deirdre hear her mother's anxious questions and lamentations on the end of a most suitable engagement.

*   *   *

Lord Harry gazed placidly out at the country fields. He saw the lone figure of a peasant standing by the bend of the road outside Hopeworth, gazing intently across the fields.

Wondering if the vicar had made his kill, Lord Harry signalled to his coachman to stop. He let down the glass and leaned out.

'Watching the hunt?' he called.

The yokel turned slowly and took some time to bring Lord Harry's face into focus.

'No, zur,' he said at last, touching his forelock. 'I bee watching the crops grow. Just watching the crops grow.'

Lord Harry waved his hand and the coach started off again.

'I wonder,' he said to himself, 'whether the crop I have planted will ever come to maturity. Waiting for things, or people, to grow up can be a tedious business.'

NINE

The vicar of St Charles and St Jude wearily wended his homeward way, slumped over the pommel of his saddle. A string of oaths floated out behind him on the evening air.

'I do believe,' he shouted over his shoulder to his coachman-cum-groom-cum-kennel-master-cum-whipper-in, John Summer, 'that there fox is an invention of the devil. I seen him, with my own two eyes. You saw him too, didn't you John?' he asked pleadingly.

'That I did, master,' said John in a comforting way. 'Saw him with my own eyes. You 'member, the first find was close to Hans Wood and from then onwards, hounds' heads were down and their voices singing well over half the afternoon. Must have run not short of twenty mile.'

'And then what happened?' mourned the vicar. 'Reynard disappears like a puff o' smoke and hounds were running round that great elm in circles. Climbed up it, didn't you? Not a whisker o' Reynard in sight and the scent as cold as last Sunday's dinner.'

'Well, I told you, master,' said John, 'foxes don't climb trees.'

'This poxy one does,' growled the vicar. 'God! I'm mortal stiff. Sharp set, too.'

Wearily, he dismounted outside the vicarage and led his weary horse to the stables.

By the time he had rubbed down his mount and covered it with a blanket, warm from the saddle-room fire, and seen to its feed, the vicar felt every muscle had been wrenched out by some giant hand and put back in all the wrong places.

Groaning heavily, he entered the small dark hall of the vicarage, shouting for Betty to come and pull off his boots. Betty was stooping over the second boot as the vicar sat on an upright chair in the hall when he had a sort of feeling he was being watched.

He glanced up and saw a huddled figure on the first landing.

He sent Betty off to bring brandy to the study and waited until the maid had gone into the kitchen and closed the door behind her.

'Come down,' said the vicar, addressing the figure on the landing.

Deirdre rose and came slowly down the stairs. His heart smote him as he saw the telltale marks of tears on her pallid cheeks.

Silently she followed him into the study. 'Don't

169

say a word,' said the vicar, vigorously poking the fire, 'until I get a drop of brandy down me.'

Deirdre slumped in a chair and the vicar sat behind his cluttered desk. Betty came in with the bottle and glass on a tray along with lemons and a jug of hot water.

She glanced curiously at Deirdre.

As soon as she had left, the vicar poured himself a large glass of brandy and tossed it off. He looked narrowly at Deirdre's woebegone face, and poured another glass down him for good measure.

'That's better,' he said, wiping his mouth with the back of his hand. 'Now, what's amiss?'

Deirdre just shook her head dismally.

She wanted to tell someone, but surely anyone was better than this brutish father.

'Well, I'll need to guess,' said the vicar. 'Let's start with Guy Wentwater.'

Deirdre turned as red as she had been pale a moment before.

'Yes,' said the vicar, tilting back his chair and putting his thumbs in his waistcoat, 'him. I think you went and asked that wastrel to elope with you because you didn't want to marry Desire. I think he turned you down that night when you went to Lady Wentwater's carrying them bandboxes. Fortunately for you, her ladyship was in residence or the worst might have happened and you would have ended up with no wedding ring to show for it. Don't you know Wentwater wants revenge?'

Deirdre looked at her father with her mouth open.

The vicar waited to see if she would say anything, and when she did not, he went on, 'And somehow Desire got wind o' it and went up to Wentwater's and brought back them bandboxes. Next thing you says you're going to marry him, but you look so mortal scared o' the man that squire and me decide he's blackmailing you. So we ups to London to try to keep you away from him as much as possible so you might guess we were on your side and tell us the truth. It came as a relief when I finally faced him and he agreed not to marry you. Now would you like to fill in the blanks in my story?'

Deirdre hung her head. She was amazed her father had guessed so much and yet was not ranting or raving.

The need to unburden herself was great, and with a little sigh, she began. She told him the whole story from beginning to end, leaving nothing out, except the last meeting.

'I'll kill him,' said the vicar savagely. 'I'll tell you why he did it.' He related the story of driving Guy out of the county. 'He's weak and vicious,' ended the vicar. 'You look as if you've had punishment enough, but, 'fore George, I cannot but wonder you were so taken in.'

Somehow, Deirdre found herself telling him of her love for Guy, of her dreams of the sort of love Minerva had found—'You know, Papa,' she ended earnestly, 'pure and spiritual without any *lust*.'

'Well, they've hardly got a marriage without passion,' said the vicar drily. 'Minerva and Sylvester are too well-bred to paw and ogle in public, but they can hardly keep their hands off each other and it's as well he married her sharpish or I would've been forced to run him up to the altar with my shotgun at his back.'

'Papa!'

'Gad's 'Oonds, daughter! How d'ye think they

171

came to have a child? 'Twas not by reading poetry to each other or by discussing the state of the nation.'

Deirdre stared at him wide-eyed, her eyes very green and sharp—'like that demned fox,' thought the vicar sourly.

He put his elbows on the desk and leaned forwards. 'You don't know what I'm talking about, do you?'

'No, Papa.'

Beads of perspiration began to appear on the vicar's brow. 'Your mother should tell you about these things,' he said crossly, 'but in truth, I don't think she knows. Eight children and she still thinks it's all the fault of the stork. You'd think she was one o' them Greeks, like Leda, to hear her, 'cept that was a swan.

'Did Wentwater kiss you?'

'Yes, Papa.'

'And what did you feel?'

'I felt as a girl in love should feel,' said Deirdre. 'Pure and spiritual and elated.'

'Hey, ho. Desire, did he kiss you?'

'Yes, Papa.'

'And how did you feel?'

'Wanton and lustful,' whispered Deirdre.

'Oh, tut, tut, *tut*,' said the vicar sarcastically.

Deirdre flared up. 'Think of the times you have preached against lust from the pulpit!'

'Aye, but I hadn't a word to say agin passion. Let's get back to Wentwater. You did not see him after the night?'

'I'm afraid I did. He ... he followed me to Green Park. I went there one morning early to think things out. He must have been watching the house. He

172

said he loved me. He said he had spurned me for my own good. I asked him to elope with me.'

The vicar clutched his hair and gave it a yank. 'Is there any more of this?' he wailed.

'Yes. I was to meet him at two in the morning in Green Park, but I did not.'

'Well, thank God for small mercies. See here Deirdre, you have been playing a dangerous game. Wentwater does not care a fig for you, never has, and never will. He is determined to get revenge, that is all. He wants to marry Emily, if anything. That way, he could anger me, and get himself a wife with a good dowry. But there is something in all this that does not add up. It looks as if Desire put the fear o' God into him, and Wentwater's mortal afraid o' me. So why does he still pursue the matter?'

He sat for a long time, buried in thought. Then he said slowly, 'We never really knew much about these Wentwaters. Lady Wentwater seems to have been missed out of the peerage. Well, we assumed she might have adopted the title and she seems harmless enough. But I wonder where the Wentwaters came from? I am going back to London.' He thought of that pesky fox and a wistful look crossed his face. 'I'll need to smoke out Guy Wentwater and make sure he never comes near Hopeworth again. None of you girls is to go near Lady Wentwater. I'll call on her myself and tell her why.'

He stopped and looked at the drooping picture of misery that was Deirdre Armitage.

'You've made a sad mull o' things,' he said in a kindly voice, 'but it's all over.' He stood up and came round his desk. 'Off to bed with you. It's late

173

and I have not yet had my supper.'

Deirdre stood up and faced him. Large tears began to roll down her cheeks.

The vicar wordlessly held out his arms and she rushed into them.

'There, now,' he said, 'it's all over.'

'But I love him, Papa,' choked Deirdre.

The vicar stiffened. 'Then you will need to get over it,' he said harshly. 'Wentwater does not set a foot in this house!'

'Oh, not him,' wailed Deirdre, crying harder than ever.

'Who, in Gad's name?'

'Lord Harry.'

The vicar's pudgy hands tightened on her shoulders. He wanted to shake her and shake her until her teeth rattled. Instead he said wearily, 'We'll talk again tomorrow. Now off to bed like a good girl.'

'Oh, Papa,' sobbed Deirdre, 'I love you, too. I have been *such* a fool.'

'You do, do you?' grinned the vicar, suddenly feeling all the troubles of the world slip from his shoulders. 'Well, that's all right. Go and say your prayers.'

He stood beaming until she had left the room. But when Mrs Armitage came in some ten minutes later to ask him whether he was going to eat his supper or not, the vicar of St Charles and St Jude was slowly banging his head rhythmically against the study wall.

Mrs Armitage assumed it was some mysterious masculine hunting ritual—men were so strange, quite like children—and retreated to tell cook and Betty that the master would no doubt be ready to

174

eat in a little while.

Deirdre was glad to have a bedroom all to herself again. She sat by the window, but this time she dreamed of seeing Lord Harry Desire walking in the lane. Why hadn't she realized she loved him before? Why had she hated her father so much? It was as if she had been looking at the world through a distorting glass, and now suddenly she saw things plain for the first time.

How bitter to realize you loved a man, right after you had successfully disengaged yourself from him.

Betty came bustling in, carrying a hot posset. 'Mr Armitage sent me up with this and says you are to go right to bed.'

'Very well, Betty,' said Deirdre. 'Perhaps I have made a mull of things but maybe I shall find a rich husband and then you and John will be able to marry.'

''Tis a pity it wasn't that Lord Harry,' said Betty. 'But he was too handsome. Quite scary in a way. And don't mind about me, miss, though it's kind of you to bother. Vicar'll make sure I marry John before next harvest is out, never fear.'

'That is wonderful, Betty. But how can you prevail upon Papa to do so?'

'There are ways,' said Betty, grinning. 'Now, I'll put the warming pan between the sheets and you slip into your nightgown.'

At last, when she was tucked up in bed, Deirdre said sleepily, 'Betty, how do I learn Latin?'

'I don't know, miss. Why not ask Mr Pettifor. He has a deal of book learning.'

'Very well, Betty. I do want to learn things.'

'You can read and write, miss, and play the pannyforty. What does a lady need with else?'

'Only, I have found I am really rather stupid, Betty.'

'Oh, not you, miss,' said Betty placidly, as she blew out the candles and lit the rushlight in its pierced canister beside the bed. 'Miss Minerva, I mean Lady Sylvester, always said as how you were the brains of the family.'

'Then she was much mistaken,' sighed Deirdre.

'Ah, you're young,' smiled Betty, tucking the bedclothes about her, 'and there ain't a body in the whole wide world that don't do stupid things when they're young. You'll feel clever again in the morning.'

And with that, she quietly left the room.

*   *   *

A deputation of angry farmers called at the vicarage in the morning to curse the reverend for hunting over their fields while the spring crops were about to sprout. Added to that the day was white with frost, so the vicar had two reasons not to tempt him to take out his hounds.

Instead of flying off to London to scour the clubs and coffee houses for Guy Wentwater, he decided to call on Squire Radford first.

Wentwater had always been on the dubious fringes of society, reflected the vicar. He was the sort of fellow who professed to know everyone, and yet no one knew him, He was unknown in White's or Brooks's or Watier's. He was never to be seen in fashionable saloons or drawing-rooms.

In the county of Berham, he was considered one of the upper set. But he only came on infrequent visits, and Lady Wentwater was considered

176

something of a recluse.

Squire Radford listened eagerly to the ramifications of the story about Deirdre.

'The thing that frightens me,' finished the vicar, 'is that she should go ahead and plan to do the same thing again, that she should ask him to elope with her a second time. Do you think she's addled in her brainbox?'

'I think she is very young for her years and that she was very unhappy. Minerva had given her a role to play, the one of highly intelligent girl. And so she played that role and believed in it. Suddenly it was not true and she felt lost and self-disgusted and silly. Sir Thomas Browne said that each man is his own executioner, and I believe that. My poor daughter chose to kill herself by running away with a wastrel. If we do not destroy ourselves, we often find someone else to do it for us. Given a short time to recover, Deirdre will discover she is actually almost as intelligent as Minerva led her to believe herself to be, but very young and sadly uninformed.'

'Aye, but that's not all, Jimmy,' said the vicar eagerly, 'she's in love with him.'

'Dear me!'

'No, not Wentwater. Desire.'

'And when did she discover this? It may be all part and parcel of her temporary madness?'

'Mayhap. Anyway, the silly jade must discover this great fact *after* Lord Harry had broken the engagement and taken his leave. All that money! Jeremy Blewett's said to be richer than Golden Ball. If I was not so worried for my daughter's sanity, I would've given her a beating. Now, there's no hope.'

'I would not say that,' ventured the squire

177

cautiously. 'I could not help observing on the journey to Hopeworth that they were remarkably at ease with each other. The air between them seemed to hold a certain intimacy.'

'Best rush her back to London then.'

'Ah, no. I think Miss Deirdre should be allowed a period of quiet and, if necessary, boredom.'

'But what if Desire goes and gets married to someone else?'

'He told you he had made enough money on 'Change and did not need his uncle's money,' pointed out the squire.

'But some woman's bound to snap him up.'

'They have not succeeded yet and he is surely about thirty years old.'

'But he was at the wars for years and years,' said the vicar. 'No one had a chance to get hold of him.'

'Well, I think we should wait, nonetheless. But to return to Guy Wentwater. It is passing strange that he should even go near Miss Deirdre. I really think we perhaps might return to London, just for a day or two, and call on Lord Harry and ask him to tell us what exactly happened when he went to pick up the bandboxes and whether he threatened Deirdre in any way.'

'She says she asked *him* to marry her.'

'I think it is no use speculating about it until we find out a little more. I've never been much worried about Guy Wentwater, strangely enough, although I fear he is a shiftless and vicious young man. I always thought him too much of a coward.'

'We could maybe start by paying a call on Lady Wentwater,' said the vicar.

Lady Wentwater was at home, as she nearly always was, sitting alone in the dingy, dark drawing-room with its cheap tallow candles, reading a novel.

'My daughters won't be reading to you again,' began the vicar, without preamble, 'on account o' that there nephew o' yours.'

'What's up with him?' asked Lady Wentwater, 'apart from your unusual views on the slave traffic.'

'He's been trying to ruin one of my daughters again,' said the vicar crossly, 'and I may tell you, my lady, that I'm going up to London to hunt him down and make sure he don't put foot in this village again.'

'Guy is always more sinned against than sinning,' said Lady Wentwater, beginning to show rare signs of animation. 'If your girls will throw themselves at him, what else do you expect him to do?'

'Look here, I'll tell you what happened,' said the vicar, 'and if you breathe a word of it, it'll be the worse for your nephew.'

Lady Wentwater listened to the tale of the abortive elopement with her large head on one side, while the ivy leaves rattled against the windows and sent fluttering shadows dancing about the room.

'Just as I thought,' she commented when the vicar had finished. 'More sinned against than sinning. If I have it right, your daughter threw herself at him, begging him to elope with her because you were forcing her into marriage to a man she did not like. He decides not to go through with it. She turns up here. He has been drinking heavily with two friends. He teases her a little to bring her to her senses, and his friends being bosky, try to make sport so she runs away. My poor Guy then fancies himself in love with her and waylays

179

her in London. Again, she begs him to elope with her, but then changes her mind and does not even send him a note to say so. Now, what is so evil and terrible about that? I would not like to be an unescorted female chancing upon you, reverend, when you are in your altitudes.'

The vicar turned red. All at once he remembered when he was much younger, drinking at a wayside inn with two of his friends. A woman had come in and quietly ordered a meal. They had all paid her broad and warm compliments until she had run out of the inn.

It had transpired later that she was a gentlewoman whose maid had fallen sick on the road and whose carriage had then broken down.

The landlord had berated the vicar most roundly and called him an insult to the cloth.

'But I don't think for a minute he's in love with her,' he howled. 'Demme, I swear he's out to get revenge.'

'That's the sort of thing you would do, vicar,' said Lady Wentwater blandly, 'but you must not judge others by yourself. Guy is a sweet and pretty young man who would not harm a fly.'

'Who was your husband, ma'am?' asked the vicar abruptly.

There was a little silence. The asthmatic clock in the corner wheezed preparatory to striking the hour.

'Sir William Wentwater,' she said finally. 'Why do you ask?'

'Never heard o' him,' said the vicar rudely.

'No, why should you? He has been dead for a long time.'

The vicar rolled his eyes in the squire's direction.

The squire coughed gently. 'Perhaps you might furnish us with Mr Wentwater's direction? We are going to London and would like to call on him.'

'I don't know where he's staying,' said Lady Wentwater. 'Try Long's or Limmer's.'

Both men rose to take their leave.

'But if you find him, give him my love,' said Lady Wentwater. Then she picked up her book and appeared to forget their existence.

When both gentlemen had walked a little way down the road, the vicar burst out with, 'I don't like it. Don't like it at all.'

'But the way Lady Wentwater put it, well, it does rather seem as if we are imagining Haymarket villains when they don't exist,' suggested the squire.

No, no, it stinks,' said the vicar. 'Everytime I look at that old bat, I see custom-house goods.'

'Custom-house goods, Charles?'

'Oh, I was talkin' cant,' said the vicar. 'Custom-house goods is the stock and trade of a prostitute, because fairly entered, don't you see.'

'Charles, you shock me.'

'There's something about her,' said the vicar, paying no heed to his friend, 'that calls to mind that Covent Garden abbess, Peggy Jones,' He gave a rich chuckle. 'There was a one. The things that woman could do with a feather duster ...'

'*Charles!* Enough! Remember your calling. What if one of your parishioners should hear you talk like this?'

'Sorry,' mumbled the vicar. 'Plaguey frost. Do you think it'll be the same tomorrow? Is spring never going to come?'

'If you are longing to go hunting, you had best dream about next season,' said the squire severely.

'I, for one, do not want my spring crops ruined by your hunt.'

'Oh, Gad!' screamed the vicar suddenly. 'Look at that!'

They were passing a thick thorn hedge which bordered part of the Hall's estates. There was a small gap in it. On the other side of the gap sat a fox, studying them with yellow-eyed insolence.

'You see it, too, don't you, Jimmy?' pleaded the vicar.

'Yes,' said the squire, staring at the fox in amazement. 'I swear that animal knows we cannot reach it because of the thorns.'

'Oh, can't we!' yelled the vicar. He threw himself like a maniac at the gap in the hedge, cursing and shouting as the thorns stabbed his face and hands.

The fox put its head on one side and looked at him curiously.

'I'll get hounds,' gasped the vicar, reeling back defeated. 'I'll *have* that beast, pads and mask and brush.'

'No, no,' said the squire. 'You cannot take hounds out in such a frost. The ground is too hard. It will cut their paws.'

'Then I'll *strangle* that Reynard myself!' howled the vicar, tears of frustration starting to his eyes.

Before the squire could stop him, he was off down the road and in at the gates of the Hall. He doubled back along the other side of the hedge.

The fox studied his approach, and then, with a flick of its brush, it was gone.

The vicar blundered through the woods, shouting and hallooing and cursing fit to wake the dead.

He was nearly shot by one of his brother's

182

gamekeepers, and by the time the squire caught up with him, he seemed fit to die of an apoplexy.

'You see, I can't leave Hopeworth now,' moaned the vicar. 'Not with that gurt beast mocking and sneering at me.'

'Well, we'll see,' said the squire. 'Here's Edwin.'

The vicar's brother, Sir Edwin, made his leisurely way towards them through the trees. He was formally dressed as usual, a contrast to his stocky brother. He raised his quizzing glass and surveyed the mess that was the vicar: bleeding hands, scratched face, dirty clothes.

'Well, Charles,' said Sir Edwin, 'I see you have returned to all your former glory of dress.' He tittered. 'Quite reassuring to see you looking your old self. May I ask what you are doing cursing and screaming about my property?'

'It's that fox,' babbled the vicar. 'It's in your grounds.'

'Well, I'm sure one of my men will shoot it.'

The vicar reeled with shock. 'Shoot it! You're talking like a coxcomb! Shoot the fox. Did you hear that, Jimmy? The man's insane. *Shoot* a fox!'

'It's my property and I can do what I like, demme,' said Sir Edwin, turning puce. 'I will not have you riding over my grounds and ruining my game, Charles, and if I have to arm men at the gates to keep you out, I will.'

'You are not a Christian. You will go to hell and fry for this wickedness,' howled the vicar, jumping up and down with rage.

'Come along, please,' said the squire, tugging the vicar's sleeve. 'No hunting can be done in such weather anyway. Come along, Charles. Calm yourself.'

183

The vicar allowed himself to be led away.

Squire Radford accepted an invitation to dinner at the vicarage, although he would have much preferred the comfort of his own home and the vicarage was hardly famous for its cuisine.

The vicar sat like a man who has sustained a severe shock. He mumbled to himself about the wickedness of his brother. He barely touched his food.

'If we are going to London tomorrow,' said the squire at last, 'I must be off home and get an early night's sleep.'

'Oh, ah,' said the vicar dismally. 'Ain't any hope of a thaw, think you, Jimmy?'

The squire shook his head.

'London!' Deirdre's green eyes lit up. 'Oh, Papa, take me with you.'

'Oh, very well,' grumbled the vicar.

'But ...' began Squire Radford, and then broke off, feeling it would be bad manners to tell the company at large why Deirdre should not go.

'I really feel this is too much,' said Mrs Armitage crossly. 'Betty must go with her, and now that you do not have the benefit of dear Lord Sylvester's carriage, then you needs must take John as well. Faith, why don't you take cook?'

'Don't be silly,' said her husband rudely. 'The only decent thing about going to London is getting away from her cooking.'

'That is not fair, Mr Armitage,' said Mrs Armitage, turning an alarming colour. 'Mrs Hammer does very well, very well indeed, on the miserly allowance you give her!'

The vicar looked as if he were about to launch into battle, but Mrs Armitage settled the score by

184

throwing one of her Spasms. Squire Radford crept off and Deirdre went up to her room to dream.

Visions of the old Deirdre running down the lane in search of Guy, meeting him in the churchyard, hating her father, flitted through her brain. It was like looking at the strange antics of another person.

A new Deirdre would go back to London, taking with her her new-found love. She did not know if it would be accepted.

But at least she could try.

*　　　*　　　*

'You have done very well indeed,' said Silas Dubois.

Guy Wentwater smirked modestly.

'Blewett's money should be coming to me soon,' went on Silas, rubbing his hands. 'He is vastly annoyed that Desire is not to be wed, and furthermore has not had the courtesy to visit him. When I saw the notice in the newspapers that the engagement was broken, I knew it was your work. How on earth did you do it?'

'I told her I loved her,' said Guy, 'and she believed me.'

Both men were sitting in Humbold's coffee house. It had been Guy's first visit to that establishment for some time. He had been hiding out, picturing his reputation in shreds. Only by chance, since he hardly ever read the newspapers, did he learn about the broken engagement. So his reputation was safe, and, not only that, Silas believed him to have been instrumental in the ending of it.

'Well, I certainly must do something to repay you,' smirked Silas.

185

'I have money enough,' said Guy.

'Oh, I didn't mean money. I feel I owe it to you to give you the news that the dear vicar and that ancient squire from Hopeworth are searching all the clubs and taverns and coffee houses for you. The vicar is crying for your blood. Dear, dear,' chortled Silas, in high good humour, 'you really must have upset the apple cart.'

Guy turned pale. He had carefully kept to places where he would not be likely to come across Lord Harry Desire. But now the hunting vicar was after him, nowhere was safe.

'I must leave,' he said, looking wildly about as if expecting to hear the vicar's halloo and see him charging through St James's with his pack of hell-hounds streaming out in front of him.

He would rusticate somewhere in the country far from Hopeworth. But one day he would return and get his revenge on the whole Armitage family, Deirdre in particular.

A Deirdre trembling with sweet love was one thing; a Deirdre so much in love with another man that she did not even seem to be aware of his presence was another.

He wanted to inflict all sorts of nasty humiliations on her. If he could only lure her as far as Bristol, there was a bawdy house he knew of where the abbess was skilled in training and breaking down the most God-fearing girl into the tricks of the trade.

A shadow fell across the doorway and Guy started from his seat like a rocketing pheasant. It turned out to be a man he had never seen before, but the shock left him trembling.

He muttered a hurried goodbye to the grinning

186

and malicious Silas and darted out of the coffee house.

Silas ordered another bottle of wine. He had never felt better. He could imagine stiff-necked Minerva wringing her hands over Deirdre's disgrace, for Silas was quite sure Guy had done something awful. And what made the joke so rich was that none of the Armitages knew of his involvement.

*   *   *

Perhaps, had Deirdre Armitage been asked, she would have said that Lady Godolphin's dinner party was the most awful thing that had, as yet, happened to her.

Lady Godolphin was giving a dinner and taking the guests to the opera afterwards.

Deirdre had looked forward to it with trembling excitement, for Lord Harry had said he *might* attend but had sent a note to Lady Godolphin, saying if he was not present by six, not to wait for him.

But Deirdre had been so sure he would come. His empty place next to her mocked her dismal eyes.

Although she had not had much time to improve her education, Deirdre had read all the newspapers she could get her hands on and had rehearsed conversation with Lord Harry Desire in which she would dazzle him with her knowledge of contemporary affairs. And she would really like to know what Lord Harry thought of the Prince Regent's latest madness. He had infuriated the Whigs by having it announced in Parliament that he was going to erect a monument in Rome, designed by ... Casanova? No, that was not right. Canova! That was it. This was to be in memory of the Stuarts. The Whigs were boiling over with rage at this glorification of the Stuarts, a family that might seem glamorous to Highland Tories and Walter Scott but did not inspire any nostalgic affection among English Whigs. Perhaps she would never have a chance to discuss it with him. Perhaps Lord Harry did not want to see her again.

The rest of the party was made up of the vicar and the squire, Lady Chester and Mr Anstey, Colonel Arthur Brian and, of course, Lady Godolphin.

The atmosphere was strained to say the least. The vicar and squire were exhausted from their day's Wentwater hunting. Mr Anstey was more effete, more mincing, and more posturing than Deirdre could remember him being before.

Lady Chester kept sending him killing glances from out of her rheumy old eyes when she was not flashing triumphant ones in Lady Godolphin's direction.

As Lady Godolphin put it, *sotto voce*, 'Asking her was a fox's paw.'

Colonel Brian looked embarrassed and kept drinking rather more wine than was good for him.

Deirdre started at every sound of carriage wheels in the square outside.

Her heart sank as the interminable dinner dragged on, and on. Of course he would not come. She had behaved so badly. How could she expect him to come? She had told him they would not suit, she had shown everyone in the world that she was afraid of him. So it was silly to keep jumping at every sound.

In fact, he was probably staying away because he heard she was to be there.

It was only a simple dinner, but the awkward atmosphere and the general lack of appetite made it seem more than it was.

Deirdre tried to keep her mind off the absent Lord Harry, by identifying and counting the dishes, until she had a large ornamental menu printed inside her brain.

First Course

Pigeons Comport
Lambs' Ears,
Forc'd
French Pye
Boil'd Turkey
Sheeps' Rumps and
Kidneys in Rice
Florendine of
Rabbits
Fish Remove
Transparent Soup
Harrico
Pork Griskins
Kidney Beans   Broccoli, etc
Mock Turtle
Bottl'd Peas   Sallad
House Lamb
Larded oysters   Ox Pallets
Beef Olives
Hare Soup
Remove Hanch of Venison
Fricas'd Chickens
Cod's Sounds like little Turkey

189

Fricando Veal
Small Ham
Sweet Breads à la Royal
Ducks alamode

Second Course

Snow balls
Fish pond
Roast Woodcocks
Pistachio Cream
Rocky Island
Pheasant
Crow fish in Savory Jelly
Pickl'd Smelts
Marbl'd Veal
Mince Pies
Stew'd cardoons
Pompadore Cream
Transparent pudding
cover'd with a silver web
Maccaroni
Stew'd Mushrooms
Crocant with Hot pippins
Collar'd Rig
Pott'd Lampreys
Snipes in savory Jelly
Roast'd Hare
Moonshine
Globes of gold web
with mottes in them
Pea chick with
Asparagus
Floating Island
Burnt Cream

190

The wines consisted of Lisbon, vintage Rhenish, champagne, claret (Château Margaux, Lafite, Pontack), old burgundy, port and sherry.

By the time the tablecloth was removed and the port and sherry, walnuts and sweetmeats stood reflected in the polished wood of the table, everyone was slightly tipsy in a silent and surly way.

'Well, it seems as if Lord Harry is not coming. Waste o' money,' grumbled Lady Godolphin who had been coerced into holding the dinner so that Deirdre could resume her acquaintanceship with Desire. Of course, she had taken the opportunity to renew her own acquaintance with Mr Anstey, fondly picturing that young man spurning Lady Chester and darting to her side.

But Lady Godolphin was clutch-fisted and Lady Chester was not, and so out of sheer pride Lady Godolphin was forced to favour her former beau, Colonel Brian, with her attentions.

Mr Anstey fingered the new ruby pin in his stock and smiled fondly on Lady Chester.

The evening was bad, but worse was to follow. No sooner had they all been set down at the opera than a stern matron descended on their party.

'Oh lor',' muttered the vicar to Deirdre. ''Tis Lady Mason, Lady Chester's daughter.'

'Mama,' said Lady Mason awfully, 'what is this I hear? Is *this* the famous Mr Anstey of whom I have heard so much? Is *this* the ne'er-do-well who preys on elderly ladies for their money? You are the laughing stock of London society.'

''Pon rep,' bleated Mr Anstey, falling back before the venom in Lady Mason's bulging eyes, 'I dote on your Mama.'

'Fustian, you mountebank, you man-milliner, you *counter jumper!*' hissed Lady Mason. 'Mason!' she called over her shoulder. Her thick-set, brutish husband came ambling up. 'Mason, this is the creature who has been battening on Mama like a leech.'

'Oh, it is, is it?' said Lord Mason with an awful glare and fingering his dress sword.

Mr Anstey looked to his party for help. Mr Armitage and Squire Radford seemed completely absorbed in watching the passing crowd outside the opera. Lady Godolphin was clutching tightly on to Colonel Brian's arm and staring straight ahead.

Lady Chester looked terrified of her daughter.

'I say,' bleated Mr Anstey, 'you musn't say things like that.'

'What are you going to do about it, hey?' sneered Lord Mason. He stripped off one glove and smacked Mr Anstey across the face with it.

'Name your seconds,' he growled.

'I won't!' screeched Mr Anstey, and he turned and fled into the crowd as fast as his spindly legs would carry him.

Lady Chester began to cry but was strong-armed off by her daughter and son-in-law.

The depleted party made their way silently to Lady Godolphin's box.

The opera was Gluck's *Orpheus and Eurydice*. Watching and listening, at first, more for Lord Harry's arrival than anything to do with what was going on on the stage, Deirdre at last became caught up in the story and the music.

And when Orpheus clasped the dead Eurydice in his arms and broke into that famous lament, 'Che faro senza Eurydice' (I have lost my Eurydice), tears poured unchecked down Deirdre's cheeks as the beautiful music rose and fell in the hushed opera house.

And then a hand appeared in front of her nose holding a large pocket handkerchief. She took it gratefully, and, only as the last note of the famous aria died away, did she remember the last time a hand had reached in front of her with a handkerchief. She twisted her head and looked up into the clear blue eyes of Lord Harry Desire who was standing behind her chair.

On stage, Eurydice was restored to life by Amor, and Deirdre was brought back to the present world by the light touch of Lord Harry's hand on her shoulder.

After the opera was finished, Lord Harry made his apologies to Lady Godolphin. 'You didn't miss anything,' said her ladyship, 'except a lot of curst scenes and historicals. That old trout, Lady Chester, was arrested by her daughter, Lady Mason.

'Mason himself challenges Anstey to a duel and Anstey runs away like the arrant, useless coward he is. My Arthur would never have behaved so cravenishly.' She pressed the Colonel's hand. Colonel Brian glowed with pleasure and murmured, 'Dear lady,' in a deprecating way.

Lord Harry took his hand from Deirdre's shoulder and she gave a shiver, as if suddenly cold.

When she thought he was not looking, Deirdre glanced up at Lord Harry. He immediately turned and looked full at her. She dropped her eyes and blushed painfully. A terrible blush. She could feel it beginning somewhere around the soles of her feet and coursing in a red tide right to the top of her head.

Inwardly, she cursed the glaring lights of the opera house. Eyes seemed to stare at her curiously from all sides. Through an embarrassed red mist, she dimly saw Lord Harry turn away and say something to Colonel Brian.

At last, they all battled down the stairs in the press of people.

'No one ever wants to sit quietly in their box until everyone else has gone,' thought Deirdre crossly. 'Being *tonnish* seems to involve a sad degree of crushing.'

Then the press of the crowd thrust her against Lord Harry, who put a protective arm about her, and Deirdre promptly forgot about everything and everyone else.

He would not hold her so if he did not care!

But her heart plummeted as she saw that his *other* arm was around Lady Godolphin's shoulder to protect *her,* Colonel Brian having been thrust back into the crowd.

But she would have an opportunity to talk a little to Lord Harry at Lady Godolphin's—for surely he would come back with them for wine and cakes— and then she might be able to judge if he had any warm feelings towards her.

But no sooner were they all in Lady Godolphin's carriage and Lord Harry had left in his own than it transpired they were all to go on to a rout at a Mr South's.

There was a little comfort in the fact that Lord Harry was to join them there.

And so after an hour of waiting in a line of other carriages, they alighted at Mr South's mansion and pushed and shoved until they had reached the top of the stairs. Lord Harry was already there, and talking to a dashing matron nearly as tall as himself. She had red hair.

Wedged in a press of bodies with a glass of wine in one hand and a biscuit in the other, Deirdre at last found herself trapped in one of those 'interesting' conversations of which she had dreamed. An intense young man, jammed up against her, subjected her to a strong lecture on the disgraceful state of the economy, the miserable harvests, the sheer ingratitude of the Luddites, and the deviousness and stupidity of the Prime Minister.

In her dreams, she had always replied wittily and intelligently, but she found herself mumbling, 'Indeed,' and 'How true,' while all the while her green eyes kept straying across to where she could see Lord Harry's handsome head.

He was looking down at his companion with a lazy, seductive, slightly predatory expression.

'And as for Napoleon,' Deirdre's companion was saying. 'He should have been beheaded on Tower Hill. Do you know he lives like a *king* on St Helena? Do you know ...?'

'I don't care,' said Deirdre rudely, 'whether he is surrounded with a harem of dancing girls and eats from gold plates. He is locked away and will never frighten the world again.'

'Good Gad,' said the young man, trying to raise his quizzing glass but finding his arms jammed to his side. 'You are a bluestocking.'

'I am not a bluestocking,' said Deirdre crossly. 'I have said nothing to give anyone that idea.'

'Young ladies,' said the young man firmly, 'should not have views on anything. Their role is to listen to men since their minds are of the inferior variety.'

'They can become bored just like any man. Oh, do excuse me,' said Deirdre, her voice rising on a note of agony as she saw Lord Harry evidently moving off with the redhead. What if he *left* with her? What if he married her?

She elbowed her way frantically through the crowd and came up against him all at once. Of his companion, there was no sign.

'You look as if you are fleeing from wolves,' said Lord Harry. 'I will find us a quiet corner.'

Magically, the crowd parted to let them through and they were soon ensconced in two chairs in a corner, half hidden from the room by a carved screen.

'Someone was talking *at* me,' said Deirdre, 'and I felt suffocated.'

'A rout must be a crush to be a success,' he laughed. 'You are not fashionable, Miss Deirdre, unless you enjoy having sharp elbows rammed in your side, and someone jumping on your feet. Why are you in London? You will become worn to a frazzle with all this junketing back and forth.'

'Papa found out about ... about Mr Wentwater. He means to hunt him down.'

'If anyone can find Mr Wentwater, Mr Armitage can. Is it so important? He behaved badly, but you did throw yourself at him, and, I think, you have had your revenge.'

Deirdre grasped her fan very tightly. He could not know of that second elopement. Papa had not time to tell him. Did he know *everything?*

To change the subject she said lightly, 'Are you still of a mind to wave your uncle's fortune goodbye?'

'I don't know,' he said seriously. 'I have to get married sometime, don't I?'

'Why?'

'Among other things, I would like a son.'

'Oh.'

'Would you like to have children?'

Deirdre knit her brows. Children. How *did* one have them? She had studied the women of the village and knew now that the baby was obviously carried inside the belly.

But how did it get *out?* She had some idea that perhaps the navel widened into a sort of door from which the baby would spring fully-clothed like Pallas Athene from the head of Zeus.

It would be all very simple if one could pull babies out of one's head.

Did having them have anything to do with all those warm sensations inside her body when Lord Harry kissed her? Like cheese being churned. Did babies *solidify* inside one after a certain amount of the right kind of kissing? And was that why one was never supposed to let a gentleman do more than press one's hand?

'You have not answered my question,' pointed out Lord Harry with an amused look at her troubled face.

'Of course I would like to have children,' said Deirdre.

'How many?'

'Do I have a choice?' asked Deirdre naïvely.

'Perhaps. My uncle is anxious for me to have children since no one else in my family shows any signs of becoming wed,' said Lord Harry. 'Of course, Silas may marry someone just to pip me at the post.'

'Silas?'

'Silas Dubois—my rival for uncle's fortune.'

'How very odd,' said Deirdre. 'I know I have heard that name before. I was passing the morning room when I was staying at Minerva's one time, and she was talking to her husband and I heard her say, "Do you ever hear anything of that dreadful Mr Dubois? I confess I sometimes still have nightmares when I think of him." I did not want to stay and eavesdrop on their conversation, so I heard no more.'

'Indeed!' Lord Harry looked curious. 'Silas has an unforgettable appearance. He is all nose with little beady eyes and he walks like a crab.'

'Why! A man just like that stopped right in front of me one day and looked into my face. Then I thought he was following me and I confess I was afraid.'

'When was this?' he asked sharply.

'Why, it was the morning when ...' Deirdre broke off and bit her lip, remembering it was the morning she had met Guy in the park. 'I forget,' she added lamely.

'There would appear to be some connection with your family,' said Lord Harry thoughtfully. 'I shall ask Lady Sylvester.'

Deirdre realized she had not yet tried to impress him with her new-found knowledge, and launched into her speech about the latest iniquities of the Prince Regent.

'Poor Prinny,' said Lord Harry with amusement, although Deirdre had a feeling he was more amused at her lecture than he was at the antics of the Prince Regent.

'But why should he suddenly fall in love with the

Stuarts?' demanded Deirdre, narrowing her eyes in what she hoped was a penetrating and intelligent look.

'He is wretched because of his own unpopularity. He is, I think, fascinated by the Stuarts because they have become such a romantic legend, and he would so much like to become a romantic legend himself. And then, the more unpopular he gets, the more determined he seems, in some perverse way, to cultivate more unpopularity.'

At that moment, Lady Godolphin came puffing up to say they were leaving.

Somehow, by the time they had all struggled down the stairs again and were waiting on the step for their carriage to be brought round, Lord Harry had disappeared. Lady Godolphin said he would not be joining them for supper, and Deirdre could not help asking, 'Did he say anything about seeing us again?' to which Lady Godolphin said crossly, 'If you mean you, miss, no he did not and I can't say I blame him.'

Deirdre flushed and hung her head.

But when they were at Lady Godolphin's and Deirdre had retired with Lady Godolphin to her boudoir where they planned to repair their appearance, Deirdre remembered about babies and about her ignorance of how they came to be conceived.

She waited impatiently until the maid had left the room. Lady Godolphin was the very person to ask. There was something so inhibiting about putting delicate questions to Minerva or Annabelle.

As soon as the door had closed behind the maid, Deirdre took a deep breath and said, 'Lady

Godolphin, how does a lady have babies? 'I mean, how does she *get* them?'

Lady Godolphin looked at Deirdre's red face with indulgent amusement. 'And you a country girl,' she laughed. 'Well, I belong to the old school and go in for plain speaking. I don't believe in gels being kept in ignorants, so I'll tell you direct. Now, sit down and listen.'

Deirdre sat down and leaned forward. Lady Godolphin looked quickly around as if expecting shocked matrons to leap out from behind the curtains.

'See here,' she said hoarsely. 'The man takes out his pinnace and puts it into her virginal and after a bit of fiddley-diddley, a baby is started.'

Deirdre looked blank.

Lady Godolphin groaned.

'I'll try again. The man, see, he takes his Shaftsbury and puts it in her private.'

'Private what?' asked Deirdre.

The maid came back into the room with a warming pan.

'Well, there you are,' said Lady Godolphin. 'I'm glad you asked me. I'm good at explaining delicate matters. In such intimate things, I don't believe anything should be left to the imagination.'

Deirdre was just as baffled as ever.

After she had returned to Minerva's and was lying in bed, still struggling with the problem, Deirdre felt she *had* to know.

Betty would know. Betty, the maid, had been present at the birth of Mrs Armstrong's boy in the village last autumn.

Deirdre decided to go to Betty's room and ask her. It did not seem quite right to ring the bell at this hour of the night—or morning, thought Deirdre with a fretful glance at the clock—but if she, Deirdre, just crept into her room and asked her softly, well, then she would know and then she could sleep.

Carrying a candle in its flat stick, she cautiously and quietly made her silent way to the maid's room, and gently pushed open the door.

She gave a gasp and the candle dropped from her hand, but there was still enough light from the rushlight beside the bed to show Miss Deirdre Armitage the splendid vista of John Summer's bare backside and Betty's startled face peering over his shoulder.

Deirdre picked up the candle and hurried off to her own room.

She fell immediately asleep, because, all at once, she did not want to think of anything at all.

TEN

Deirdre was feeling very tired. Her father was making return-to-Hopeworth noises. Her sister Annabelle had scooped her up early in the day— eleven o'clock was early by *tonnish* standards—and had taken her on a shopping expedition.

Annabelle still had all her old love of new gowns and ribbons and gewgaws. They had spent at least two hours in Harding, Hoswell & Co.'s premises in Schoenberg House in Pall Mall. Unflagging, Annabelle had moved on to Bond Street, very much a masculine preserve with its hotels and apartments, tailors, wig-makers and bookshops, although it had lately become quite *comme il faut* for a lady to shop there. Annabelle had also spent quite a deal of time at Jane Taylor & Son, 'China and Glass Sellers to His Royal Highness ye Prince of Wales' at the Feathers, Pall Mall which sold 'all sorts of China ware, Cutt and Plain Glass,' although she had so far bought nothing at all, and seemed to have endless reserves of energy left to explore Bond Street.

Past the Clarendon Hotel they trudged with Annabelle's maid in stolid attendance. The Clarendon Hotel, famed for its enormously expensive dinners, was run by Monsieur Jacquier, who had been chef to Louis XVIII. It was in the narrow part of the street, known as the Bond Street Straits, and it was there both ladies met Lord Harry Desire, ambling towards them in a leisurely way.

Deirdre had never noticed before her sister's infuriating propensity to flirt with any handsome man she met. Annabelle chattered on breathlessly and Deirdre reflected that she was too forward by half. Of course, Lord Harry was only being polite to pay such complete attention to Annabelle's prattle, but Deirdre could not help wishing her sister's hair was not quite so golden or her eyes quite so blue.

'I am taking my little sister on a tour of the shops,' said Annabelle gaily, and Deirdre could have killed her for that patronizing remark. 'You know how it is, my lord,' went on Annabelle, 'these young things will get up to mischief if one does not keep them truly occupied.'

Lord Harry's calm blue gaze turned on Deirdre.

'And what mischief have you been getting up to, Miss Deirdre?' he said.

'Nothing at all,' mumbled Deirdre, feeling like a

gauche schoolgirl.

'Then we shall have to invent some for you,' he said. 'I am going to the Jamesons' masked ball tonight. Would that supply you with mischief enough?'

'I have not been invited,' said Deirdre.

'But *I* have and I can escort you, with your father's permission, of course.'

'You cannot take her without a chaperone,' exclaimed Annabelle, turning from flirtatious matron to stern matron all in a moment.

'Of course not,' said Lord Harry. 'A respectable chaperone will be provided.'

'Oh, in that case,' said Annabelle brightly, 'I can supply my little sister with a domino. It is blue which is not exactly your colour, Deirdre, but 'twill suffice.'

Lord Harry said he would call on Mr Armitage and make all the arrangements, then he made both ladies a magnificent bow, and strolled off.

'What a man!' said Annabelle, watching his well-tailored back retreating down Bond Street. 'Oh, you are such a fool to turn him down, Deirdre!'

'Ooooh! I wish you would stop putting on airs the whole time, Annabelle, and patronizing me in that stupid way. "My little sister," indeed! *And* you were making sheep's eyes at him in front of everyone in Bond Street. I have a good mind to tell Brabington of your behaviour.'

'That's just what a spiteful little cat like you *would* do,' said Annabelle, tossing her curls. 'If you say anything at all to Brabington, I shall pull your disgusting carroty hair out bit by bit.'

'You are very vulgar and common, Annabelle,'

said Deirdre haughtily. 'You have learned no manners at *all.*'

'And *you* have learned no sense, you widgeon. Imagine letting such a prize as Desire get away. Of course, you are so countrified, such a rustic, you no doubt gave the poor man a disgust of you.'

'If he has such a disgust of me, then why is he taking me to a masked ball?'

'Because it *is* a *masked* ball and he won't have to look at your insipid little face.'

Breathing hard through her nose with rage, Deirdre stamped on Annabelle's toe. Annabelle rammed the ivory tip of her parasol into Deirdre's instep.

Deirdre kicked Annabelle in the shins and Annabelle drew off and punched Deirdre in the midriff.

All this they performed with rigid social smiles pinned on their faces.

Then Annabelle began to giggle, and put an arm around Deirdre's waist. 'I haven't changed, have I?' she laughed. 'Come along and I will get us ices at Gunter's and I will behave myself.'

Deirdre grinned back and they moved off arm in arm down Bond Street. Deirdre wondered whether she should ask Annabelle about babies. But it was well known in the Armitage family that Annabelle desperately wanted a baby and so far nothing had happened. How odd! Perhaps she did not kiss her husband enough.

Deirdre was in such good spirits by the time she returned to Minerva's house in St James's Square that she was able to accept the fact that Lady Godolphin was to be her chaperone without demur. Deirdre was fond of Lady Godolphin, but found her embarrassingly eccentric and often wondered at Lord Harry's very obvious affection for her.

Minerva was delighted that Deirdre should be seeing Lord Harry so soon again. Of course, it had been different when Deirdre had appeared afraid of the man, but now she was not, well, there was no denying that Lord Harry would be a delightful addition to the Armitage family.

Deirdre had seen Betty in the morning before she had left with Annabelle, but had been too embarrassed to ask the maid any questions.

But as Betty was helping her dress for the masked ball Deirdre at last blurted out, 'I'm sorry I went to your room like that, Betty.'

'I'm sorry too, miss,' said Betty, putting the curling tongs on their little spirit stove to heat.

'What were you doing?' asked Deirdre. 'I mean ... I ...' Her voice tailed away.

'Well, miss, seeing as how vicar is never going to let John and me marry, we decided to force his hand. So we were making a baby.'

'Oh.' Deirdre thought furiously. But her thoughts seemed to be dominated by the memory of the nakedness and size of John Summer's bare bottom.

'Oh, so that is how it is done,' she said at last.

'Please don't talk about such things, miss,' said Betty earnestly. 'It is not fitting that a young girl like yourself should know of such matters. I am that ashamed you saw us.'

'I won't tell anyone, Betty,' said Deirdre. 'If one takes off all one's clothes and goes to bed, does that mean one gets a baby?'

'Like as not, miss. Please don't talk about it. What if Lady Sylvester were to hear you?'

'Very well, Betty,' said Deirdre, knitting her brow. One green eye swivelled in the direction of Betty's stomach.

'Is the baby in there now?' she asked. 'I'll not ask you anything else.'

'Maybe it is and maybe it isn't,' said Betty, finally turning brick red. 'Now, be a good girl and say no more.'

'Just like bulls and cows,' said Deirdre at last. *'Ouch!* That hurts. You are burning the back of my neck, Betty."

'You a vicar's daughter!' exclaimed Betty, tears starting to her eyes. 'I just know you're going to come out with one of them remarks when you oughtn't.'

No, no, Betty, I promise. But you see it is all very curious.'

'Curiosity kills,' said Betty. 'Now, Lady Peter sent round that domino, and Miss Minerva—I mean, Lady Sylvester says she has a pretty mask. I'll just go and fetch it.'

'It's all right, Betty, I'll go. I feel too restless to sit around.'

Deirdre went along the passageway, the dark blue taffeta skirts of her gown rustling as she walked.

But instead of going directly to Minerva's room, Deirdre sat down at the top of the stairs and propped her chin in her hands. She always sat on landings when she was upset. It seemed a suitably in-between world. Stepping into an actual room seemed to mean she had to take some sort of action.

If she took off all her clothes and went into Lord Harry's bed, she would get a baby and then he

206

would be pleased. Naturally, he would marry her. But perhaps only the lower orders got babies that way. How odd to think of the *ton* cavorting about like beasts of the fields.

Deirdre gave a little sigh. That must be it. Mrs Armitage was always saying, 'Only very common people do that,' referring to everything from eating peas with your knife to crossing your legs. Therefore, it followed that perhaps one went about having babies in a more genteel way.

Lady Godolphin's lecture had been worse than useless. Her many malapropisms made her quite unintelligible at the best of times.

Then, take the stately Minerva for instance. And her supremely cool and elegant husband. They could *never* ... No, it must be something else.

With a little sigh, Deirdre rose and went to Minerva's boudoir, absent-mindedly forgetting to scratch at the door first.

Minerva was locked in her husband's arms. He was only in his breeches and Minerva was clad in the scantiest of petticoats. Her hair was tumbled about her flushed face. Lord Sylvester was kissing her with single-minded passion. Both were completely unaware they were observed.

Deirdre closed the door and stood gasping. She felt as if she had just been slapped in the face.

So it was all the same for everybody!

She went slowly back to her room and mumbled to Betty to fetch the mask 'but not now, later.'

By the time she was to go downstairs and meet Lord Harry. Deirdre was in a strung-up, excited state. Her eyes shone green in her pointed face. Her brushed and pomaded hair flamed above her delicately flushed features.

Erotic visions danced through her brain making her go hot and cold by turns.

She fervently hoped Lord Harry would not read her mind as he seemed able to do from time to time.

Grateful for Minerva's blue velvet mask, Deirdre entered the drawing-room to find Lord Harry being entertained by her father and the squire.

The vicar was in high good humour, quite obviously seeing a new fortune about to join the Armitage family.

Lord Harry was wearing a black velvet mask with a black silk domino slung over his shoulders. He no longer looked easy and amiable but quite Satanic. His breeches were moulded to his thighs.

He really had very good legs, thought Deirdre, studying them carefully. Would his bare bottom be as huge and round as John's, or would it ...?'

Shocked rigid by her thoughts, Deirdre blushed so much that her sympathetic father helped her solicitously to a chair, convinced her garters had fallen down. In the vicar's great experience, that was the only thing that made a girl blush when no one had said a word to embarrass her.

Minerva entered the room on her husband's arm and poor Deirdre blushed again.

Before they were about to leave, Minerva drew Deirdre a little away from the others.

'It seems you do not hold Lord Harry in dislike,' she whispered.

Deirdre shyly shook her head.

'Then remember to be modest and well-behaved,' said Minerva. 'Gentlemen do not like *fast* young misses, nor do they like girls who encourage liberties.'

'Oh, really,' rejoined Deirdre sarcastically. 'I shall behave just like you.'

'Thank you,' said Minerva simply, failing to notice the sarcasm in her sister's voice. 'I hope I set a good example.'

Lord Harry strolled up to say they were leaving.

'The Jamesons are a rather wild couple,' cautioned Lord Sylvester. 'I believe the company is to be of the most select, but I do not need to tell you, Deirdre, that the most respectable people can behave in the oddest manner when they are in costume.'

'Then there will be nothing in either my dress or Miss Deirdre's to incite us to wild behaviour,' laughed Lord Harry, 'for our only concession to fancy dress is our masks and dominoes.'

It showed the low state of Lady Godolphin's mind that she, too, was wearing ordinary evening dress and carrying a mask on a cane in front of her face, for usually, Lady Godolphin dearly loved fancy dress. Colonel Brian had not even a mask, and from the way the elderly pair were glaring at each other it looked as if they had been rowing quite ferociously before Lord Harry and Deirdre arrived.

It transpired, however, when they arrived at the Jamesons' in Soho that the rest of the guests were less inhibited. A duke was dressed as an Hungarian Hussar, a knight as a double-man, half-miller, half-chimney sweep. A captain went as a gamester with cards sewn all over his clothes; a countess was an Indian Sultana with one hundred thousand pounds' worth of diamonds on her head-dress; one duchess appeared as a running footman and another as the Witch of Endor.

209

But there never was a masquerade without its sensation and this time a certain Major Humphries of the Guards provided it. His effort was received with much disapproval. As the *Gentleman's Magazine* later reported: 'A figure of Adam, the unavoidable indelicacy of the dress, flesh-coloured silk with an apron of fig leaves worked in it fitting the body to the utmost nicety, rendered it the contempt of the whole company.'

Or as one wit described it:

'When we entered this paradise, judge, my dear
    madam,
With what pleasure we met our first ancestor
    Adam,
Good God! 'twas so awful to see whence we
    sprung,
For the dress to his body most prettily clung.'

But although the company pretended to be shocked the Major's scandalous costume seemed to spice the ball with an air of licence. The guests drank quantities of wine more quickly than usual; they flirted and ogled through the slits of their masks with gay abandon.

One gentleman had arrived dressed as a thatched cottage complete with the insurance company's badge on the front which prompted one noisy party to set it on fire 'since it was covered' and it was fortunately put out with several bottles of champagne before the poor inhabitant of the cottage was incinerated.

Lord Harry twice had to rescue Deirdre from a dancing partner who had become over warm in his attentions.

'I really should not have brought you,' he said. 'Now, I have lost Lady Godolphin.'

No matter,' said Deirdre, delighted to have him by her side again. 'Perhaps, my lord, if it should please you, we could move a little way away from the press of dancers.'

'By all means. There is an empty box over in that corner. If we are very quick, we shall reach it before anyone else decides to take it up.'

The ballroom was formed by a chain of saloons. Round the edge of each saloon boxes had been erected, made of flimsy garlanded lattice work.

Lord Harry helped her into the vacant box and then said he would fetch them some refreshment. The arrangement of the garlands, which were made of silk flowers, afforded a certain shelter from the eyes of the dancers at the ball.

Some couples were making the most of the semi-privacy and were cavorting about in such a manner as to leave Deirdre in little doubt as to how the aristocracy made love.

A young man vaulted into her box and swept her into his arms.

Deirdre let out a scream and tried to push him away but her scream was drowned in all the noise.

His mouth was about to descend on her own, twist her head as she might, when, suddenly, she was free.

Lord Harry lifted the young man bodily out of the chair next to Deirdre and flung him on to the dance floor.

'And I didn't spill a drop,' he said cheerfully, placing a bottle and two glasses on the little table in front of them.

'It is very strange,' said Deirdre, looking about

211

her, 'that one should receive so many lectures about how to go on in society, and then to have to look at ... all this.'

'Society is very two-faced,' said Lord Harry. 'I was amazed to find you returning to Town so quickly.'

'Papa would have me go with him.'

'Ah, you must be his favourite daughter.'

His newest marriageable daughter, thought Deirdre. 'He is fond of us all, I think,' she said aloud.

'Do you wish me to volunteer to return with you to Hopeworth on a visit so that you may escape Town? I fear Mr Armitage still views me in the light of a future son-in-law.'

'No, we shall be returning in a few days' time, perhaps.'

She felt uneasy with him. His masked face turned him into a stranger. She was painfully aware of his closeness.

He was looking about him, his eyes glittering through the slits of his mask. 'I think I should take you away from here,' he said. 'Things are liable to get out of hand. Goodness knows what has happened to Lady Godolphin. If I leave you to go in search of her, I may find you being attacked when I return. And if we *both* look for Lady Godolphin, we shall be sadly jostled in the press.

'Then it is not exactly *convenable* to escort you back in a closed carriage without a chaperone, but I feel your family would not like to see you here in such surroundings. So I think escaping with me is the better of two evils.'

'Do let us go,' said Deirdre who did not like to confess the behaviour of the guests shocked her in case she seemed too unsophisticated, and was glad to think she should be alone with him, away from this riot, if only for a short space of time.

As they threaded their way through the saloons Deirdre suddenly saw Lady Godolphin, sitting in a box with Colonel Brian. They seemed to be having a heated argument. Her step faltered.

'What is it?' asked Lord Harry, looking down at her. 'Have you seen Lady Godolphin?'

'No,' lied Deirdre, turning her head determinedly in the wrong direction.

Once alone with him in the darkness of the carriage, Deirdre found his silence almost unbearable.

All at once, she was afraid she was going to be handed over to Minerva while the night was still young.

And perhaps, after that, she might not see him again.

'It is only eleven o'clock,' she ventured. She gave a little laugh which sounded false in her own ears. 'It is very early to be thinking of going to bed.'

'I agree,' said Lord Harry, 'but since *I* have now become your chaperone, 'twould be best if I took you straight to Lady Sylvester.'

'Where do you live?'

'In lodgings, in Bond Street, near where I met you.'

'Are you comfortable there?'

'Very comfortable.' His voice sounded amused.

'I would like to visit them one day.'

'Gladly.'

'I could visit them *now*.'

'You shock me, Miss Deirdre. You cannot be contemplating visiting my bachelor lodgings at this time of night.'

'No one would know, except your servants. I do not want to go to bed so early.'

'Now, when do you go to bed when you are at home?'

'Hopeworth? About nine o'clock in the winter, later in the summer.'

'Then it is already long past your bedtime.'

'But no one goes to bed here before dawn, no one in the whole world,' said Deirdre, meaning the world bounded by St James's Square and Grosvenor Square.

'Are you not afraid of what might happen to you were you to be alone with me in my lodgings?'

'I am sure you would behave like a gentleman.'

'I might be tempted to kiss you, Deirdre.'

'Well,' faltered Deirdre, 'that would not do at all since we are not to be wed.'

'No. On the other hand, I really should like to marry *someone*, you know, and, as I told you, I am very lazy. The thought of pursuing females and meeting their families exhausts me. I have already met *your* family and you have met mine. What a pity we cannot get married. It would save a great deal of trouble, although this time I don't think anyone would accept the invitation or send us a present. They would say it is all a hum.'

'Yes,' said Deirdre.

The coach stopped outside the Comfreys' residence in St James's Square. The tall house was in darkness. Deirdre peered out. 'I cannot even ask you to accompany me inside,' she said sadly. 'It appears everyone has gone to bed.'

A footman opened the carriage door.

'Close it,' said Lord Harry lazily. 'We are not yet

214

ready to get down.'

The servant closed the door.

'Where were we?' said Lord Harry. 'Ah, we were talking of marriage. Of course, I was quite cast down when your father and Lord Sylvester pointed out you were afraid of me. Now, I ask you, what is there to be afraid of? I am clean, house-trained, have all my own teeth, and am in good coat.'

'It is very hard to explain ...'

'Do try. My *amour propre* was quite ruined.'

'I found your attentions ... you treated me to an excess of civility.'

'So I did. Do you still sleep-walk?'

'No.'

'Pity. I like it when you walk in your sleep. Very well, I did kiss you. Was that so very frightening? The last time I did so you did not even struggle.'

'My own feelings frightened me, my lord,' said Deirdre.

'In what way?'

'Oh, I cannot *explain*,' said Deirdre, exasperated. 'Besides,' she added primly, 'I have forgotten.'

'That is easily remedied. Now if I take you in my arms, like this, and kiss you, like this, what do you feel?'

'Breathless and shaken.'

'That sounds unpleasant, perhaps we had better try again ...'

Although they were sitting side by side, it was odd how he seemed to manage to get most of her body pressed against his own, how every rushing emotion seemed to be centred in her lips. But if she married him, she would need to lie naked with him in that peculiar way that John was behaving with Betty and she could not.

215

He felt her body go rigid and quickly released her.

'You *are* frightened of me,' he said gently. 'What is it?'

Overset by all her emotions, Deirdre blurted out a disjointed, rambling, tearful explanation about John and Betty and she could not do *that,* and if *that* was part of marriage then she would die an old maid.

Lord Harry rapped on the roof with his cane. 'Home!' he called up to the coachman.

'Then I will not touch you again,' he said firmly. 'My servants are very discreet so you may examine my lodgings and then I will return you here.'

So that was that, thought Deirdre. How irrational her feelings were! All she now wanted was him to take her in his arms again and kiss away all her fears.

Lord Harry's Swiss made a startled appearance as his master entered the apartment.

'Bruno!' said Lord Harry. 'I know you have been longing for a night off. Now is your opportunity.'

'At nearly midnight, milor'?'

'The perfect time to go roistering,' said Lord Harry firmly.

'Very good, milor',' said Bruno in a hollow voice.

'Well, what do you think of my abode?' asked Lord Harry when his servant had left.

He swung his domino from his shoulders and threw it over a chair. Then he took off his mask.

'Very comfortable,' said Deirdre, looking about her curiously.

'I'll take you on a guided tour,' said Lord Harry. 'This is my living-room.' It was a small cluttered room, full of books and papers which spilled over various seats and tables.

'And this,' he said, leading the way and holding up a candle, 'is my boudoir.'

Clothes seemed to be lying all over the place. A toilet table was crammed with everything except toiletries; magazines, blacking, snuff boxes, a decanter of wine, a card rack, and a pile of letters.

'And beyond that is the bedroom. You have seen it all.'

'All?' said Deirdre in surprise. 'I always thought lords lived in large houses.'

'Not this one. But since I am become rich of late, I plan to find myself a mansion and stretch my legs. Would you care for a glass of wine?'

Deirdre nodded and he grasped the decanter and carried it back into the living-room where he made space for her to sit down by shovelling several books and journals from a chair.

'Your servant does not clean very well,' said Deirdre shyly.

'Bruno's a good sort and can valet me better than any gentleman's gentleman in London. He loves to clean, but I will not let him disturb my things. Once he has been house-cleaning, I cannot find anything. I am not a domesticated animal.'

He poured Deirdre a glass of wine and helped himself to one.

'Please sit down, my lord,' said Deirdre. 'You make me nervous, looming over me like that. Also, I am doing a very wicked thing. I should not be here with you.'

'It would be very wicked indeed if I took advantage of the situation,' he pointed out. 'And I have no intention of doing so. My servants will not talk, so you may be easy.'

217

Some devil seemed to prompt Deirdre to move the conversation on to a more intimate footing.

'When I told you about Betty and John,' she said boldly, 'you did not seem shocked.'

'I don't know the parties, except as your servants,' he said. 'Since they are to be married and have found a means to make Mr Armitage marry them, I cannot really say anything much about it. Are they in love?'

'Yes, very much.'

'Then what they were doing was only natural. Other people's lovemaking always looks highly *unnatural,* of course, while one's own does not.'

'But how can *any* lady ... it is different for servants, surely.'

'Deirdre, talking of such things—I do not know if you are doing it deliberately—is forcibly bringing to my mind the intimacy of our situation. If you go on, I shall be tempted to break my promise.'

'You are right,' said Deirdre, standing up. 'We should go.'

'Aren't you hot with that mask on?'

'Yes, I am a little.' She put up her hands and untied the strings and tucked the velvet mask into her reticule.

'That is better. Masks make the most innocent people look wicked. Now you look like a country virgin.'

'Thank you, sir,' said Deirdre, although she was not sure it was a compliment.

'Well ...' she said, moving from one foot to the other, 'I should return.'

'Of course. Oh, God!' he suddenly screamed. 'Look at that!'

The terror in his voice and face were so real that

Deirdre gave a startled shriek and flung herself into his arms, babbling, 'What is it? Oh, is it a *ghost?*'

She hugged him close and buried her face in his chest.

'I am sorry to have alarmed you,' he said mildly. 'I saw my cravat in the looking glass and it had a *spot* on it.'

'You tricked me,' accused Deirdre, her voice muffled in his waistcoat.

'Not I,' he replied softly. 'Do look up and say you forgive me. You see, I have kept my promise. Your arms are about me, but mine are by my side.'

She looked up and opened her mouth to accuse him again of trickery, but the words died on her lips. His blue eyes were dark in the candlelight, no longer calm and childlike, but blazing down at her with a certain intensity that kept her wide gaze trapped in his.

He stood very still.

She gave a little sigh and stood on tiptoe and kissed him gently on the mouth.

Still, his arms remained at his sides, but his mouth burned and clung, and she kissed him with increasing passion. His mouth slid to the lobes of her ears, then the tip of her nose, then her eyelids, and then ...

'Ow!' yelped Deirdre, her eyes wide with alarm and a hand flying to her neck. 'You *bit* me!'

'Oh, I am so sorry,' he said, drawing back. 'Are you *sure?* I told you Bruno was not allowed to clean. Now only see. It is quite obvious. I have fleas.'

'Sir, this was not a flea bite,' said Deirdre, as cold as she had been hot a moment before. 'I do not understand you. Please take me home.'

'Very well,' he said mildly.

Deirdre kept a very stiff demeanour on the road to St James's Square, her back straight, her face averted from him.

This time, the house in St James's Square was ablaze with lights.

'Confusion,' said Lord Harry, as he helped Deirdre to alight. 'I fear Lady Godolphin has returned and has started an alarm as to your whereabouts. I must think of a good excuse.'

Deirdre and Lord Harry walked into the drawing-room to face a battery of accusing eyes. Ranged up in front of them were Lady Godolphin, Colonel Brian, Minerva and Lord Sylvester, and the vicar and Squire Radford.

'Where have you been?' asked Lord Sylvester.

'We could not find Lady Godolphin,' said Lord Harry easily, 'and I became concerned because the masquerade turned out not to be suitable for a lady of tender years such as Miss Deirdre. In fact, it was not suitable for any *lady*. Lord Sylvester, I assure you, it was like Rome before the Fall. I decided the best thing I could do was to remove Miss Deirdre from the Jamesons' as soon as possible.'

'Forgive me for being a septic,' said Lady Godolphin drily. 'But I do not think you looked very hard.'

'We looked for you at eleven o'clock,' put in Colonel Brian, 'and could not find you anywhere. When we asked at the entrance, we were told you had left a little *before* eleven. Since you did not send the carriage back, I had to escort poor Lady Godolphin here in a hack.'

'We were sitting in the carriage discussing the works of Shakespeare,' said Lord Harry, 'and quite forgot the time. As you can see, Miss Deirdre has come to no harm.'

'Come here, girl,' barked the vicar suddenly, 'And stop lurking in the doorway.'

Deirdre walked forwards, her hand to her throat.

'Is Lord Harry telling the truth?' demanded the vicar.

'Yes, Papa,' said Deirdre.

'Come closer.'

The vicar stared at his daughter's face, and then suddenly his arm shot out and he dragged Deirdre's hand down from her neck.

All eyes fastened on the subsequently exposed purple bruise.

The vicar's eyes were like two black diamonds in his flushed face.

'Where did you come by that?' he asked softly.

'Wh ... what?' Deirdre tried to look innocent and only succeeded in looking miserably guilty.

'You, answer,' snarled the vicar, rounding on Lord Harry.

'No, I will answer,' said Deirdre quickly. 'A man jumped into our box at the masquerade when Lord Harry was fetching us refreshments, and ... he tried to kiss me, and in the struggle, I came by this bruise.'

'Such a reason fair pisses my goose,' said the vicar coldly.

'Papa!' shrieked Minerva. 'Such language.'

'Get used to it,' said the vicar. 'There's worse to come, I think. Well, Desire, what's your explanation?'

Lord Harry spread his hands in a deprecating manner, and shot a rueful glance in Deirdre's direction.

'I find it very hard to lie,' he said. 'The truth is, I

221

was holding your daughter in my arms and kissing her and I regret to say I forgot myself.'

'Where did this take place, sirrah? In the carriage?'

Clear as a bell, Lord Harry's voice seemed to ring through the drawing-room.

'In my lodgings, Mr Armitage.'

Green eyes gleaming, Lord Sylvester made a quick move towards Lord Harry. Deirdre threw herself between them.

'It was all my fault,' she gasped. 'I *flirted* with him, quite shamefully. I led him on.'

Lord Harry dropped his hands lightly on her shoulders and pulled her against him.

Then he rested his chin on top of her head and surveyed the outraged company with amused eyes.

Despite all her fright and confusion, Deirdre, nonetheless leaned gratefully back against him, thinking with one little part of her brain that it was the first time she had ever seen Minerva struck speechless.

'So there it is,' said Lord Harry. 'I have sadly compromised your daughter. We will need to be married as soon as possible.'

'That you will,' growled the vicar. 'Come with me, Lord Harry. You have a great deal of talking to do.'

Lord Harry raised Deirdre's hand to his lips and kissed it.

She looked up at him in a dazed and bewildered way. She loved him. He was to marry her, after all. The picture of John and Betty making love surfaced in her mind and she shuddered. How could she be so in love with the man, and yet so frightened of the idea of her wedding night?

222

ELEVEN

Silas Dubois turned a little cloisonné snuff box over in his hands. It had cost a lot of money, and Silas did not like spending money—on anyone other than himself.

He was waiting in a gloomy downstairs saloon in Mr Blewett's residence; waiting to be ushered into the presence.

Mr Blewett had told Silas that he had definitely changed his will in Silas's favour. That was good. But on that last visit, Mr Blewett kept saying eagerly that Silas should inform Lord Harry of this fact.

Cat and mouse games, thought Silas sourly.

The snuff box was an expensive trinket to remind Mr Blewett that his moneybags were to go to the one who appreciated him most.

Silas Dubois had not seen Lord Harry for some time, and had no intention of seeing him now and telling him about the changed will.

For what if Desire should come hot foot to his uncle's bedside and charm the old fool into changing his will again?

A footman entered and told Silas Dubois that Mr Blewett was ready to see him.

'Physician called today?' asked Silas eagerly as he mounted the stairs behind the servant.

'Yes, sir.'

'And what is the verdict?'

'I am sure I do not know, sir,' said the footman haughtily.

Silas glared at his liveried back. Jackanapes!

'You'll be the first to go—and without a reference,' he thought, 'just as soon as I get my hands on Blewett's estate.'

Mr Blewett was propped up against the pillows. He looked as usual. That is, he looked at death's door.

He was clutching a copy of the *Morning Post* and his eyes were bright with malicious humour.

'Well, here's confusion,' he said as Silas sidled up to his bedside. 'You have seen today's newspapers?'

Silas shook his head.

'Desire is to be wed to that Armitage chit after all! I knew he would do what I wanted in the end. I'd no intention of leaving him my money while he was bent on being single. But a wife will settle him down.'

Silas Dubois' fingers curled round the snuff box. 'Do you mean to tell me,' he grated, 'that this engagement of Desire's alters things? You are surely not contemplating changing your will again.'

'Why not?' demanded Mr Blewett pettishly. 'It's my will and my money and I can do what I like with it.'

Silas slid the snuff box into his pocket. He noticed in a detached kind of way that his hands were trembling.

'I would not change your will so soon,' he said forcing a smile. 'The wedding could be off again.'

'Well, I'll confess that's a possibility,' said Mr Blewett cheerfully. 'But I have sent for Desire and expect him directly.'

Silas Dubois thought furiously. He thought of tall and handsome Lord Harry, strolling in and charming this old curmudgeon into changing his will, Lord Harry who was reported to be making money hand over fist on the Stock Exchange.

And then he saw the eager, malicious look on Mr Blewett's face.

'You don't look very comfortable,' said Silas, forcing a smile. 'Allow me to arrange your pillows.'

'Leave them alone,' snapped Mr Blewett. 'I don't like you hovering about me like a demned vulture.' He gave a senile giggle. 'Demme, if you don't look like a vulture with that great nose of yours.'

Well, it was only the matter of a moment to whip the pillow out from under the old man and ram it down on his face.

Silas pressed down with all his strength and tried to think of something else. Who was it who had apologized because he had been an unconscionable time dying? Charles II, that was it.

The frail body on the bed jerked once more and was still. Silas gently removed the pillow and looked down at the contorted face on the bed.

He composed his features into a suitable expression of mourning and reached for the bell rope.

No. He would go downstairs and make his announcement in soft tones to the butler.

He walked slowly towards the door.

A scrabbling sound behind him made the blood freeze in his veins.

He whipped round and a chamber pot struck him full in the face.

'You don't get rid of me that easily,' cackled Mr Blewett. He tugged the bell rope.

Silas reeled and staggered out of the door. A footman came running up the stairs.

'Murder!' shouted Mr Blewett from the room in an amazingly strong voice. *'Murder!'*

225

The game was up. Silas took to his heels and fled.

Mr Blewett's house was in Streatham. With hard riding, he, Silas, could reach his lodgings in Brook Street before the Bow Street Runners came to call.

'And no China Street pig is going to haul me off to the cells,' muttered Silas as he spurred his horse.

His one thought was to reach the sanctuary of his lodgings and pack a portmanteau. He had a small fortune in diamonds carefully hoarded away under the floorboards. He had to get out of England as soon as possible.

He hurtled into his lodgings and sent his servant to reserve two seats on the mail coach. 'I have to leave the country,' he gabbled. 'Urgent business. Don't stand there gawking, man. Go to it!'

Once alone, he sank down on a chair and bit his knuckles, his eyes darting this way and that like a cornered rat.

Then all at once, he rose and began to pack feverishly. He prised up a floorboard in the dark corner of his sitting-room and pulled out a heavy wash leather bag of diamonds and thrust them into a corner of his portmanteau.

He had very little time.

Blewett's servants would have set out after him as soon as they got their wits together.

He heard a quick, light step on the stairs as he fastened the clasp of the portmanteau. His servant had been quick. The door opened.

'Well, don't stand there like a fool. Take this bag,' snapped Silas.

And then he looked up.

Guy Wentwater stood framed in the doorway, a pistol in his hand.

'So Desire is to be married,' said Guy Wentwater, 'and you are going to blab all over London. You are going to ruin me, heh?'

'No,' screamed Silas. 'Not I. Sit down, dear boy, and put that pistol away.'

'Very well. I'll hear what you have to say.' Guy Wentwater strolled forwards.

'I knew you would see sense,' said Silas mopping his brow. 'A drink. That's what we both need.' He crossed to the sideboard and seized a decanter of brandy.

Guy took careful aim and shot Silas Dubois through the head, quickly averting his eyes from the subsequent mess. Then he coolly put his smoking pistol away in one of his capacious pockets and made for the door.

All at once, his legs seemed to give way from under him and he collapsed in a heap on the floor. He buried his face in his hands and sobbed bitterly for the wreck of his life and ambitions. He would never become the honoured figure of society he had longed to be. He would be a fugitive, travelling the Continent, living on his wits. He had not even tried to disguise himself and several people must have seen him enter the lodgings.

Damn those Armitages to hell, the whole pack of them.

He finally dried his eyes and crawled to his feet. And then he heard the cries of 'Murder! Murder!' from the street outside. How could anyone know so soon?

Heavy feet sounded on the stairs and two Bow Street Runners backed by Mr Blewett's servants appeared on the landing.

'Mr Dubois?' asked one. Guy waved his hand in

227

the direction of Mr Dubois' body and stood, waiting for his arrest.

'Well, you've saved the law a hanging,' said one of the officers, straightening up. 'Did he attack you?'

Guy had not the faintest idea what was going on but he began to see a glimmer of hope.

'Yes,' he said. 'I came to call on him and he cursed and flew at me, and I shot him, for I feared he was about to kill me.'

'Don't look so put about, master,' said the Bow Street Runner who stood next to Guy. 'He deserved what he got. Trying to kill an old man. Shameful. Now, if you'll just step along o' us to Bow Street, we'll put all the facts before the magistrate. You'll feel better when you get some fresh air. Come along, now.'

* * *

By the time Lord Harry arrived to call on Mr Blewett it was much later that day. Mr Blewett was in a high state of excitement over his own cleverness. The minute he had felt the pillow over his face, he said, he had decided to fake dying, relying on the fact that Dubois would obviously think him weaker than he was.

'And I fooled him!' crowed Mr Blewett.

'And you sent him to the gallows or transportation by playing on his greed,' sighed Lord Harry.

'He's dead. Marvellous thing. Chap called Wentwater shot him. My servants told me,' giggled Mr Blewett.

'What!' Lord Harry was shaken out of his usual

228

urbane calm.

'Yes, seems this young friend called at his lodgings and Silas attacked him, no doubt thinking this Wentwater knew about the attempted murder. So Wentwater shot him.'

Lord Harry sat deep in thought, deaf to Mr Blewett's voice. Minerva had told him of the duel between Dubois and her husband, fought because Dubois and his friends had tried to ruin her. Deirdre had told of the strange man who had looked so closely at her on the day she had gone out walking alone and had then met Guy Wentwater in Green Park. It seemed as if Guy Wentwater and Silas Dubois had been joining forces to attack the Armitage family. That Dubois and Wentwater knew each other came as no surprise to Lord Harry after some more thought. Dubois seemed to have known every weak and shiftless wastrel on the fringes of society.

Lord Harry suddenly decided to call at Bow Street and find an address in London where he could reach Guy Wentwater. That young man had a great deal of explaining to do.

He left Mr Blewett, who was still chortling and chattering over his escape from death, and rode back into London.

But at Bow Street he was informed that Mr Wentwater had announced his intention of leaving the country on business. There had, naturally, been no charges against him. The Runners appeared to think he had acted promptly and bravely.

Lord Harry returned to his own lodgings and told his Swiss to re-hire the watchdog to look after Miss Deirdre Armitage; then he took himself off to see the vicar.

But the vicar was in a bad mood. He said he could not understand any of it, and then glared at Lord Harry and remarked acidly he trusted *he* was not leaving London since his wedding was in two weeks' time and by special licence.

'For you'll have to marry her now,' said the vicar crossly, 'after what you did to her.'

'Yes,' agreed Lord Harry sadly, and Deirdre who was sitting on the other side of the drawing-room looked at him with troubled eyes and wondered if he felt he had been coerced into the marriage.

'Papa,' she said suddenly, '*nothing* happened between myself and Lord Harry.'

'How would *you* know,' said the vicar gloomily. 'Just be guided by your father, and we'll have a respectable matron made of you as soon as possible.'

Deirdre looked pleadingly at Lord Harry but he only smiled blandly back at her.

'Nonetheless, sir,' said Lord Harry, returning to the subject of Guy Wentwater, 'I feel none of your family is safe until we find out exactly where he is. I suggest we get all our servants, that is, mine, the Comfreys', the Brabingtons' and Lady Godolphin's, to search the whole of London.'

'He'll not dare show his face again,' said the vicar.

'On the contrary, I think he will. He is by way of being a sort of hero over the shooting of Dubois.'

'Just think about your marriage,' growled the vicar. 'I am disappointed in you, Desire. Now, I've got the cost of a wedding on my hands, not to mention Mrs Armitage and the girls arriving. Then, there's the boys to fetch from Eton. And the whole world and his wife speculating about the speed of the marriage.'

'It is all very sad,' agreed Lord Harry amiably.

Deirdre studied Lord Harry covertly. All these marriage arrangements were bursting about her head. He had bitten her. Bitten! What other unknown horrors lay waiting for her on the marriage bed. She did not know this man *at all*.

Squire Radford was brought into the discussion, Lord Sylvester arrived, and soon everyone seemed to be speculating about the connection between Guy Wentwater and Silas Dubois.

At last Lord Harry rose to leave. Deirdre stood up as well.

'I would like to have a few words with my fiancé, Papa,' she said, 'in private.'

The vicar scowled awfully. 'I s'pose you're both beyond needin' a chaperone. You may go to the library, but leave the door open, mind!'

Lord Harry held the door open for Deirdre and she walked towards him, aware of the accusing eyes of her father.

'What ails you?' asked Lord Harry, leading her into the library and absent-mindedly closing the door.

'The shame of it all,' said Deirdre breathlessly. 'We did nothing, and yet you allowed everyone to think you had.'

'I knew they would not believe otherwise,' he said, looking down at her. A red curl had escaped from its moorings and he carefully tucked it back into place on the top of her head. 'Don't you want to marry me?' he asked, noticing the way she flinched from his touch.

'I am afraid, sir,' said Deirdre, hanging her head.

'Of me?'

'You shocked me. You *bit* me.'

'Ah, shameless that I am.'

'It is not a joking matter,' said Deirdre, raising anxious, worried eyes to his. 'It is just that there are a lot of things I do not know about you.'

'It is our wedding night,' he said. *'That* is what troubles you.'

Deirdre hung her head again.

He took her gently in his arms. 'I am a very wicked man,' he said huskily. 'There is something I must tell you ...'

'Ho!' said the vicar, wrenching open the door and glaring at them with his hands on his hips. 'You'll now wait until you're married, the pair of you. Deirdre! You are coming back with me to Hopeworth and you will return with your mother in a week's time.'

'My dear sir ...' began Lord Harry, still keeping his arms about Deirdre.

'No, that's final,' said the vicar. 'I'll not rest in my bed o' nights until I see you two *legalized.'*

He stood there glaring until Lord Harry left. Deirdre wondered miserably what wickedness Lord Harry had been about to confess to.

*   *   *

Deirdre was to look back on the days before her marriage as a rushed series of comings and goings between Hopeworth and London.

The fact that she did not seem particularly elated about her marriage was, this time, firmly ignored by the Armitage family. She should consider herself lucky she was to be married and not parcelled off to the Continent to live out her shameful days in the

232

obscurity of some genteel spa.

Even Minerva and Annabelle, who should surely have been the ones to be tolerant of pre-marital experiments, privately felt that in their case, it had all been different.

The wedding was to be held in a small church in Islington. Only members of each family were to be present with the exception of a very few close friends.

The newspapers had broadcast the bravery of Guy Wentwater in shooting down Silas Dubois. But a diligent search of London by the staff of the various households had refused to unearth that young man.

The vicar was heartily weary of daughters and marriage. He washed his hands of the whole messy business, he said loudly. The rest could all die old maids for all he cared.

Daphne was secretly disappointed in Deirdre. Deirdre was the last one of them, thought Daphne, that one would ever have thought would allow herself to be rushed into marriage by any man.

She added to Deirdre's uncertainty and distress by treating her like an invalid, talking softly in her presence, and getting cook to make nourishing broths and possets.

Numbly, Deirdre listened to the gossip about the wedding preparations. She was to wear Annabelle's wedding gown which had been refurbished for the occasion and her younger sisters were to wear the bridesmaids gowns they had worn for Annabelle's wedding.

The boy's silk suits were sent to the tailors to be altered to fit their increased size.

A simple wedding breakfast was to be served at

an inn near the church.

By the time the whole family set out for London, Deirdre felt crushed. All those tumultuous feelings Lord Harry had caused seemed a vague memory. At times, she was hard put to remember his face. She had feared him and hated him, then she had loved him, and now she was frightened of him again. But this time, no one seemed to care. Her downcast looks were judged to be entirely suitable in a maiden who had fallen from the pinnacle of virginity before her marriage.

Lady Godolphin did not help matters by being eaten up with jealousy because Colonel Brian had finally turned his attentions elsewhere and was reported to be courting a buxom matron, widow of a City merchant, who was only forty years old.

'Men are disgusting,' said Lady Godolphin to Deirdre. 'I should have warned you. When you asked me about having babies, I should not have told you, but how was I to know you would go and lose your virginal? Well, I shall attend your nipples, but if you was expecting Colonel Brian, you will be disappointed. He is flirting with a Cit. Horrible great fat thing. What can he see in her? Oh, follicles!'

And with that Lady Godolphin burst into tears and turned a deaf ear to all Deirdre's pleas of innocence.

Betty was small comfort. The maid shook her head over Deirdre's shame.

'But *you* are not waiting until you get married,' said Deirdre.

'It's different for such as me,' said Betty. 'I had to do it.'

234

'Well, I did *not!*' howled Deirdre, breaking the sticks of the fan she was holding in her agitation. 'Yes, I went to his lodgings but nothing *happened!*'

'Oh, come, miss, and you with that great bruise on your neck.'

'It just happened. He just ... oh, what's the use,' said Deirdre wretchedly. 'Everyone is creeping about me as if I am going to a funeral, and then there is this havey-cavey wedding, tucked away in the fields of Islington. And now with everyone in the family being so shocked, it has got about London, and *this* was in a print shop in Bond Street.'

She reached over to a small table and held up a coloured cartoon.

Betty looked at it, her eyes wide with horror. In it, Deirdre Armitage in a state of undress was sitting on Lord Harry Desire's knees.

Underneath there was a poem. It read:

'The wedding's on, the wedding's off,
Says capricious Miss D.A.
But Desire by name
Desire by fame,
Must needs go have his way

Now whether she desire it,
Or whether she say nay,
Our flighty miss,
Needs wedded bliss,
For Desire has had his way.'

'Oh, *miss,*' said Betty. 'It's a *mercy* he is going to marry you.'

'I cannot understand why he should not make

an effort to convince Papa that nothing happened,' said Deirdre fretfully. 'Oh, God. Would that I had never met him!'

'Well, there's nothing you can do about it now,' said Betty, picking up the hairbrush. 'Them gossips will have forgot the whole thing in another few weeks.'

But Deirdre worried and worried. Her father seemed to think that if she saw her fiancé at the wedding rehearsal, then it would be soon enough.

She could not talk openly about it, for the scandal had to be kept from the twins and from Frederica and Diana. Also, it was as if she were to be punished by the parsimony of the wedding arrangements, and she was kept busy, endlessly making and stitching petticoats and handkerchiefs.

The wedding rehearsal was a solemn affair, more like a funeral.

The church was small and dark and smelly. The vicar who was to perform the service was an old University friend of Mr Armitage.

He was one of those muscular Christians who pride themselves on the ease with which they can talk freely on all sorts of delicate subjects, and he teased the young couple jovially about their haste to be married, and was only silenced when Lord Harry Desire roused himself from his reverie and threatened to call the parson out.

'Thank goodness that part's over,' sighed the vicar, after Deirdre had been firmly marched away from Lord Harry and into the family carriage. 'Now we've only got tomorrow to worry about.'

'Yes,' agreed Mrs Armitage. 'It is all very unfortunate. We had two grand weddings already,

236

Mr Armitage, and that is something to be grateful for. Town depresses me these days and I have a monstrous severe pain in my hip. I confess I shall be glad to return to Hopeworth when this is all over.'

'Why are you getting married in such a poky church?' asked Diana, after a whispered consultation with Frederica.

'Shh!' reproved Mrs Armitage. 'There are things it is better you should not know.'

Suddenly a fit of rebellion assailed Deirdre. She was *not* going to be meekly marched to the altar on the morrow and handed over to Lord Harry Desire. She *must* know what he had been about to confess. What if it were something terrible? There was still a chance to escape. The only way to escape was to ask him.

And, if it were something too terrible, then she would escape this time by facing up to her family.

There was no Guy Wentwater to elope with. What a fool she had been over him. At least she wasn't going to be married to *him*. Deirdre briefly wondered where he was.

*   *   *

At that moment, Guy Wentwater was sitting in a hostelry in Bristol waiting for the tide. He signed his name to the foot of the letter he had just written, and then read it over to make sure there were no mistakes in grammar or spelling.

He read: 'My dear Miss Emily, By the time this reaches you, I shall be on the High Seas, bound for the West Indies. I have a certain deal of Business there. As you will have perused in the journals,

I am accounted as something of a Hero, by virtue of having struck down one Silas Dubois. They praise me more than I deserve since I was merely protecting my person from a vicious, savage, and armed murderer. He was great and powerful and quite brutal in his madness and I am relieved to have defended myself so ably.

'Give my warmest regards to Yr. Family. I hope to return to further our acquaintance. Meanwhile, I remain, Yr. Humble and Devoted Servant, G.W.'

Guy looked at what he had written and frowned. Should he, perhaps, have said something about hoping she would wait for him? Then he laughed. With such a face, Miss Emily would still be unwed by the time he returned.

TWELVE

Deirdre found herself more worried and agitated than ever as evening arrived. At last she summoned Betty.

'Betty,' said Deirdre, 'I wish you to do something for me. Pray put on your bonnet and cloak and take one of the footmen with you and call on Lord Harry and tell him I must speak to him.'

'Mr Armitage won't like it,' said Betty. 'Nor will Lady Sylvester.'

'Papa is at some coffee house with Squire Radford, Mama, the girls, and the twins have gone to make a brief call on Lady Godolphin, and Minerva and Sylvester are gone to the play. *Please*, Betty. You will be ruining my life if you do not.'

238

Betty hesitated. In truth, she was sorry for Miss Deirdre. The wedding was to be a poky little affair.

'I'll go, miss,' she said at last. 'But you must get him to say he called round of his own accord.'

'I will, Betty. I promise. Now wait there until I write something.'

Betty waited patiently until Deirdre had scribbled a letter. 'Tell him to return with you, if possible,' urged Deirdre, 'for Mama will be coming home soon.'

When Betty had left, Deirdre changed the simple gown she was wearing for one of her best. She went downstairs and sat by the drawing-room window, waiting to see when Lord Harry would arrive.

At last, when she felt she could not bear to wait any longer, a carriage drew up, the door opened and Lord Harry's tall figure alighted on the pavement.

Deirdre flew into the hall and opened the door herself.

'Come in quickly,' she whispered. 'I do not want the servants to know you are here. Come into the library.'

As she led the way, Deirdre noticed Lord Harry was wearing evening dress and had his chapeau bras tucked under his arm.

She realized she would need to say her piece quickly. He was obviously en route for the opera.

Deirdre lit the fire which had been made up and then turned and faced him.

'There is something I must know, my lord ...' she began.

'How severe you look. And will you not call me Harry?'

'Very well ... Harry. Please sit down.'

He sat down in an armchair and Deirdre sat on a chair facing him on the other side of the fire and studied him intently.

'Do you love me?' she asked.

'With all my heart,' he answered in his usual light manner.

'I feel ... I feel you might have tried to make Papa understand that nothing at all happened between us,' said Deirdre miserably, all her worries beginning to come out in a rush. 'And you bit me. And you said you had something to tell me about wickedness, but Papa interrupted us and now I don't know what to expect, and I am to have this poky little wedding as if I were in disgrace, and no one but family is to attend.

'And I am to wear Annabelle's old wedding gown, and *I am frightened.*'

She looked at him, trembling a little, waiting for him to answer.

He got up and walked to her, and, with one swift movement, gathered her up in his arms. Then he returned to his chair and arranged her comfortably on his knees.

Deirdre was reminded of the cartoon. 'And, oh Harry, they have the most awful drawings of us in the print shop,' she wailed.

'I will begin at the beginning,' he said, holding her tightly and giving her a little shake, 'and you will listen patiently.'

'Now, I saw you nearly two years ago in the Park with your sister, Annabelle. You were laughing and teasing her and I could not rest until I discovered who you were. I found out you were very young. Your sister had just become married to Brabington. I had to go to the wars but somehow I was determined that when I returned, I would seek you out.

'Shortly after my return your father visited me at White's. You can imagine my amazement. I was being offered marriage to you. I still thought you too young and thought it disgraceful of your father to push you into an unwanted marriage, and so I amused myself by telling him I didn't like girls with red hair and I didn't like clever ones either.

'I wanted you to fall in love with me, but when you really seemed so frightened and miserable and I had ascertained you no longer had any warm feelings towards Wentwater, I decided to agree to a termination of the engagement and then to wait and hope that you would come to miss me.

'Imagine my surprise when I found you back in London so soon! I was persuaded you were not indifferent to me. I was afraid you might run away from me again and so I compromised you—with your help, of course, my love. And you are not to have a poky little wedding. Your father will find I have made other arrangements for the-wedding breakfast since I have invited all London society from Brummell to the Prince Regent.

'And the church is to be especially decorated and my army friends will form a guard of honour and society will talk about it for years.'

'Why didn't you tell Papa?'

'I couldn't be bothered,' said Lord Harry lazily. 'I am paying for it, but he would bluster and shout so much before I got a chance to tell him and that does make my head ache.'

Deirdre played shyly with his top waistcoat button. 'You are so generous, and I am sure I love you, only it is a pity,' she said in a low voice, 'that love-making could not be like this ... just being together and being comfortable.'

'Oh, it is, most of the time. I am sorry I bit you. I was simply making my mark, you know, like putting a gold mark on things, except I do not yet have gold teeth. You are naturally afraid of the intimacies of marriage. It would be strange if you were not. When I said I had been wicked, I simply meant that I had not told you I had been in love with you for a long time.'

'Do we ... do we need to go in for any intimacies right away?' asked Deirdre. 'I mean, could we not become better acquainted first?'

'Of course,' he said, sinking down into the depths of the chair and arranging her head comfortably on his shoulder. 'We could sit many evenings just like this. It would not trouble you if I merely kissed you?'

Deirdre shyly shook her head.

He bent his head and kissed her gently. Deirdre felt the stirrings of passion and decided since he had been so generous, it would only be courteous to kiss him back with some of the enthusiasm she felt.

With equal generosity, Lord Harry replied in kind. Deirdre finally broke free and sat up on his knees and looked down into his blue eyes.

'I love you Harry,' she said simply.

He mutely held out his arms and she threw herself against his chest with such force that the chair overbalanced and decanted them both on to the library floor.

And then somehow Deirdre could not seem to stop kissing him, and clothes were becoming an increasing irritation, and when his hand moved down the front of her gown and held one firm

242

breast, it seemed the most natural thing in the world.

Upstairs, Betty waited patiently. The hours passed. The family had long since gone to bed. She had told Lady Sylvester that Deirdre was asleep with the headache and did not want to be disturbed.

She had not taken a footman with her and so she hoped the rest of the servants were not aware of what was going on and that his lordship had had the sense to lock the library door.

At last Betty fell asleep, sitting in a chair beside the fire in Deirdre's bedroom.

She was awakened at five in the morning by Miss Deirdre Armitage creeping into the room.

Betty struggled out of the chair. 'Oh, Miss Deirdre,' she said crossly, 'you do take advantage of a body's kindness. Now into bed this minute or I'll never get you up in time to go to church.'

*   *   *

The wedding was hailed as an outstanding success. People talked for months about the glory of the choir and the beauty of the flower arrangements, of the reception in striped marquees on Islington Fields and of how the Prince Regent himself had put in an appearance and had danced with Deirdre. The vicar, once he got over his first stunned shock at seeing so many fashionable guests, began to fret and gnaw his nails and worry about the cost of everything and say he always knew Desire was an idiot.

When he was told Lord Harry was paying for everything, Mr Armitage's admiration and gratitude knew no bounds.

'Arranged marriages are just the thing,' he told Squire Radford gleefully. 'If it hadn't been for all my work, this would never have come about.'

'Perhaps,' mused the squire, 'except I have a feeling Desire tricked us and really meant to marry Deirdre all along.'

'Not he! Fine fellow, but ain't got much upstairs.'

'Deirdre is happy at last,' said the squire, watching the new Lady Desire's glowing face. 'You are a lucky man, Charles. Three daughters wed, and all to men they love.'

'Aye, and it was all my doing,' said the vicar, puffing out his chest. 'And His Royal Highness here as well. Edwin's so jealous, he's near fit to burst.'

The vicar strutted off.

Squire Radford sighed and watched him go. Charles was about to become vain and puffed up again. It was as well Daphne was still young or the vicar would be arranging a marriage for her on the spot, despite his protestations to the contrary.

That young lady was surrounded by a crowd of admirers. She did not do anything to attract them, noticed the squire, but simply stood there, like some beautiful statue.

The squire shook his head. It would not be long before Mr Armitage turned his attention in Daphne's direction.

The vicar was not the man to let a beautiful daughter lie fallow in Hopeworth when he might be adding another illustrious name to the family tree.

Lady Godolphin waddled up, spilling champagne down the front of her gown.

She looked once more her old self, painted and wigged, and dressed in a frivolous white merino gown with broad scarlet stripes.

'My servants had wind o' Wentwater,' she said to the squire. 'Got on a boat bound for the West Indies. We won't be seeing him again. Bad cess to the man. Never could abide him.'

'I did not think you had ever met him,' pointed out the squire.

'Doesn't matter,' sighed Lady Godolphin. 'Heard enough about him. I ain't going to have anything to do with men again, Mr Radford. I am going to remain chased the way a woman's supposed to be. I don't care whether it's Mr Armitage, or Desire, or Comfrey, or Brabington, or that fickle, useless Colonel Brian.

'Men are all just a load of follicles!'

'Ah, you must not be so bitter,' said the squire in his kindly way. 'Our newly-weds are just leaving. Allow me to escort you, Lady Godolphin. It is not every day an old stick like myself can have the pleasure of escorting such a diamond of the first water.'

'Naughty man!' murmured Lady Godolphin, ogling him quite awfully, and tapping his hand with her fan.

They walked arm in arm to where Deirdre and Lord Harry were getting into the open carriage that was to carry them off to the new town house Lord Harry had bought as one of his many wedding surprises.

Deirdre stood up and tossed her bouquet into the crowd, and then sank down laughing beside Lord Harry.

'Who caught it?' he asked. 'One of your sisters?'

'No. I threw it towards Daphne, and it was caught by a *young man* standing next to her. She held out her hand for it but he was admiring

245

the flowers so much, he didn't even notice. Poor Daphne. It is the first time she has been so ignored.'

'Except by me,' said Lord Harry. 'I only ever saw you.'

'Oh, Harry, how beautiful of you to say so ... Harry! You must not kiss me in an open carriage with everyone looking! Oh, *Harry!*'